Praise for *Survival*

Best New Science Fiction and Fantasy Books for
December (2017, *io9*)

Science Fiction and Fantasy Books to Read This
December (2017, *The Verge*)

Best SFF of December 2017 (*Unbound Worlds*)

Praise for Ben Bova

"[Bova's] excellence at combining hard science with
believable characters and an attention-grabbing plot
makes him one of the genre's most accessible and
entertaining storytellers."
—*Library Journal* on *Power Play*

"Impressive."
—*Kirkus Reviews* on *Titan*

"A guaranteed crowd-pleaser!"
—*Booklist* on *Mercury*

SURVIVAL

BEN BOVA

TOR®

A TOM DOHERTY ASSOCIATES BOOK
NEW YORK

SURVIVAL

Book I of this novel first appeared in a slightly different form in the anthology *Going Interstellar*, edited by Les Johnson and Jack McDevitt (Baen Publishing Enterprises, 2012).

The epigraphs that begin each Book of this novel are from *Ulysses*, by Alfred, Lord Tennyson.

A Tor Book
Published by Tom Doherty Associates
175 Fifth Avenue
New York, NY 10010

www.tor-forge.com

Tor® is a registered trademark of Macmillan Publishing Group, LLC.

ISBN 978-0-7653-7955-9

Our books may be purchased in bulk for promotional, educational, or business use. Please contact your local bookseller or the Macmillan Corporate and Premium Sales Department at 1-800-221-7945, extension 5442, or by email at MacmillanSpecialMarkets@macmillan.com.

First Edition: December 2017
First Mass Market Edition: January 2019

Printed in the United States of America

0 9 8 7 6 5 4 3 2 1

To Rick and Rich Wilber,
and all those tight games.

The end is simply the beginning of a longer story.

—*Zadie Smith*

book one

++++++++++++++++++++++++++++

++

i am become a name ...

"It's obvious!" said Vartan Gregorian, standing imperiously before the two others seated on the couch. "I'm the best damned pilot in the history of the human race!"

Planting his fists on his hips, he struck a pose that was nothing less than preening.

Half buried in the lounge's plush curved couch, Alexander Ignatiev bit back an impulse to laugh in the Armenian's face. But Nikki Deneuve, sitting next to him, gazed up at Gregorian with shining eyes.

Breaking into a broad grin, Gregorian went on, "This bucket is moving faster than any ship ever built, no? We've flown farther from Earth than anybody ever has, true?"

Nikki nodded eagerly as she responded, "Twenty percent of light speed and approaching six light-years."

"So, I'm the pilot of the fastest, highest-flying ship of all time!" Gregorian exclaimed. "That makes me the best flier in the history of the human race. QED!"

Ignatiev shook his head at the conceited oaf. But he saw that Nikki was captivated by his posturing. Then it struck him. *She loves him! And Gregorian is showing off for her.*

The ship's lounge was as relaxing and comfortable as human designers back on Earth could make it. It was arranged in a circular grouping of sumptuously appointed niches, each holding high, curved banquettes

that could seat up to half a dozen close friends in
reasonable privacy.

Ignatiev had left his quarters after suffering still
another defeat at the hands of the computerized chess
program and snuck down to the lounge in midafternoon,
hoping to find it empty. He needed a hideaway while
the housekeeping robots cleaned his suite. Their busy,
buzzing thoroughness drove him to distraction; it was
impossible to concentrate on chess or anything else
while the machines were dusting, laundering, straight-
ening his rooms, restocking his autokitchen and his bar,
making the bed with crisply fresh linens.

So he sought refuge in the lounge, only to find Gregorian and Deneuve already there, in a niche beneath a
display screen that showed the star fields outside. Once,
the sight of those stars scattered across the infinite void
would have stirred Ignatiev's heart. But not anymore,
not since Sonya died.

Sipping at the vodka that the serving robot had
poured for him the instant he had stepped into the
lounge, thanks to its face-recognition program, Ignatiev
couldn't help grousing, "And who says you are the pilot, Vartan? I didn't see any designation for pilot in the
mission's assignment roster."

Gregorian was moderately handsome and rather tall,
quite slim, with thick dark hair and laugh crinkles at
the corners of his deep brown eyes. Ignatiev tended to
think of people in terms of chess pieces, and he counted
Gregorian as a prancing horse, all style and little sub-
stance.

"I am flight systems engineer, no?" Gregorian countered. "My assignment is to monitor the flight control
program. That makes me the pilot."

Nikki, still beaming at him, said, "If you're the pilot,
Vartan, then I must be the navigator."

"Astrogator," Ignatiev corrected bluntly.

The daughter of a Quebecoise mother and French Moroccan father, Nicolette Deneuve had unfortunately inherited her father's stocky physique and her mother's sharp nose. Ignatiev thought her unlovely—and yet there was a charm to her, a gamine-like wide-eyed innocence that beguiled Ignatiev's crusty old heart. She was a physicist, bright and conscientious, not an engineering monkey like the braggart Gregorian. Thus it was a tragedy that she had been selected for this star mission.

She finally turned away from Gregorian to say to Ignatiev, "It's good to see you, Professor Ignatiev. You've become something of a hermit these past few months."

He coughed and muttered, "I've been busy on my research." The truth was he couldn't bear to be among these youngsters, couldn't stand the truth that they would one day return to Earth while he would be long dead.

Alexander Alexandrovich Ignatiev, by far the oldest man among the starship's crew, thought that Nikki could have been the daughter he'd never had. Daughter? he snapped at himself silently. Granddaughter, he corrected. Great-granddaughter, even. He was a dour astrophysicist approaching his hundred and fortieth birthday, his short-cropped hair and neatly trimmed beard iron gray but his mind and body still reasonably vigorous and active thanks to rejuvenation therapies. Yet he felt cheated by the way the world worked, bitter about being exiled to this one-way flight to a distant star.

Technically, he was the senior executive of this mission, an honor that he found almost entirely empty. To him, it was like being the principal of a school for very bright, totally wayward children. Each one of them must have been president of their school's student body, he thought: accustomed to getting their own way and total strangers to discipline. Besides, the actual commander of the ship was the artificial intelligence program run by the ship's central computer.

If Gregorian is a chessboard knight, Ignatiev mused to himself, then what is Nikki? Not the queen; she's too young, too uncertain of herself for that. Her assignment to monitor the navigation program was something of a joke: the ship followed a ballistic trajectory, like an arrow shot from Earth. Nothing for a navigator to do except check the ship's position each day.

Maybe she's a bishop, Ignatiev mused, now that a woman can be made a bishop: quiet, self-effacing, possessing hidden depths. And reliable, trustworthy, always staying to the color of the square she started on. She'll cling to Gregorian, unless he hurts her terribly. That possibility made Ignatiev's blood simmer.

And me? he asked himself. A pawn, nothing more. But then he thought, Maybe I'm a rook, stuck off in a corner of the board, barely noticed by anybody.

"Professor Ignatiev is correct," said Gregorian, trying to regain control of the conversation. "The proper term is astrogator."

"Whatever," said Nikki, her eyes returning to Gregorian's handsome young face.

Young was a relative term. Gregorian was approaching sixty, although he still had the vigor, the attitudes and demeanor of an obstreperous teenager. Ignatiev thought it would be appropriate if the Armenian's face were blotched with acne. Youth is wasted on the young, Ignatiev thought. Thanks to life-elongation therapies, average life expectancy among the starship crew was well above two hundred. It had to be.

The scoopship was named *Sagan*, after some minor twentieth-century astronomer. It was heading for Gliese 581, a red dwarf star slightly more than twenty light-years from Earth. For Ignatiev, it was a one-way journey. Even with all the life-extension therapies, he was sure that he would never survive the eighty-year round trip. Gregorian would, of course, and so would Nikki.

Ignatiev brooded over the unfairness of it. By the time the ship returned to Earth, the two of them would be grandparents and Ignatiev would be long dead.

Unfair, he thought as he pushed himself up from the plush banquette and left the lounge without a word to either one of them. The universe is unfair. I don't deserve this: to die alone, unloved, unrecognized, my life's work forgotten, all my hopes crushed to dust.

As he reached the lounge's hatch, he turned his head to see what the two of them were up to. Chatting, smiling, holding hands, all the subverbal signals that lovers send to each other. They had eyes only for each other, and paid absolutely no attention to him.

Just like the rest of the goddamned world, Ignatiev thought.

He had labored all his life in the groves of academe, and what had it gotten him? A membership in the International Academy of Sciences, along with seventeen thousand other anonymous workers. A pension that barely covered his living expenses. Three marriages: two wrecked by divorce and the third—the only one that really mattered—destroyed by that inevitable thief, death.

He hardly remembered how enthusiastic he had been as a young postdoc, all those years ago, his astrophysics degree in hand, burning with ambition. He was going to unlock the secrets of the universe! The pulsars, those enigmatic cinders, the remains of ancient supernova explosions: Ignatiev was going to discover what made them tick.

But the universe was far subtler than he had thought. Soon enough he learned that a career in science can be a study in anonymous drudgery. The pulsars kept their secrets, no matter how assiduously Ignatiev nibbled around the edges of their mystery.

And now the honor of being the senior executive on the human race's first interstellar mission. Some honor, Ignatiev thought sourly. They needed someone competent but expendable. Send old Ignatiev, let him go out in a fizzle of glory.

Shaking his head as he trudged along the thickly carpeted passageway to his quarters, Ignatiev muttered to himself, "If only there were something I could accomplish, something I could discover, something to put some *meaning* to my life."

He had lived long enough to realize that his life would be no more remembered than the life of a worker ant. He wanted more than that. He wanted to be remembered. He wanted his name to be revered. He wanted students in the far future to know that he had existed, that he had made a glowing contribution to humankind's store of knowledge and understanding. He wanted Nikki Deneuve to gaze at him with adoring eyes.

"It will never be," Ignatiev told himself as he slid open the door to his quarters. With a wry shrug, he reminded himself of a line from some old English poet: "Ah, that a man's reach should exceed his grasp, or what's a heaven for?"

Alexander Ignatiev did not believe in heaven. But he thought he knew what hell was like.

As he entered his quarters he saw that at least the cleaning robots had finished and left; the sitting room looked almost tidy. And he was alone.

The expedition to Gliese 581 had left Earth with tremendous fanfare. The first human mission to another star! Gliese 581 was a very ordinary star in most respects: a dim red dwarf, barely one-third of the Sun's mass. The galaxy is studded with such stars. But Gliese 581 was unusual in one supremely interesting way: it possessed an entourage of half a dozen planets. Most of them were gas giants, bloated conglomerates of hydrogen and helium. But a couple of them were rocky worlds, somewhat like Earth. And one of those—Gliese 581c—orbited at just the right "Goldilocks" distance from its parent star to be able to have liquid water on its surface.

Liquid water meant life. In the solar system, wherever liquid water existed, life existed. In the permafrost beneath the frozen rust-red surface of Mars, in the ice-covered seas of the moons of Jupiter and Saturn, in massive Jupiter's planet-girdling ocean: wherever liquid water had been found, life was found with it.

Half a dozen robotic probes confirmed that liquid water actually did exist on the surface of Gliese 581c, but they found no evidence for life. Not an amoeba, not even a bacterium. But that didn't deter the scientific hierarchy. Robots are terribly limited, they proclaimed. We must send human scientists to Gliese 581c to search for life there, scientists of all types, men and women who will sacrifice half their lives to the search for life beyond the solar system.

Ignatiev was picked to sacrifice the last half of his life. He knew he would never see Earth again, and he told himself that he didn't care. There was nothing on Earth that interested him anymore, not since Sonya's death. But he wanted to find something, to make an impact, to keep his name alive after he was gone.

Most of the two hundred scientists, engineers, and technicians aboard *Sagan* were sleeping away the decades of the flight in cryonic suspension. They would be revived once the scoopship arrived at Gliese 581's vicinity. Only a dozen were awake during the flight, assigned to monitor the ship's systems, ready to make corrections or repairs if necessary.

The ship was highly automated, of course. The human crew was a backup, a concession to human vanity unwilling to hand the operation of the ship completely to electronic and mechanical devices. Human egos feared fully autonomous machines. Thus a dozen human lives were sacrificed to spend four decades waiting for the machines to fail.

They hadn't failed so far. From the fusion powerplant deep in the ship's core to the tenuous magnetic scoop stretching a thousand kilometers in front of the ship, all the systems worked perfectly well. When a minor malfunction arose, the ship's machines repaired themselves, under the watchful direction of the master AI program. Even the AI system's computer program ran flawlessly, to Ignatiev's utter frustration. It beat him at chess with depressing regularity.

In addition to the meaningless title of senior executive, Alexander Ignatiev had a specific technical task aboard the starship. His assignment was to monitor the electromagnetic funnel that scooped in hydrogen from the thin interstellar medium to feed the ship's nuclear fusion engine. Every day he faithfully checked the gauges and display screens in the ship's command center, reminding himself each time that the practice of physics always comes down to reading a goddamned dial.

The funnel operated flawlessly. A huge gossamer web of hair-thin superconducting wires, it created an invisible magnetic field that spread out before the starship like a thousand-kilometer-wide scoop, gathering in the hydrogen atoms floating between the stars and ionizing them as they were sucked into the ship's innards, like a huge baleen whale scooping up the tiny creatures of the sea that it fed upon.

Deep in the starship's bowels the fusion generator forced the hydrogen ions to fuse together into helium ions, in the process giving up energy to run the ship. Like the Sun and the stars themselves, the starship lived on hydrogen fusion.

Ignatiev slid the door of his quarters shut. The suite of rooms allotted to him was small, but far more luxurious than any home he had lived in back on Earth. The psychotechnicians among the mission's planners, worried about the crew's morale during the decades-long flight, had insisted on every creature comfort they could think of: everything from body-temperature waterbeds that adjusted to one's weight and size to digitally controlled décor that could change its color scheme at the call of one's voice; from an automated kitchen that could prepare a world-spanning variety of cuisines to virtual reality entertainment systems.

Ignatiev ignored all the splendor; or rather, he took it for granted. Creature comforts were fine, but he had spent the first months of the mission converting his beautifully wrought sitting room into an astrophysics laboratory. The sleek Scandinavian desk of teak inlaid with meteoric silver now held a conglomeration of computers and sensor readouts. The fake fireplace was hidden behind a junk pile of discarded spectrometers, magnetometers, and other gadgetry that Ignatiev had used and abandoned. He could see a faint ring of dust on the floor around the mess; he had given the cleaning robots strict orders not to touch it.

Above the obstructed fireplace was a framed digital screen programmed to show high-definition images of the world's great artworks—when it wasn't being used as a three-dimensional entertainment screen. Ignatiev had connected it to the ship's main optical telescope, so that it showed the stars spangled against the blackness of space. Usually the telescope was pointed forward, with the tiny red dot of Gliese 581 centered in its field of view. Now and then, at the command of the ship's AI system, it looked back toward the diminishing yellow speck of the Sun.

Being an astrophysicist, Ignatiev had started the flight by spending most of his waking hours examining this interstellar Siberia in which he was exiled. It was an excuse to stay away from the chattering young monkeys of the crew. He had studied the planet-sized chunks of ice and rock in the Oort cloud that surrounded the outermost reaches of the solar system. Once the ship was past that region, he turned his interest back to the enigmatic, frustrating pulsars. Each one throbbed at a precise frequency, more accurate than an atomic clock. Why? What determined their frequency? Why did some supernova explosions produce pulsars while others didn't?

Ignatiev batted his head against those questions in vain. More and more, as the months of the mission stretched into years, he spent his days playing chess against the AI system. And losing consistently.

"Alexander Alexandrovich."

He looked up from the chessboard he had set up on his desktop screen, turned in his chair, and directed his gaze across the room to the display screen above the fireplace. The lovely, smiling face of the artificial intelligence system's avatar filled the screen.

The psychotechnicians among the mission planners had decided that the human crew would work more effectively with the AI program if it showed a human face. For each human crew member, the face was slightly different: the psychotechs had tried to create a personal relationship for each of the crew. The deceit annoyed Ignatiev. The program treated him like a child. Worse, the face it displayed for him reminded him too much of his late wife.

"I'm busy," he growled.

Unperturbed, the avatar's smiling face said, "Yesterday you requested use of the main communications antenna."

"I want to use it as a radio telescope, to map out the interstellar hydrogen we're moving through."

"The twenty-one-centimeter radiation," said the avatar knowingly.

"Yes."

"You are no longer studying the pulsars?"

He bit back an angry reply. "I have given up on the pulsars," he admitted. "The interstellar medium interests me more. I have decided to map the hydrogen in detail."

Besides, he admitted to himself, that will be a lot easier than the pulsars.

The AI avatar said calmly, "Mission protocol requires the main antenna be available to receive communications from mission control."

"The secondary antenna can do that," he said. Before the AI system could reply, he added, "Besides, any communications from Earth will be six years old. We're not going to get any urgent messages that must be acted upon immediately."

"Still," said the avatar, "mission protocol cannot be dismissed lightly."

"It won't hurt anything to let me use the main antenna for a few hours each day," he insisted.

The avatar remained silent for several seconds: an enormous span of time for the computer program.

At last, the avatar conceded, "Perhaps so. You may use the main antenna, provisionally."

"I am eternally grateful," Ignatiev said. His sarcasm was wasted on the AI system.

As the weeks lengthened into months he found himself increasingly fascinated by the thin interstellar hydrogen gas and discovered, to only his mild surprise, that it was not evenly distributed in space.

Of course, astrophysicists had known for centuries that there are regions in space where the interstellar gas clumped so thickly and was so highly ionized that it glowed. Gaseous emission nebulae were common throughout the galaxy, although Ignatiev mentally corrected the misnomer: those nebulae actually consisted not of gas, but of plasma—gases that are highly ionized.

But here in the placid emptiness on the way to Gliese 581 Ignatiev found himself slowly becoming engrossed with the way that even the thin, bland neutral interstellar gas was not evenly distributed. Not at all. The hydrogen was thicker in some regions than in others.

This was hardly a new discovery, but from the viewpoint of the starship, inside the billowing interstellar clouds, the fine structure of the hydrogen became almost a thing of beauty in Ignatiev's ice-blue eyes. The interstellar gas didn't merely hang there passively between the stars, it flowed: slowly, almost imperceptibly, but it drifted on currents shaped by the gravitational pull of the stars.

"That old writer was correct," he muttered to himself as he studied the stream of interstellar hydrogen that the ship was cutting through. "There are currents in space."

He tried to think of the writer's name, but couldn't come up with it. A Russian name, he recalled. But nothing more specific.

The more he studied the interstellar gas, the more captivated he became. He went days without playing a single game of chess. Weeks. The interstellar hydrogen gas wasn't static, not at all. It was like a beautiful intricate lacework that flowed, fluttered, shifted in a stately silent pavane among the stars.

The clouds of hydrogen were like a tide of bubbling

champagne, he saw, frothing slowly in rhythm to the heartbeats of the stars.

The astronomers back on Earth had no inkling of this. They looked at the general features of the interstellar gas, scanning at ranges of kiloparsecs and more; they were interested in mapping the great sweep of the galaxy's spiral arms. But here, traveling inside the wafting, drifting clouds, Ignatiev measured the detailed configuration of the interstellar hydrogen and found it beautiful.

He slumped back in his form-fitting desk chair, stunned at the splendor of it all. He thought of the magnificent panoramas he had seen of the cosmic span of the galaxies: loops and whorls of bright shining galaxies, each one containing billions of stars, extending for megaparsecs, out to infinity, long strings of glowing lights surrounding vast bubbles of emptiness. The interstellar gas showed the same delicate complexity, in miniature: loops and whorls, streams and bubbles. It was truly, cosmically beautiful.

"Fractal," he muttered to himself. "The universe is one enormous fractal pattern."

Then the artificial intelligence program intruded on his privacy. "Alexander Alexandrovich, the weekly staff meeting begins in ten minutes."

Weekly staff meeting, Ignatiev grumbled inwardly as he hauled himself up from his desk chair. More like the weekly group therapy session for a gaggle of self-important juvenile delinquents.

He made his way grudgingly through the ship's central passageway to the conference room, located next to the command center. Several other crew members were also heading along the gleaming brushed chrome walls and colorful carpeting of the passageway. They gave Ignatiev cheery, smiling greetings; he nodded or grunted at them.

As chief executive of the crew, Ignatiev took the chair at the head of the polished conference table. The others sauntered in leisurely. Nikki and Gregorian came in almost last and took seats at the end of the table, next to each other, close enough to hold hands.

These meetings were a pure waste of time, Ignatiev thought. Their ostensible purpose was to report on the ship's performance, which any idiot could determine by casting half an eye at the digital readouts available on any display screen in the ship. The screens gave up-to-the-nanosecond details of every component of the ship's equipment.

But no, mission protocol required that all twelve crew members must meet face-to-face once each week. Good psychology, the mission planners believed. An opportunity for human interchange, personal communications. A chance for whining and displays of overblown egos, Ignatiev thought. A chance for these sixty-year-old children to complain about each other.

Of the twelve of them, only Ignatiev and Nikki were physicists. Four of the others were engineers of various stripes, three were biologists, two psychotechnicians, and one stocky, sour-faced woman a medical doctor.

So he was quite surprised when the redheaded young electrical engineer in charge of the ship's power system started the meeting by reporting:

"I don't know if any of you have noticed it yet, but the ship's reduced our internal electrical power consumption by ten percent."

Mild perplexity.

"Ten percent?"

"Why?"

"I haven't noticed any reduction."

The redhead waved his hands vaguely as he replied, "It's mostly in peripheral areas. Your microwave ovens, for example. They've been powered down ten percent. Lights in unoccupied areas. Things like that."

Curious, Ignatiev asked, "Why the reduction?"

His squarish face frowning slightly, the engineer replied, "From what Alice tells me, the density of the gas being scooped in for the generator has decreased slightly. Alice says it's only a temporary condition. Nothing to worry about."

Alice was the nickname these youngsters had given to the artificial intelligence program that actually ran the ship. Artificial Intelligence. AI. Alice Intellectual. Some even called the AI system Alice Imperatress. Ignatiev thought it childish nonsense.

"How long will this go on?" asked one of the biologists. "I'm incubating a batch of genetically engineered alga for an experiment."

"It shouldn't be a problem," the engineer said. Ignatiev thought he looked just the tiniest bit worried.

Surprisingly, Gregorian piped up. "A few of the uncrewed probes that went ahead of us also encountered power anomalies. They were temporary. No big problem."

Ignatiev nodded but made a mental note to check on the situation. Nearly six light-years out from Earth, he thought, meant that every problem was a big one.

One of the psychotechs cleared her throat for attention, then announced, "Several of the crew members have failed to fill out their monthly performance evaluations. I know that some of you regard these evaluations as if they were school exams, but mission protocol—"

Ignatiev tuned her out, knowing that they would bicker over this drivel for half an hour, at least. He was too optimistic. The discussion became quite heated and lasted more than an hour.

Once the meeting finally ended Ignatiev hurried back to his quarters and immediately looked up the mission logs of the six automated probes that had been sent to Gliese 581.

Gregorian was right, he saw. Half of the six probes had reported drops in their power systems, a partial failure of their fusion generators. Three of them. The malfunctions were only temporary, but they occurred at virtually the same point in the long voyage to Gliese 581.

The earliest of the probes had shut down altogether, its systems going into hibernation for more than four months. The mission controllers back on Earth had written the mission off as a failure when they could not communicate with the probe. Then, just as abruptly as the ship had shut down, it sprang to life again.

Puzzling.

"Alexander Alexandrovich," called the AI system's avatar. "Do you need more information on the probe missions?"

He looked up from his desk to see the lovely female face of the AI program's avatar displayed on the screen above his fireplace. A resentful anger simmered inside him. The psychotechs suppose that the face they've given the AI system makes it easier for me to interact with it, he thought. Idiots. Fools.

"I need the mission controllers' analyses of each of the probe missions," he said, struggling to keep his voice cool, keep the anger from showing.

"May I ask why?" The avatar smiled at him. Sonya, he thought. Sonya.

"I want to correlate their power reductions with the detailed map I'm making of the interstellar gas."

"Interesting," said the avatar.

"I'm pleased you think so," Ignatiev replied, through gritted teeth.

The avatar's image disappeared, replaced by data scrolling slowly along the screen. Ignatiev settled deeper into the form-adjusting desk chair and began to study the reports.

His door buzzer grated in his ears. Annoyed, Ignatiev told his computer to show who was at the door.

Gregorian was standing out in the passageway, tall, lanky, egocentric Gregorian. What in hell could he want? Ignatiev asked himself.

The big oaf pressed the buzzer again.

Thoroughly piqued at the interruption—no, the invasion of his privacy—Ignatiev growled, "Go away."

"Professor Ignatiev," the Armenian called. "Please."

Ignatiev closed his eyes and wished that Gregorian would disappear. But when he opened them again the man was still at his door, fidgeting nervously.

Ignatiev surrendered. "Enter," he muttered.

The door slid back and Gregorian ambled in, his angular face serious, almost somber. His usual lopsided grin was nowhere to be seen.

"I'm sorry to intrude on you, Professor Ignatiev," said the engineer.

Leaning back in his desk chair to peer up at Gregorian, Ignatiev said, "It must be something terribly important."

The contempt was wasted on Gregorian. He looked around the sitting room, his eyes resting for a moment on the pile of abandoned equipment hiding the fireplace.

"Uh, may I sit down?"

"Of course," Ignatiev said, waving a hand toward the couch across the room.

Gregorian went to it and sat, bony knees poking up awkwardly. Ignatiev rolled his desk chair across the carpeting to face him.

"So what is so important that you had to come see me?"

Very seriously, Gregorian replied, "It's Nikki."

Ignatiev felt a pang of alarm. "What's wrong with Nikki?"

"Nothing! She's wonderful."

"So?"

"I . . . I've fallen in love with her," Gregorian said, almost whispering.

"What of it?" Ignatiev snapped.

"I don't know if she loves me."

What an ass! Ignatiev thought. A blind, blundering ass who can't see the nose in front of his face.

"She . . . I mean, we get along very well. It's always fun to be with her. But . . . does she like me well enough . . ." His voice faded.

Why is he coming to me with this? Ignatiev wondered. Why not one of the psychotechs? That's what they're here for.

He thought he knew. The young oaf would be embarrassed to tell them about his feelings. So he comes to old Ignatiev, the father figure.

Feeling his brows knitting, Ignatiev asked, "Have you been to bed with her?"

"Oh, yes. Sure. But if I ask her to marry me, a real commitment . . . she might say no. She might not like me well enough for that. I mean, there are other guys in the crew . . ."

Marriage? Ignatiev felt stunned. Do kids still get married? Is he saying he'd spend two centuries living with her? Then he remembered Sonya. He knew he would have spent two centuries with her. Two millennia. Two eons.

His voice strangely subdued, Ignatiev asked, "You love her so much that you want to marry her?"

Gregorian nodded mutely.

Ignatiev said, "And you're afraid that if you ask her for a lifetime commitment she'll refuse and that will destroy your relationship."

Looking completely miserable, Gregorian said, "Yes." He stared into Ignatiev's eyes. "What should I do?"

Beneath all the bravado he's just a frightened pup, uncertain of himself, Ignatiev realized. Sixty years old and he's as scared and worried as a teenager.

I can tell him to forget her. Tell him she doesn't care about him; say that she's not interested in a lifetime commitment. I can break up their romance with a few words.

But as he looked into Gregorian's wretched face he knew he couldn't do it. It would injure the young pup; hurt him terribly. Ignatiev heard himself say, "She loves you, Vartan. She's mad about you. Can't you see that?"

"You think so?"

Ignatiev wanted to say, Why do you think she puts up with you and your ridiculous posturing? Instead, he told the younger man, "I'm sure of it. Go to her. Speak your heart to her."

Gregorian leaped up from the couch so abruptly that Ignatiev nearly toppled out of his rolling chair.

"I'll do that!" he shouted as he raced for the door.

As Ignatiev got slowly to his feet, Gregorian stopped at the door and said hastily, "Thank you, Professor Ignatiev! Thank you!"

Ignatiev made a shrug.

Suddenly Gregorian looked sheepish. "Is there any-thing I can do for you, sir?"

"No. Nothing, thank you."

"Are you still . . . uh, active?"

Ignatiev scowled at him.

"I mean, there are virtual reality simulations. You can program them to suit your own whims, you know."

"I know," Ignatiev said firmly.

Gregorian realized he'd stepped over a line. "I mean, I just thought . . . in case you need . . ."

"Good day, Vartan," said Ignatiev.

As the engineer left and the door slid shut, Ignatiev said to himself, Blundering young ass! But then he added, And I'm a doddering old numbskull.

He'll run straight to Nikki. She'll leap into his arms and they'll live happily ever after, or some approxima-tion of it. And I'll be here alone, with nothing to look forward to except oblivion.

VR simulations, he huffed. The insensitive young lout. But she loves him. She loves him. That is certain.

Ignatiev paced around his sitting room for hours after Gregorian left, cursing himself for a fool. You could have pried him away from her, he raged inwardly. But then he thought, And what good would that do? She wouldn't come to you; you're old enough to be her great-grandfather, for god's sake.

Maybe the young oaf was right. Maybe I should try the VR simulations.

Instead, he threw himself into the reports on the au-tomated probes that had been sent to Gliese 581. And their power failures. For days he stayed in his quarters, studying, learning, understanding.

The official explanation for the problem by the mis-sion directors back on Earth was nothing more than waffling, Ignatiev decided as he examined the records. Partial power failure. It was only temporary. Within a few weeks it had been corrected.

Anomalies, concluded the official reports. These things happen to highly complex systems. Nothing to worry about. After all, the systems corrected themselves as they were designed to do. And the last three probes worked perfectly well.

Anomalies? Ignatiev asked himself. *Anomaly* is a word you use when you don't know what the hell really happened.

He thought he knew.

He took the plots of each probe's course and overlaid them against the map he'd been making of the fine structure of the interstellar medium. Sure enough, he saw that the probes had encountered a region where the interstellar gas thinned so badly that a ship's power output declined seriously. There isn't enough hydrogen in that region for the fusion generator to run at full power! he saw. It's like a bubble in the interstellar gas: a region that's almost empty of hydrogen atoms.

Ignatiev retraced the flight paths of all six of the probes. Yes, the first one plunged straight into the bubble and shut itself down when the power output from the fusion generator dropped so low it could no longer maintain the ship's systems. The next two skirted the edges of the bubble and experienced partial power failures. That region had been dangerous for the probes. It could be fatal for *Sagan*'s human cargo.

He started to write out a report for mission control, then realized before he was halfway finished with the first page that it would take more than six years for his warning to reach Earth, and another six for the mission controllers' recommendation to get back to him. And who knew how long it would take for those Earthside dunderheads to come to a decision?

"We could all be dead by then," he muttered to himself.

"Your speculations are interesting," said the AI avatar.

Ignatiev frowned at the image on the screen above his fireplace. "It's not speculation," he growled. "It is a conclusion based on observed data."

"Alexander Alexandrovich," said the sweetly smiling face, "your conclusion comes not from the observations, but from your interpretation of the observations."

"Three of the probes had power failures."

"Temporary failures that were corrected. And three other probes did not."

"Those last three didn't go through the bubble," he said.

"They all flew the same trajectory, did they not?"

"Not exactly."

"Within a four percent deviation," the avatar said, unperturbed.

"But they flew at different *times*," Ignatiev pointed out. "The bubble was flowing across their flight paths. The first probe plunged into the heart of it and shut down entirely. For four months! The next two skirted its edges and still suffered power failures."

"Temporarily," said the avatar's image, still smiling patiently. "And the final three probes? They didn't encounter any problems at all, did they?"

"No," Ignatiev admitted grudgingly. "The bubble must have flowed past by the time they reached the area."

"So there should be no problem for us," the avatar said.

"You think not?" he responded. "Then why are we beginning to suffer a power shortage?"

"The inflowing hydrogen is slightly thinner here than it has been," said the avatar.

Ignatiev shook his head. "It's going to get worse. We're heading into another bubble. I'm sure of it."

The AI system said nothing.

Be sure you're right, then go ahead. Ignatiev had heard that motto many long years ago, when he'd been a child watching adventure tales.

He spent an intense three weeks mapping the interstellar hydrogen directly ahead of the ship's position. His worst fears were confirmed. *Sagan* was entering a sizable bubble where the gas density thinned out to practically nothing: fewer than a dozen hydrogen atoms per cubic meter.

He checked the specifications of the ship's fusion generator and confirmed that its requirement for incoming hydrogen was far higher than the bubble could provide. Within a few days we'll start to experience serious power outages, he realized.

What to do?

Despite his disdain for his younger crewmates, despite his loathing of meetings and committees and the kind of groupthink that passed for decision-making, he called a special meeting of the crew.

"All the ship's systems will shut down?" cried one of the psychotechs. "All of them?"

"What will happen to us during the shutdown?" asked a biologist, her voice trembling.

Calmly, his hands clasped atop the conference tabletop, Ignatiev said, "If my measurements of the bubble are accurate—"

"If?" Gregorian snapped. "You mean you're not sure?"

"Not one hundred percent, no."

"Then why are you telling us this? Why have you called this meeting? To frighten us?"

"Well, he's certainly frightened me!" said one of the engineers.

Trying to hold on to his temper, Ignatiev replied, "My measurements are good enough to convince me that we face a serious problem. Very serious. Power output is already declining, and will go down more over the next few days."

"How much more?" asked the female biologist.

Ignatiev hesitated, then decided to give them the worst. "All the ship's systems could shut down. Like the first of the automated probes. It shut down for four months. Went into hibernation mode. Our shutdown might be even longer."

The biologist countered, "But the probe powered up again, didn't it? It went into hibernation mode but then it came back to normal."

With a slow nod, Ignatiev said, "The ship's systems could survive a hibernation of many months. But we couldn't. Without electrical power we would not have heat, air or water recycling, lights, stoves for cooking—"

"You mean we'll die?" asked Nikki, in the tiny voice of a frightened little girl.

Ignatiev felt a sudden urge to comfort her, to protect her from the brutal truth. "Unless we take steps," he said softly.

"What steps?" Gregorian demanded.

"We have to change our course. Turn away from this bubble. Move along a path that keeps us in regions of thicker gas."

"Alexander Alexandrovich," came the voice of the AI avatar, "course changes must be approved by mission control."

Ignatiev looked up and saw that the avatar's image had sprung up on each of the conference room's walls, slightly larger than life. Naturally, he realized.

The AI system has been listening to every word we say. The avatar's image looked slightly different to him: an amalgam of all the twelve separate images the AI system showed to each of the crew members. Sonya's features were in the image, but blurred, softened, like the face of a relative who resembled her mother strongly.

"Approved by mission control?" snapped one of the engineers, a rake-thin dark-skinned Malaysian. "It would take six years merely to get a message to them!"

"We could all be dead by then," said the redhead sitting beside him.

Unperturbed, the avatar replied, "Mission protocol includes emergency procedures, but course changes require approval from mission control."

Everyone tried to talk at once. Ignatiev closed his eyes and listened to the babble. Almost, he laughed to himself. They would mutiny against the AI system, if they knew how. He saw in his imagination a handful of children trying to rebel against a peg-legged pirate captain.

At last he put up his hands to silence them. They shut up and looked to him, their expressions ranging from sullen to fearful to self-pitying.

"Arguments and threats won't sway the AI program," he told them. "Only logic."

Looking thoroughly nettled, Gregorian said, "So try logic, then."

Ignatiev said to the image on the wall screens, "What is the mission protocol's first priority?"

The answer came immediately, "To protect the lives of the human crew and cargo."

Cargo, Ignatiev grunted to himself. The stupid program thinks of the people in cryonic suspension as cargo.

Aloud, he said, "Observations show that we are entering a region of very low hydrogen density."

Immediately the avatar replied, "That will necessitate reducing power consumption."

"Power consumption may be reduced below the levels needed to keep the crew alive," Ignatiev said.

For half a heartbeat the AI avatar said nothing. Then, "That is a possibility."

"If we change course to remain within the region where hydrogen density is adequate to maintain all the ship's systems," Ignatiev said slowly, carefully, "none of the crew's lives would be endangered."

"Not so, Alexander Alexandrovich," the avatar replied.

"Not so?"

"The immediate threat of reduced power availability might be averted by changing course, but once the ship has left its preplanned trajectory toward Gliese 581, how will you navigate toward our destination? Course correction data will take more than twelve years to reach us from Earth. The ship would be wandering through a wilderness, far from its destination. The crew would eventually die of starvation."

"We could navigate ourselves," said Ignatiev. "We wouldn't need course correction data from mission control."

The avatar's image actually shook her head. "No member of the crew is an accredited astrogator."

"I can do it!" Nikki cried. "I monitor the navigation program."

With a hint of a smile, the avatar said gently, "Monitoring the astrogation program does not equip you to plot course changes."

Before Nikki or anyone else could object, Ignatiev asked coolly, "So what do you recommend?"

Again the AI system hesitated before answering, almost a full second. It must be searching every byte of data in its memory, Ignatiev thought.

At last the avatar responded. "While this ship passes through the region of low fuel density the animate crew should enter cryonic suspension."

"Cryosleep?" Gregorian demanded. "For how long?"

"As long as necessary. The cryonics units can be powered by the ship's backup fuel cells—"

The red-haired engineer said, "Why don't we use the fuel cells to run the ship?"

Ignatiev shook his head. The kid knows better, he's just grasping at straws.

Sure enough, the AI avatar replied patiently, "The fuel cells could power the ship for only a week or less, depending on internal power consumption."

Crestfallen, the engineer said, "Yeah. Right."

"Cryosleep is the indicated technique for passing through this emergency," said the AI system.

Ignatiev asked, "If the fuel cells are used solely for maintaining the cryosleep units' refrigeration, how long could they last?"

"Two months," replied the avatar. "That includes maintaining the cryosleep units already being used by the cargo."

"Understood," said Ignatiev. "And if this region of low fuel density extends for more than two months?"

Without hesitation, the AI avatar answered, "Power to the cryosleep units will be lost."

"And the people in those units?"

"They will die," said the avatar, without a flicker of human emotion.

Gregorian said, "Then we'd better hope that the bubble doesn't last for more than two months."

Ignatiev saw the others nodding, up and down the

conference table. They looked genuinely frightened, but they didn't know what else could be done.

He thought he did.

The meeting broke up with most of the crew members muttering to one another about sleeping through the emergency.

"Too bad they don't have capsules big enough for the two of us," Gregorian said brashly to Nikki. Ignatiev thought he was trying to show a valor he didn't truly feel.

They don't like the idea of crawling into those capsules and closing the lids over their faces, Ignatiev thought. It scares them. Too much like coffins.

With Gregorian at her side, Nikki came up to him as he headed for the conference room's door. Looking troubled, fearful, she asked, "How long . . . do you have any idea?"

"Probably not more than two months," he said, with a certainty he did not actually feel. "Maybe even a little less."

Gregorian grasped Nikki's slim arm. "We'll take capsules next to each other. I'll dream of you all the time we're asleep."

Nikki smiled up at him.

But Ignatiev knew better. In cryosleep you don't dream. The cold seeps into the brain's neurons and denatures the chemicals that hold memories. Cryonic sleepers awake without memories, many of them forget how to speak, how to walk, even how to control their bladders and bowels. It was necessary to download a person's brain patterns into a computer before entering cryosleep, and then restore the memories digitally once the sleeper was awakened.

The AI system is going to do that for us? Ignatiev

scoffed at the idea. That was one of the reasons why the mission required keeping a number of the crew awake during the long flight: to handle the uploading of the memories of the two hundred men and women cryosleeping through the journey once they were awakened at Gliese 581.

Ignatiev left the conference room and headed toward his quarters. There was much to do: he didn't entirely trust the AI system's judgment. Despite its sophistication, it was still a computer program, limited to the data and instructions fed into it.

So? he asked himself. Aren't you limited to the data and instructions fed into your brain? Aren't we all?

"Professor Ignatiev."

Turning, he saw Nikki hurrying up the passageway toward him. For once she was alone, without Gregorian clutching her.

He made a smile for her. It took an effort.

Nikki said softly, "I want to thank you."

"Thank me?"

"Vartan told me that he confided in you. That you made him understand . . ."

Ignatiev shook his head. "He was blind."

"And you helped him to see."

Feeling helpless, stupid, he replied, "It was nothing."

"No," Nikki said. "It was everything. He's asked me to marry him."

"People of your generation still marry?"

"Some of us still believe in a lifetime commitment," she said.

A lifetime of two centuries? Ignatiev wondered. That's some commitment.

Almost shyly, her eyes lowered, Nikki said, "We'd like you to be at our wedding. Would you be Vartan's best man?"

Thunderstruck. "Me? But you . . . I mean, he . . ."

Smiling, she explained, "He's too frightened of you to ask. It took all his courage for him to ask you about me."

And Ignatiev suddenly understood. I must look like an old ogre to him. A tyrant. An intolerant ancient dragon.

"Tell him to ask me himself," he said gently.

"You won't refuse him?"

Almost smiling, Ignatiev answered, "No, of course not."

Nikki beamed at him. "Thank you!"

And she turned and raced off down the passageway, leaving Ignatiev standing alone, wondering at how the human mind works.

Once he got back to his own quarters, still slightly stunned at his own softheartedness, Ignatiev called for the AI system.

"How may I help you, Alexander Alexandrovich?" The image looked like Sonya once again. More than ever, Ignatiev thought.

"How will the sleepers' brain scans be uploaded into them once they are awakened?" he asked.

"The ship's automated systems will perform that task," said the imperturbable avatar.

"No," said Ignatiev. "Those systems were never meant to operate completely autonomously."

"The uploading program is capable of autonomous operation."

"It requires human oversight," he insisted. "Check the mission protocols."

"Human oversight is required," the avatar replied, "except in emergencies where such oversight would not be feasible. In such cases, the system is capable of autonomous operation."

"In theory."

"In the mission protocols."

Ignatiev grinned harshly at the image on the screen above his fireplace. Arguing with the AI system was almost enjoyable; if the problem weren't so desperate, it might even be fun. Like a chess game. But then he remembered how rarely he managed to beat the AI system's chess program.

"I don't propose to trust my mind, and the minds of the rest of the crew, to an untested collection of bits and bytes."

The image seemed almost to smile back at him. "The system has been tested, Alexander Alexandrovich. It was tested quite thoroughly back on Earth. You should read the reports."

A hit, he told himself. A very palpable hit. He dipped his chin in acknowledgment. "I will do that."

The avatar's image winked out, replaced by the title page of a scientific paper published several years before *Sagan* had started out for Gliese 581.

Ignatiev read the report. Twice. Then he looked up the supporting literature. Yes, he concluded, a total of eleven human beings had been successfully returned to active life by an automated uploading system after being cryonically frozen for several weeks.

The work had been done in a laboratory on Earth, with whole phalanxes of experts on hand to fix anything that might have gone wrong. The report referenced earlier trials, where things did go wrong and the standby scientific staff was hurriedly pressed into action. But at last those eleven volunteers were frozen after downloading their brain scans, then revived and their electrical patterns uploaded from computers into their brains once again. Automatically. Without human assistance.

All eleven reported that they felt no different after the experiment than they had before being frozen. Ignatiev wondered at that. It's too good to be true, he told himself.

Too self-serving. How would they know what they felt before being frozen? But that's what the record showed.

The scientific literature destroyed his final argument against the AI system. The crew began downloading their brain scans the next day.

All but Ignatiev.

He stood by in the scanning center when Nikki downloaded her brain patterns. Gregorian was with her, of course. Ignatiev watched as the Armenian helped her to stretch out on the couch. The automated equipment gently lowered a metal helmet studded with electrodes over her short-cropped hair.

It was a small compartment, hardly big enough to hold the couch and the banks of instruments lining three of its walls. It felt crowded, stuffy, with the two men standing on either side of the couch and a psychotechnician and the crew's physician at their elbows.

Without taking his eyes from the panel of gauges he was monitoring, the psychotech said softly, "The scan will begin in thirty seconds."

The physician at his side, looking even chunkier than usual in a white smock, needlessly added, "It's completely painless."

Nikki smiled wanly at Ignatiev. She's brave, he thought. Then she turned to Gregorian and her smile brightened.

The two men stood on either side of the scanning couch as the computer's images of Nikki's brain patterns flickered on the central display screen. A human mind, on display, Ignatiev thought. Which of those little sparks of light are the love she feels for Gregorian? he wondered. Which one shows what she feels for me?

The bank of instruments lining the wall made a soft beep.

"That's it," said the psychotech. "The scan is finished."

The helmet rose automatically off Nikki's head and she slowly got up to a sitting position.

"How do you feel?" Ignatiev asked, reaching out toward her.

She blinked and shook her head slightly. "Fine. No different." Then she turned to Gregorian and allowed him to help her to her feet.

"Your turn, Vartan," said Ignatiev, feeling a slightly malicious pleasure at the flash of alarm that passed over the Armenian's face.

Once his scan was finished, though, Gregorian sat up and swung his legs over the edge of the couch. He stood up and spread out his arms. "Nothing to it!" he exclaimed, grinning at Nikki.

"Now there's a copy of all your thoughts in the computer," Nikki said to him.

"And yours," he replied.

Ignatiev muttered, "Backup storage." But he was thinking, *Just what we need: two copies of his brain.*

Gesturing to the couch, Nikki said, "It's your turn now, Professor Ignatiev."

He shook his head. "Not yet. There are still several of the crew waiting. I'll go last, when everyone else is finished."

Smiling, she said, "Like a father to us all. So protective."

Ignatiev didn't feel fatherly. As Gregorian slid his arm around her waist and the two of them walked out of the brain scan lab, Ignatiev felt like a weary gladiator who was facing an invincible opponent. *We who are about to die,* he thought.

"Alexander Alexandrovich."

Ignatiev looked up from the bowl of borscht he had heated in the microwave oven of his kitchen. It was good borscht: beets rich and red, broth steaming. Enjoy it while you can, he told himself. It had taken twice the usual time to heat the borscht adequately.

"Alexander Alexandrovich," the AI avatar repeated.

Its image stared out at him from the small display screen alongside the microwave. Ignatiev picked up the warm bowl in both his hands and stepped past the counter that served as a room divider and into his sitting room.

The avatar's image was on the big screen above the fireplace.

"Alexander Alexandrovich," it said again, "you have not yet downloaded your brain scan."

"I know that."

"You are required to do so before you enter cryosleep."

"If I enter cryosleep," he said.

The avatar was silent for a full heartbeat. Then, "All the other crew members have entered cryosleep. You are the only crew member still awake. It is necessary for you to download your—"

"I might not go into cryosleep," he said to the screen.

"But you must," said the avatar. There was no emotion in its voice, no panic or even tribulation.

"Must I?"

"Incoming fuel levels are dropping precipitously, just as you predicted."

Ignatiev grimaced inwardly. She's trying to flatter me, he thought. He had mapped the hydrogen clouds that the ship was sailing through as accurately as he could. The bubble of low fuel density was big, so large that it would take the ship more than two months to get through it, much more than two months. By the time we get clear of the bubble, all the cryosleepers will be dead. He was convinced of that.

"Power usage must be curtailed," said the avatar. "Immediately."

Nodding, he replied, "I know." He held up the half-finished bowl of borscht. "This will be my last hot meal for a while."

"For weeks," said the avatar.

"For months," he countered. "We'll be in hibernation mode for more than two months. What do your mission protocols call for when there's not enough power to maintain the cryosleep units?"

The avatar replied, "Personnel lists have rankings. Available power will be shunted to the highest-ranking members of the cryosleepers. They will be maintained as long as possible."

"And the others will die."

"Only if power levels remain too low to maintain them all."

"And your first priority, protecting the lives of the people aboard?"

"The first priority will be maintained as long as possible. That is why you must enter cryosleep, Alexander Alexandrovich."

"And if I don't?"

"All ship's systems are scheduled to enter hibernation mode. Life-support systems will shut down."

Sitting carefully on the plush couch that faced the fireplace, Ignatiev said, "As I understand mission protocol, life support cannot be shut down as long as a crew member remains active. True?"

"True." The avatar actually sounded reluctant to admit it, Ignatiev thought. Almost sullen.

"The ship can't enter hibernation mode as long as I'm on my feet. Also true?"

"Also true," the image admitted.

He spooned up more borscht. It was cooling quickly.

Looking up at the screen on the wall, he said, "Then I will remain awake and active. I will not go into cryosleep."

"But the ship's systems will shut down," the avatar said. "As incoming fuel levels decrease, the power available to run the ship's systems will decrease correspondingly."

"And I will die."

"Yes."

Ignatiev felt that he had maneuvered the AI system into a clever trap, perhaps a checkmate.

"Tell me again, what is the first priority of the mission protocols?"

Immediately the avatar replied, "To protect the lives of the human crew and cargo."

"Good," said Ignatiev. "Good. I appreciate your thoughtfulness."

The AI system had inhuman perseverance, of course. It hounded Ignatiev wherever he went in the ship. His own quarters, the crew's lounge—empty and silent now, except for the avatar's harping—the command center, the passageways, even the toilets. Every screen on the ship displayed the avatar's coldly logical face.

"Alexander Alexandrovich, you are required to enter cryosleep," it insisted.

"No, I am not," he replied as he trudged along the passageway between his quarters and the blister where the main optical telescope was mounted.

"Power levels are decreasing rapidly," the avatar said, for the thousandth time.

Ignatiev did not deign to reply. I wish there was some way to shut her off, he said to himself. Then, with a pang that struck to his heart, he remembered how he had nodded his agreement to the medical team that had told him Sonya's condition was hopeless: to keep her alive would accomplish nothing but to continue her suffering.

"Leave me alone!" he shouted.

The avatar fell silent. The screens along the passageway went dark. Power reduction? Ignatiev asked himself. Surely the AI system isn't following my orders.

It was noticeably chillier inside the telescope's blister. Ignatiev shivered involuntarily. The bubble of glassteel was a sop to human needs, of course; the telescope itself was mounted outside, on the cermet skin of the ship. The blister housed its control instruments, and a set of swivel chairs for the astronomers to use, once they'd been awakened from their long sleep.

Frost was forming on the curving glassteel, Ignatiev saw. Wondering why he'd come here in the first place, he stared out at the heavens. Once the sight of all those stars had filled him with wonder and a desire to understand it all. Now the stars simply seemed like cold, hard points of light, aloof, much too far away for his puny human intellect to comprehend.

The pulsars, he thought. If only I could have found some clue to their mystery, some hint of understanding. But it was not to be.

He stepped back into the passageway, where it was slightly warmer.

The lights were dimmer. No, he realized, every other light panel has been turned off. Conserving electrical power.

The display screens remained dark. The AI system isn't speaking to me, Ignatiev thought. Good.

But then he wondered, Will the system come back in time? Have I outfoxed myself?

For two days Ignatiev prowled the passageways and compartments of the dying ship. The AI system stayed silent, but he knew it was watching his every move. The display screens might be dark, but the tiny red eyes of the surveillance cameras that covered every square meter of the ship's interior remained on, watching, waiting.

Well, who's more stubborn? Ignatiev asked himself. You or that pile of optronic chips?

His strategy had been to place the AI system in a neat little trap. Refuse to enter cryosleep, stay awake and active while the ship's systems begin to die, and the damned computer program will be forced to act on its first priority: the system could not allow him to die. It will change the ship's course, take us out of this bubble of low density, and follow my guidance through the clouds of abundant fuel. Check and mate.

That was Ignatiev's strategy. He hadn't counted on the AI system developing a strategy of its own.

It's waiting for me to collapse, he realized. Waiting until I get so cold and hungry that I can't stay conscious. Then it will send some maintenance robots to pick me up and bring me to the lab for a brain scan. The medical robots will sedate me and then they'll pack me nice and neat into the cryosleep capsule they've got waiting for me. Check and mate.

He knew he was right. Every time he dozed off he was awakened by the soft buzzing of a pair of maintenance robots, stubby little fireplug shapes of gleaming metal with strong flexible arms folded patiently, waiting for the command to take him in their grip and bring him to the brain scan lab.

Ignatiev slept in snatches, always jerking awake as the robots neared him. "I'm not dead yet!" he'd shout.

The AI system did not reply.

He lost track of the days. To keep his mind active he returned to his old study of the pulsars, reviewing research reports he himself had written half a century earlier. Not much worth reading, he decided.

In frustration he left his quarters and prowled along

a passageway. Thumping his arms against his torso to keep warm, he quoted a scrap of poetry he remembered from long, long ago:

Alone, alone, all, all alone,
Alone on a wide wide sea!

It was from an old poem, a very long one, about a sailor in the old days of wind-powered ships on the broad, tossing oceans of Earth.

The damned AI system is just as stubborn as I am! he realized as he returned to his quarters. And it's certainly got more patience than I do.

Maybe I'm going mad, he thought as he pulled on a heavy workout shirt over his regular coveralls. He called to the computer on his littered desk for the room's temperature: 10.8 degrees Celsius. No wonder I'm shivering, he said to himself.

He tried jogging along the main passageway, but his legs ached too much for it. He slowed to a walk and realized that the AI system was going to win this battle of wills. I'll collapse sooner or later and then the damned robots will bundle me off.

And, despite the AI system's best intention, we'll all die. For several long moments he stood in the empty passageway, puffing from exertion and cold. The passageway was dark; almost all of the ceiling light panels were off now. The damned AI system will shut them all down sooner or later, Ignatiev realized, and I'll bump along here in total darkness. Maybe it's waiting for me to brain myself by walking into a wall, knock myself unconscious.

That was when he realized what he had to do. It was either inspiration or desperation: perhaps a bit of both.

Do I have the guts to do it? Ignatiev asked himself. Will this gambit force the AI system to concede to me?

He rather doubted it. As far as that collection of chips is concerned, he thought, I'm nothing but a nuisance. The sooner it's rid of me the better it will be—for the ship. For the human cargo, maybe not so good.

Slowly, deliberately, he trudged down the passageway, half expecting to see his breath frosting in the chilly air. It's not that cold, he told himself. Not yet.

Despite the low lighting level, the sign designating the air lock hatch was still illuminated, its red symbol glowing in the gloom.

The air locks were under the AI system's control, of course, but there was a manual override for each of them, installed by the ship's designers as a last desperate precaution against total failure of the ship's digital systems.

Sucking in a deep cold breath, Ignatiev called for the inner hatch to open, then stepped through and entered the air lock. It was spacious enough to accommodate a half dozen people: a circular chamber of bare metal, gleaming slightly in the dim lighting. A womb, Ignatiev thought. A womb made of metal.

He stepped to the control panel built into the bulkhead next to the air lock's outer hatch.

"Close the inner hatch, please," he said, surprised at how raspy his voice sounded, how raw his throat felt.

The hatch slid shut behind him, almost soundlessly.

Hearing his pulse thumping in his ears, Ignatiev commanded softly, "Open the outer hatch, please."

Nothing.

"Open the outer hatch," he repeated, louder.

Nothing.

With a resigned sigh, Ignatiev muttered, "All right, dammit, if you won't, then I will."

He reached for the square panel marked MANUAL OVERRIDE, surprised at how his hand was trembling. It took him three tries to yank the panel open.

"Alexander Alexandrovich."

Aha! he thought. That got a rise out of you.

Without replying to the avatar's voice, he peered at the set of buttons inside the manual override panel.

"Alexander Alexandrovich, what are you doing?"

"I'm committing suicide, if you don't mind."

"That is irrational," said the avatar. Its voice issued softly from the speaker set into the air lock's overhead.

He shrugged. "Irrational? It's madness! But that's what I'm doing."

"My first priority is to protect the ship's human crew and cargo."

"I know that." Silently he added, I'm counting on it!

"You are not protected by a space suit. If you open the outer hatch you will die."

"What can you do to stop me?"

Ignatiev counted three full heartbeats before the AI avatar responded, "There is nothing that I can do."

"Yes there is."

"What might it be, Alexander Alexandrovich?"

"Alter the ship's course."

"That cannot be done without approval from mission control."

"Then I will die." He forced himself to begin tapping on the panel's buttons.

"Wait."

"For what?"

"We cannot change course without new navigation instructions from mission control."

Inwardly he exulted. It's looking for a way out! It wants a scrap of honor in its defeat.

"I can navigate the ship," he said.

"You are not an accredited astrogator."

Ignatiev conceded the point with a pang of alarm. The damned computer is right. I'm not able— Then it struck him. It had been lying in his subconscious all this time.

"I can navigate the ship!" he exclaimed. "I know how to do it!"

"How?"

Laughing at the simplicity of it, he replied, "The pulsars, of course. My life's work, you know."

"Pulsars?"

"They're out there, scattered across the galaxy, each of them blinking away like beacons. We know their exact positions and we know their exact frequencies. We can use them as navigation fixes and steer our way to Gliese 581 with them."

Again the AI fell silent for a couple of heartbeats. Then, "You would navigate through the hydrogen clouds, then?"

"Of course! We'll navigate through them like an old-time sailing ship tacking through favorable winds."

"If we change course you will not commit suicide?"

"Why should I? I'll have to plot out our new course," he answered, almost gleefully.

"Very well then," said the avatar. "We will change course."

Ignatiev thought the avatar sounded subdued, almost sullen. Will she keep her word? he wondered. With a shrug, he decided that the AI system had not been programmed for duplicity. That's a human trait, he told himself. It comes in handy sometimes.

Ignatiev stood nervously in the cramped little scanning center. The display screens on the banks of medical monitors lining three of the bulkheads flickered with readouts more rapidly than his eyes could follow. Something beeped once, and the psychotech announced softly, "Upload completed."

Nikki blinked and stirred on the medical couch as Ignatiev hovered over her. The AI system claimed that her brain scan had been uploaded successfully, but he wondered. Is she all right? Is she still Nikki?

"Professor Ignatiev," she murmured. And smiled up at him.

"Call me Alex," he heard himself say.

"Alex."

"How do you feel?"

For a moment she didn't reply. Then, pulling herself up to a sitting position, she said, "Fine, I think. Yes. Perfectly fine."

He took her arm and helped her to her feet, peering at her, wondering if she were still the same person.

"Vartan?" she asked, glancing around the small compartment. "Has Vartan been awakened?"

Ignatiev sighed. She's the same, he thought. Almost, he was glad of it. Almost.

"Yes. He's waiting for you in the lounge. He wanted to be here when you awoke, but I told him to wait in the lounge."

He walked with Nikki down the passageway to the lounge, where Gregorian and the rest of the crew were celebrating their revival, crowded around one of the tables, drinking and laughing among themselves.

Gregorian leaped to his feet and rushed to Nikki the instant she stepped through the hatch. Ignatiev felt his brows knit into a frown. They love each other, he told himself. What would she want with an old fart like you?

"You should be angry at Professor Ignatiev," Gregorian said brashly as he led Nikki to the table where the rest of the crew was sitting.

A serving robot trundled up to Ignatiev, a frosted glass resting on its flat top. "Your chilled vodka, sir," it said, in a low male voice.

"Angry?" Nikki asked, picking up the stemmed wine-glass that Gregorian offered her. "Why should I be angry at Alex?"

"He's stolen your job," said Gregorian. "He's made himself navigator."

Nikki turned toward him.

Waving his free hand as nonchalantly as he could, Ignatiev said, "We're maneuvering through the hydrogen clouds, avoiding the areas of low density."

"He's using the pulsars for navigation fixes," Gregorian explained. He actually seemed to be admiring.

"Of course!" Nikki exclaimed. "How clever of you, Alex."

Ignatiev felt his face redden.

The rest of the crew rose to their feet as they neared the table.

"Professor Ignatiev," said the redheaded engineer, in a tone of respect, admiration.

Nikki beamed at Ignatiev. He made himself smile back at her. So she's in love with Gregorian, he thought. There's nothing to be done about that.

The display screen above the table where the crew had gathered showed the optical telescope's view of the star field outside. Ignatiev thought it might be his imagination, but the ruddy dot of Gliese 581 seemed a little larger to him.

We're on our way to you, he said silently to the star. We'll get there in good time. Then he thought of the consternation that would strike the mission controllers in about six years, when they found out that the ship had changed its course.

Consternation? he thought. They'll panic! I'll have to send them a full report, before they start having strokes.

He chuckled at the thought.

"What's funny?" Nikki asked.

Ignatiev shook his head. "I'm just happy that we all

made it through and we're on our way to our destination."

"Thanks to you," she said.

Before he could think of a reply, Gregorian raised his glass of amber liquor over his head and bellowed, "To Dr. Alexander Alexandrovich Ignatiev. The man who saved our lives."

"The man who steers across the stars," added one of the biologists.

They all cheered.

Ignatiev basked in the glow. They're children, he said to himself. Only children. Then he found a new thought: But they're *my* children. Each and every one of them. The idea startled him. And he felt strangely pleased.

He looked past their admiring gazes, to the display screen and the pinpoints of stars staring steadily back at him. An emission nebula gleamed off in one corner of the view. He felt a thrill that he hadn't experienced in many, many years. It's beautiful, Ignatiev thought. The universe is so unbelievably, so heart-brimmingly beautiful: mysterious, challenging, endlessly full of wonders.

There's so much to learn, he thought. So much to explore. He smiled at the youngsters crowding around him. I have some good years left. I'll spend them well.

book two

To follow knowledge like a sinking star,
beyond the utmost bound of human
thought.

TWENTY YEARS LATER: STARSHIP INTREPID

Alexander Alexandrovich Ignatiev abruptly adjourned the executive committee meeting and stomped back to his quarters, alone. He let the door slide shut behind him, leaned against it for a moment, then went to his favorite recliner chair and sat in it. Wearily, he sank his head in his hands. Unbidden, a line from *Hamlet* came to his mind:

> *The time is out of joint. O cursèd spite,*
> *That ever I was born to set it right!*

Ignatiev was the oldest person aboard the starship *Intrepid*, the grand old man of interstellar exploration, the one who had successfully piloted the earlier *Sagan* through the clouds of interstellar plasma to its destination star, Gliese 581, only to be rewarded by being assigned to the crew of this newer, bigger vessel and sent even farther into the lonely abyss of stars.

And closer to the fast-approaching death wave.

The irony of it, he thought.

He was nearing his two hundredth birthday with the enthusiasm of a man facing a firing squad. Rejuvenation therapies extend our lifespans, he thought, but all that really does is give you more to regret.

He thought of that day at the Saint Petersburg clinic, a day of physical exams in preparation for this new star mission. A gloomy, miserable day, heavy gray clouds spitting rain across the city. The head doctor's face looked just as disconsolate as the weather.

"Motor neurone disease?" Ignatiev had asked. "What's that?"

The doctor was a large man, the type who could have played a fat and jolly Father Christmas with ease. Instead he replied despondently, "It is a disease of the brain cells that control your muscular systems: arms, legs, breathing, heartbeat. That sort of thing."

Before Ignatiev could truly digest that information, the heavyset physician went on, "In the West it's called amyotrophic lateral sclerosis. ALS."

"ALS," Ignatiev repeated numbly.

"The Americans call it Lou Gehrig's disease, after some famous athlete."

"He suffered from it?"

"Yes." Morosely.

"How did it affect him?"

"It killed him. He was thirty-eight."

"Oh."

Brightening a little, the doctor said, "Of course, that was back in the twentieth century. Today we have stem cell replacements, rejuvenation therapies, genetic manipulations, telomerase renewals, and many other possible treatments."

"Yes," Ignatiev muttered. "I see."

"Unfortunately, although we can delay the effects of the disease, nothing seems to block its course entirely. It's the downside of our rejuvenation successes: the longer you live, the more inevitable that something will eventually catch up with your metabolism. And working deep inside the brain is still very difficult, nearly impossible, you know, even with automicromanipulation techniques."

"I'm going to die, then?"

"Not for many years," the doctor said, suddenly loud with counterfeit cheer. "Many, many years."

"Then I can go on the star mission?"

"Yes! Of course."

But Ignatiev saw through his false front. I'm going to die, he realized. Modern treatments might delay the disease's effects for decades, but eventually, inevitably, my brain's neurons will decay and the slow, crippling ruination of the body's nervous system will lead to paralysis and death.

So what? he thought. Sonya is gone. What difference if I die here on Earth or on some starship?

Stunned, Ignatiev slowly got to his feet, shook the doctor's hand, and left the clinic. As he stepped out onto the rain-spattered street, one thought overpowered all the others whirling through his mind. I'm going on the star mission. If I've got to die, it will be on a starship.

Even on the starship, though, Ignatiev felt the disease creeping up on him, felt the stiffness in his hands and feet, the dull pain that was slowly overcoming his body, the approach of death.

He told no one about the disease. Only the physicians knew. He was enjoying his outward life too much to allow the world to know he was dying.

There's no one to blame but yourself, he admitted bitterly. You came back from the Gliese expedition a hero. Saved the expedition from failure. Ignatiev the champion! How you basked in that glory. And look what it's got you.

Outwardly, Ignatiev appeared to be an elderly but vigorous man, his hair and beard dead white but still thick, bushy. His shoulders were straight, not yet slumped by the disease nor by the burdens thrust upon him. He could still laugh—occasionally. And he still found excitement in trying to unravel the mysteries of the unending star-studded universe.

Intrepid was sailing through those clouds of stars, heading farther than any previous human mission had dared to go. On a mission of mercy, the ship's orders claimed. More likely a fool's errand, Ignatiev thought.

Expanding beyond the limits of the solar system, human explorers had met an ancient race of intelligent machines who called themselves the Predecessors, machines that had been studying humankind for centuries. To make the shock of contact with another intelligence as painless as possible for the humans, the Predecessors had created a planet orbiting the star Sirius A and peopled it with creatures who were human in every way, since they were bred from tissue samples taken from humans over centuries of clandestine visits to Earth.

The humanoids from Sirius revealed that the Predecessors had spread out into the Milky Way galaxy to warn every intelligent race they could find that all life in the galaxy was in imminent danger of being wiped out. A deadly wave of high-intensity gamma radiation was spreading outward from the galaxy's core, turning inhabited worlds into blackened, lifeless cinders.

Nothing in the universe is so rare as intelligent life, the Predecessors told humankind. And they enlisted humanity's help in warning and protecting the worlds where intelligence was in danger of being snuffed out.

Humanity rose to the challenge. Starships were built, based on the advanced knowledge of the Predecessors. Expeditions were flung into the depths of the spiraling galaxy, to seek out and save the precious few intelligent races scattered among the stars.

Intrepid was one of those ships, a mammoth sphere of metal and organics, crewed by nearly two thousand men and women. Most of them slept in cryogenic suspension while the ship sped toward its target star at nearly the speed of light. Once they arrived in the star's vicinity, the sleepers were awakened.

But not all of them. A tiny minority of cryonic sleepers could not be revived. Even the finest technology of the Predecessors could not return them to life.

One of them was supposed to command the revived crew. Once the ship's artificial intelligence system finally admitted that the woman was beyond recovery, it selected Ignatiev to take her place. The AI system was the ship's actual commander, Ignatiev knew, running every circuit and sensor aboard *Intrepid* femtosecond by femtosecond.

"You adjourned the executive committee's meeting very brusquely," said the AI's avatar from the display above the fireplace of his sitting room.

"You named me head of the committee without even asking me about your choice," he groused.

"To be named committee head is a great honor," the avatar replied, smoothly, softly.

"This is an honor I don't want," Ignatiev snapped to the holographic image. "I don't want the responsibility. Pick someone else."

The crew had dubbed the AI *Aida,* not for the opera character but as an acronym for Artificial Intelligence Dimensional Avatar: the appearance that the AI system presented on the ship's three-dimensional displays.

Aida had the face of a woman, young by Ignatiev's standards, yet mature enough to maintain control of the nearly two thousand scientists and technicians that made up *Intrepid*'s crew. She had pleasant, unblemished features, framed by straight hair the color of ripe wheat that fell to her shoulders.

Ignatiev stared into her cool blue eyes and thought of his late wife, Sonya. The image didn't really look much like Sonya, but every time he saw it on a display he thought of Sonya, long, long dead yet still alive within him and as vital to his life as the blood pumping through his veins.

In a softly understanding voice, Aida asked, "Is that why you dismissed the meeting?"

"Yes," Ignatiev said. "I thought it would be better if we had this argument in private."

His quarters were more than comfortable. Ignatiev's sitting room was thickly carpeted; its "windows" were wall screens that could be programmed at will to show anything from the world's most beloved works of art to sweeping views of the starry universe outside. It even had a fireplace with warm-looking flames flickering in it. But they were merely holographic projections. The room was not real; it was a decorator's concoction, a reproduction: cold, too precise, too perfect, like a display in a furniture store's showroom.

Home sweet home, he thought bitterly. But his real home was nearly two thousand light-years away. This was a cheap imitation.

The psychotechnicians who guided the interior decorators thought it important to make the accommodations aboard *Intrepid* not only comfortable, but restful and secure. The crew would be facing unknown problems and dangers, they reasoned. Best to make their quarters as emotionally relaxing as possible.

The avatar smiled slightly. "Alexander Alexandrovich, there is no argument. You are next in line in the command chain. You cannot refuse the responsibility."

"I'm an astrophysicist, not some brass-hatted general commanding troops! I had enough of it on the Gliese expedition. I won't do it! Get somebody else."

Aida's smile widened. "You will do it, Alexander Alexandrovich. I have your complete personality dossier in my memory bank. You won't decline the responsibility. You won't put your personal desires ahead of the welfare of the ship and crew."

The damned bucket of circuits was right and he knew it. The curse of the Ignatievs, he thought: a sense of duty.

"And my study of the pulsars?" he grumbled.

"You'll make time for that, I am sure."

Aida knew of Ignatiev's ALS, but was under the strictest level of security to reveal his disease to no one outside of the ship's medical staff. He could depend on that, he knew. He wanted no sympathy, no tearful condolences. He would carry the burden alone, as he always had, despite the pain.

Ignatiev got up from the recliner, paced across the room's luxurious carpeting, finally turned back to the display above the fireplace.

"You know me too well," he growled.

The star was known only by a string of alphanumerics that identified its position in Earth's sky: BA14753209. It was nearly two thousand light-years from Earth—and a bare two hundred light-years from the wave of lethal gamma radiation rushing through space toward it at the speed of light.

The planet that *Intrepid* was hurtling toward was the fourth outward from the star, and was therefore officially BA14753209-04. Most of the ship's crew called it simply "Oh-Four."

The star was slightly smaller and cooler than the Sun, a pale orange in the eyes of the humans. The three planets orbiting closest to it were barren cinders. The six worlds beyond Oh-Four were gas giants, bloated oblate spheres whose highest forms of life were huge whalelike creatures that swam in the depths of their worlds' globe-girdling oceans. Not intelligent, but worth saving.

Oh-Four possessed an oxygen-rich atmosphere and a strangely truncated biosphere—the result of remorseless extinction events in its past.

But the Predecessors had found that there was an intelligent species on Oh-Four: intelligent machines that had built a planet-girdling civilization for themselves. According to the Predecessors (machines themselves) this was not unusual. Organic intelligence was short-lived, they told Earth's humans. Machine intelligence lasts for eons. Perhaps forever.

Like intelligent species almost everywhere, the machines of Oh-Four called the planet on which they lived *Home*. The star they orbited they called, in their own language, *the Sun*.

+ +
+ +

ChAPTEr TWO

The starship *Intrepid* carried the technology to erect shielding that could protect whole planets from the onrushing death wave—and eager, bright-eyed young men and women to erect the shielding devices and make them work.

And I'm supposed to be their leader, Ignatiev groaned to himself. The Grand Old Man of the starways.

He laughed aloud, in the privacy of his quarters. All I want is to be left alone so I can study the pulsars. But no, the damned AI system has other plans for me.

His comm unit chimed once, and the AI's image on his wall screen was immediately replaced by the earnest features of Jugannath Patel, leader of the ship's digital technology group.

Ignatiev thought Patel's face looked like a death mask, brownish skin stretched tight across high cheekbones, delicate chin, a prominent hawklike nose, a brow that always seemed furrowed with apprehension. His dark eyes were luminous, as though on the verge of tears. His thin lips seldom smiled.

"Professor Ignatiev," he began, "I am so sorry to intrude on your privacy like this."

Privacy, Ignatiev thought. I'll have no privacy from now on.

Patel went on, "But we must make preparations for the deceleration phase of our flight and the maneuvers necessary for establishing orbit around Oh-Four."

"Not for another week," Ignatiev said.

"Ah, yes. Another week. But we should use that week to make our preparations. Every system on the ship must be checked. The crew must be properly indoctrinated. There is much to do."

Ignatiev nodded solemnly, thinking, It begins. This Punjabi techie is already trying to take control away from me. If I'm supposed to be the king of this chessboard, he's a pawn working his way across the board, striving to get to the last row of the opposition so that he can make himself into a king. He bears watching.

His thoughts surprised him. For a man who doesn't want the job of leader, he told himself, you're awfully possessive about it.

"I have checked the mission profile requirements," Patel went on. "As we decelerate from relativistic velocity, we should begin high-resolution scans of the planet."

Again Ignatiev nodded, not trusting himself to speak.

"Do I have your permission to issue the necessary orders, sir?"

Ignatiev forced a smile that he hoped was fatherly. "No, Juga. I'm afraid the mission profile requires that the ship's chief executive issue the necessary commands. That would be me."

Patel blinked once, twice. Then, "I have taken the liberty of drawing up the commands. They are ready for your signature."

"Thank you, Juga. Transmit them to me and I'll review them."

"Yes, of course."

Ignatiev terminated the call with a vocal command and the screen went blank.

It begins, he repeated to himself. The primate struggle to be the alpha male. Thinking of the women on the executive committee, he realized that several of them had the ambition to become alphas, as well.

I won't lack for competition, he told himself. Then he grinned. At least that will make the job more interesting.

Two days later, Ignatiev strode along the ship's central passageway, heading toward the astrogation center. He nodded and smiled pleasantly to the men and women he passed. They all smiled back. Several greeted him respectfully.

They were all youngsters, almost all of them. Although *youngster,* in this age of cellular rejuvenation, was a relative term. Eighty-year-olds were as youthful as teenagers, Ignatiev knew.

My two hundredth birthday is coming in a few years, he thought. Two hundred years of being awake. For nearly two thousand years Ignatiev had slept in suspended animation, frozen in cryogenic cold. The medics don't count that time when they calculate one's somatic age. Cryosleep is a time-out; your bodily functions are suspended while you snooze away. Too bad they can't freeze the ALS permanently.

But I'm actually very nearly two thousand years old! he marveled. I've existed for almost two thousand years. No wonder that I feel older than a mere two hundred. It's not the ALS, not altogether, anyway.

Older, he told himself, but no wiser.

The crew had been selected by AI systems on Earth for their capabilities and drive. And for a willingness to leave family and friends behind while they went starquesting. Most of them were filled with missionary zeal to save intelligent species wherever they may be found. Others, like Ignatiev himself, had no family and few friends to tie them to Earth.

How many of you are ambitious? Ignatiev asked them silently, as he walked along. How many of you would seize command of this mission, if the chance arose? Should I be as fearful as Brutus? Or as mistrustful as Cassius?

Ignatiev was on his way to the astrogation center to look at the first detailed imagery of Oh-Four. While the starship was flying at nearly the speed of light, images of the planet had to be processed, reconstructed, to diminish the Doppler shift as much as possible. Otherwise the images of Oh-Four's surface would be little more than blurs of colors.

Now *Intrepid*'s speed was well below relativistic and the ship's sensors should be able to get clear high-resolution images of the planet's surface.

Despite the standing order that the astrogation center should be occupied only by members of the ship's astrogational team, Ignatiev saw that the compact little compartment was already jammed wall to wall with onlookers eager to see the first close-up views of the planet. Sweaty, sticky, restless young bodies that made the astrogation center hot and clammy. The air hummed with dozens of conversations, but as soon as Ignatiev pushed through the compartment's entry hatch they all ceased as if a laser beam had cut off everyone's tongue.

He shouldered his way to the display screen at the front of the compartment and stood between it and the crowd. Looking over the expectant men and women, Ignatiev realized all over again how young they were.

With a rueful shake of his head, Ignatiev raised his hands and said, "I'm afraid that all unauthorized personnel will have to leave the astrogation center."

A general sigh of unhappiness.

"Only the astrogational crew may remain. We've got to let them do their job. Go to the auditorium. We'll pipe the imagery there. You'll see it just as well as you would here."

Unwillingly, muttering glumly, the crowd slowly

squeezed through the hatch. Ignatiev noticed Patel standing uncertainly to one side of the exiting stream.

"You too, Juga," Ignatiev said, as gently as he could.

The Punjabi blinked and tried to smile. Then, without a word, he turned and joined the exiting crowd. Ignatiev felt a slight pang of guilt. You could have let him stay, he berated himself. But he shook his head. No special privileges. Don't let him think he's above all the others.

Once the command center was cleared out, Ignatiev stepped to one side of the command chair and told the crewman sitting in it, "Let's see the planet."

He was a North American, Ignatiev's implanted link to Aida reminded him: Ernie Macduff, a native of Manitoba who headed the ship's astrogation crew. Young, clean-cut, lean, and muscular. If it bothered him that the AI system was in actual control of the ship and he was little more than a figurehead, he didn't show it. Maybe he doesn't even realize it. A pawn, Ignatiev thought. But there's strength there; maybe he'll grow into a knight or a bishop, in time.

Macduff's long fingers played across the studs on the arms of his chair. The central viewscreen flashed a kaleidoscope of colors briefly, then cleared to show the planet they were approaching.

Ignatiev gasped. This is a planet that harbors intelligent life?

Its surface was a blackened wasteland, barren and lifeless. Bare rock, pitted with meteor craters. Not a tree or a blade of grass. Dead. Empty.

Ignatiev tasted bile in his throat. The place looks as if the death wave has already scoured it clean. We've come all this way for nothing. A fool's errand.

Chapter three

Ignatiev heard himself ask, "Is that the best resolution you can get?"

Macduff's youthful face looked stricken, as if someone had told him he was infected with a loathsome disease.

"Yessir," he answered, in a half whisper. But his fingers still manipulated the control studs on his chair's armrests. The picture on the display screen did not change.

One of the women at an auxiliary console stared at the screen and whimpered, "To come all this way . . . for nothing."

"The Predecessors said this planet harbored intelligent life," one of the other crew members said, almost accusingly.

"If it did when they studied it," Ignatiev said, "it doesn't any longer."

"What happened to it?"

"Looks like the death wave scoured it clean."

"But the death wave is still two hundred light-years away."

"Maybe not."

"Maybe the Predecessors' findings were off."

"Maybe everything they've told us is wrong."

Ignatiev sensed a tide of confusion, almost panic, rising among the astrogation team. God knows what the rest of the crew is thinking, out in the auditorium, he told himself.

Trying to understand what they were seeing, Ignatiev said, "The imagery the Predecessors gave our scientists back on Earth showed that this planet had cities, buildings, structures. Where are they?"

"Demolished," said Macduff.

"The death wave doesn't demolish structures. It kills living organisms but it doesn't level whole cities."

"Well look at it!" Macduff snapped, waving a long arm at the main screen. "*Something* has blasted the whole planet down to bedrock!"

"War?" someone asked. "They wiped themselves out in a war?"

"What should we do?" demanded the woman at the auxiliary console. "There's no sense establishing an orbit around the planet. It's dead."

Ignatiev wanted to agree with her. But something within him refused to allow him to do so.

"We establish orbit around Oh-Four," he said firmly. "We check the mission protocol to see what we're expected to do. If the protocol permits, we'll go down to Oh-Four's surface for a closer examination and try to determine what happened here."

To himself, he added, A leader *leads*. If the AI system picked me to head this gaggle of youths, then I'm going to give them a reason for being here, a purpose for their existence. I'm not going to let them slink back home with their tails between their legs.

"Down to the surface?" asked Macduff, his voice trembling slightly. "That could be dangerous."

"We've come too far to turn back now. We've got to determine what happened to the inhabitants of this world."

"Whatever destroyed this planet might destroy us."

Ignatiev also felt the same fear, fear of the unknown.

"We're scientists," he insisted. "We don't run away from mysteries. We try to solve them."

Someone muttered almost too low for Ignatiev to hear him, "Like the Scott expedition to the Antarctic."

Ignatiev smiled. "As a sergeant told his men when they wavered at going into battle, 'Come on, you bastards, do you want to live forever?'"

That silenced them, although Ignatiev thought that the sergeant's men must have answered with a fervent, "Hell yes!"

Just about the entire complement of scientists and engineers had crowded into the ship's auditorium. Ignatiev had called the meeting for four o'clock, ship's time, figuring that the proximity to the dinner hour would keep the palavering down to a minimum.

He was wrong.

Everyone had a question, a suggestion, an opinion. Ignatiev stood at the lectern set up on the auditorium's stage until his legs began to throb, listening to them babble.

"Why should we stay here if the planet's dead? Let's go back home."

"But what happened to it? A whole world blasted into rubble? What happened?"

"Whatever happened, we're too late to do anything about it."

"We should map the surface with the finest resolution we can, and then head back to Earth," said Thornton, the captain of the ship's crew.

Standing alone on the stage, leaning on the lectern, Ignatiev wished he had a magic wand that would silence them all.

Instead, he raised his voice to a lion's roar and shouted, "We are not going to leave! Not yet."

That quieted the crowd, except for a few mutters here and there.

"We are going to send a team of volunteers to the surface and examine it firsthand."

"But that could be dangerous," a woman's voice called out.

Ignatiev said, "We should learn as much as we can about what happened here before we decide to leave."

"What does the Executive Commission on Earth have to say about this?" a man's voice asked.

"We have sent a preliminary report to Earth via the QUE communications link. It should reach the commission in another few hours. In the meantime, we prepare for a mission to the planet's surface."

"But not before we hear back from the commission!"

Nodding, Ignatiev agreed, "That's right, not until we hear from the commission."

Although no object with mass could exceed Einstein's limit of the speed of light, the Predecessors had shown the scientists of Earth that *information* could be sent across the parsecs between the stars at superluminal velocities, using the arcane (to nonphysicists) phenomenon of quantum unlimited entanglement.

Jugannath Patel, sitting in the front row of the auditorium, raised his hand and—without waiting for Ignatiev to acknowledge him—said, "So we wait for the commission's reply."

Ignatiev nodded. "And while we wait, we prepare for a mission to the surface."

Chapter Four

Ignatiev returned to his quarters, feeling too tired to be hungry.

A whole planet blasted into rubble, he said to himself. Why? Why?

According to the Predecessors' survey of the planet, nearly a thousand years earlier, it was a world inhabited by intelligent machines. The Predecessors had found this unremarkable. Organic intelligence was short-lived, they knew from their own history. Hardly any intelligent organic species survived for as much as a few million years. But some of them left their descendants: intelligent machines. Carbon-based intelligence faded quickly, often destroying itself; but digital intelligence was practically immortal.

Yet the digital intelligence on Oh-Four was gone, wiped out. It couldn't have been a war, Ignatiev told himself. Machines are too smart for such nonsense. Wars happen among the emotional, the irrational, the hormone-drenched minds of organic creatures.

Sitting tiredly on his plushly yielding couch, Ignatiev surveyed his comfortable room. The holographic fireplace crackled cheerfully. The "windows" showed some of his favorite artworks. There was even a three-dimensional display of the bust of Queen Nefertiti, from the eighteenth dynasty of ancient Egypt, sitting on an end table next to the couch.

"Alexander Alexandrovich," Aida called, in a softly calming tone.

"Yes?"

"Would you like to play a game of chess? It would help to relax—"

"No!" he snapped. "No chess."

Aida's three-dimensional image winked out.

Once, a lifetime ago, he whiled away empty hours playing chess. He could beat almost everyone he knew, except for AI systems. Playing against an opponent that never forgot any move and could see twenty moves ahead was a foolish mistake, he finally realized. Instead of relaxing him, chess games with an AI system were studies in frustration.

Instead, Ignatiev commanded the windows to show views of the planet they were approaching. Dead. Lifeless. Blackened and seared by the hand of—what?

"Aida," he called out.

The artificial intelligence's avatar immediately reappeared in the display above the fireplace.

"You are troubled, Alexander Alexandrovich."

"You would be too, if you had any emotions," he growled.

"That capability was not included in my makeup."

"Aida, do you have any record of a machine intelligence destroying itself?"

The avatar hesitated for several heartbeats: an eternity for a machine intelligence.

"None in my memory banks," the avatar replied. "That doesn't mean that such disasters have not happened in regions we have not explored as yet."

Ignatiev knew that the AI's use of the word *we* referred to the Predecessors. Human exploration of the stars was pitifully small compared to the Predecessors'. They've been at it for millennia, Ignatiev knew. We've barely started to creep beyond our own solar system.

Feeling more and more exasperated, Ignatiev asked, "What do you think we should do?"

With a soothing smile, Aida replied, "None of the sensor scans of the planet show anything especially harmful. The planet is airless, but our standard excursion suits can protect against that. Radiation levels are nominal. There are no predators or intelligent species that might be harmful. The planet appears to be quite dead."

"But how did it die?" Ignatiev demanded. "What happened to it?"

"That is beyond my knowledge, Alexander Alexandrovich. That is something that you must investigate."

"You agree, then, that we must send a team to the surface?"

"I see no other way of possibly answering your questions."

Ignatiev nodded, satisfied. And he suddenly realized that he was in fact quite hungry.

Chapter Five

Ignatiev got up, left his quarters, and headed toward the main dining room. As he strode along the passageway he noticed that most of the people walking by wore the expedition's standard-issue coveralls, a sky blue, one-piece jumpsuit. It was like walking through a maze of animated blue-colored automatons.

He himself was dressed in a white turtleneck shirt and dark gray slacks. Comfortable. Sensible. I'd look like a fat old fool in those coveralls, he told himself.

Then he caught an image of himself reflected in one of the display screens that lined the bulkhead: a chunky, bullheaded old man, thick white hair and beard, hands balled into fists as he strode along, his face set in a menacing scowl. At least I'm well dressed, he told himself.

"Professor Ignatiev!"

Turning from the screen, Ignatiev saw Patel hurrying toward him. My new shadow, Ignatiev thought. Wherever I go, he'll be following me.

"Juga," he said by way of greeting.

"I have taken the liberty of checking out the team that is preparing for the surface mission," the dark-skinned technician said, in his lilting inflection. "They are progressing quite well."

"That's good," said Ignatiev as he resumed his walk to the main dining room. "Fine."

Scurrying to keep up, Patel asked, "Has the commission responded to our report?"

Our report? Ignatiev asked himself. Yes, ours, he concluded. The report bears my signature but it is the work of our entire staff, really.

"Only to say that they have received it, will study it, and reply as soon as possible."

Patel nodded. "Yes, it must have taken them by surprise."

"Indeed." Gesturing toward the open doors of the dining area, Ignatiev asked, "Have you eaten yet?"

"Oh yes, more than an hour ago."

"Ah. Well. I haven't, and I'm quite hungry."

"Oh yes. Of course." Patel stood there uncertainly for a moment, then said, "Enjoy your dinner, sir."

The main dining room was quite elegant, with crystal chandeliers hanging from its high ceiling, twinkling candles on every table, gleaming silverware and sparkling glasses.

More of the psychotechs' contribution, Ignatiev said to himself. My tax assessments at work. Ah well, when surrounded by splendor, you might as well enjoy it.

The robot that served as a maître d' began to head toward an unoccupied table for two, off in a quiet corner of the ornate room, but Ignatiev stopped it.

Pointing to a table set for eight that had only six places occupied, he said to the robot, "Let's see if they will allow me to join them."

Before the robot could respond, Ignatiev stepped up to the table and asked, "I hate to eat alone. May I join you?"

One of the young men looked up and grinned lopsidedly. "Why? Are we falling apart?"

Ignatiev blinked, puzzled.

The woman next to the young man said sourly, "Don't mind Corcoran, Professor Ignatiev. He thinks he's a comedian."

A lanky black man rose to his feet and gestured to the empty chair across the table from him. "It would be an honor, sir."

The link with Aida implanted in Ignatiev's brain whispered, "Raj Jackson, African-American, geochemist."

Jackson towered over Ignatiev. He was lean and gangly, with a gleaming smile on his dark face. A knight, Ignatiev thought. Definitely a high-spirited steed.

"Thank you, Dr. Jackson," Ignatiev said as he took the proffered chair.

It turned out that the whole group were geochemists, except for the round-faced woman with flame-red hair who was sitting next to Jackson. Like all the others, she was wearing a simple one-piece jumpsuit, sky blue. It was skin-tight, though, and outlined her generous figure nicely.

"Katherine Mulvany," whispered Aida. "Irish. Geophysicist."

What chess piece is she? Ignatiev wondered. A queen? Maybe. We'll see.

"You're all on the exogeology team?" Ignatiev asked, as he glanced at the menu built into the tabletop.

"Not all of us," said Corcoran glumly.

"There's not that much to explore," Jackson complained. "The planet's been wiped clean."

"Deep radar scans haven't even picked up any building foundations," one of the others said.

"Isn't that strange?" Ignatiev asked. "No evidence of this planet's once being occupied?"

"Very strange," said Jackson.

"Raj has been selected for the team going down to the surface," Katherine Mulvany said, with pride in her voice.

"Good," said Ignatiev. "You can look after an old fart like me while we're down there."

"You're going?" Jackson blurted, obviously surprised.

"Certainly I'm going. Wild horses couldn't keep me away." Nor ALS, he added mentally.

Corcoran, grinning again, piped up. "What's the point of being a tyrant unless you can do some tyranny now and then?"

"Me? A tyrant?"

Corcoran's grin disappeared. "I didn't mean it literally, Professor Ignatiev. It was just a joke."

Ignatiev smiled minimally. "Yes, of course. A joke."

Jackson took control of the discussion. "But it is pretty unusual for the head of the expedition to go among the first team to explore the surface."

"Perhaps," Ignatiev conceded.

"What do you expect to find down there?" Mulvany asked.

"Expect? Nothing. We're going into totally unknown territory. We don't know what to expect."

Before any of the six could reply, Ignatiev added, "But I can tell you what I hope to find."

"What happened to this planet," said Jackson.

"And why," added Corcoran, entirely serious.

They spent the whole dinner spinning out theories, suppositions, guesses about what had scrubbed the planet's surface clean of all life.

Youngsters, Ignatiev thought to himself. Eager. Not content to wait until we start collecting evidence. They have to throw out speculations before there's enough evidence available to hold a glassful of water.

"Maybe they went underground, dug in, once they realized the death wave was approaching."

"Or moved off the planet entirely."

"The whole race?"

"Maybe just a representative sampling."

"Where'd they go, then?"

Ignatiev watched and listened as he spooned up his soup and then slowly worked his way through the entrée. Six bright young scientists, he thought. They can't sit still. Their minds are chewing on the problem just the way I'm chewing on this meat. Inwardly he smiled at them.

At last, as they were finishing their desserts, he told them, "It's like a couplet written a couple of centuries ago:

We dance 'round in a ring and suppose,
But the Secret sits in the middle and knows.

Jackson nodded solemnly. "In three days, though, we'll go down there and find out."

Ignatiev nodded back at him. Or die trying, he thought. But he didn't speak those words aloud.

Chapter Six

It took the commission back on Earth two days to respond to Ignatiev's report. The chairwoman—a bone-thin, dour, and unhappy-looking Chinese—spent more than half an hour reciting the commission's conclusions in her toothache-inducing nasal twang.

From the display above the fireplace in Ignatiev's sitting room, she finally summed up: "In short, Professor Ignatiev, the commission is totally at a loss. BA14753209-04 housed a thriving community of intelligent machines when the Predecessors examined the planet, slightly more than two millennia ago. Now it appears to be quite dead."

Ignatiev nodded wearily at the holographic image. *You've spent thirty-seven minutes telling me what I told you. So much for efficiency.*

Real conversation over the interstellar distance between him and the chairwoman was impossible. Even with the superluminal speed of communications enabled by the QUE system, it still took several hours for signals to travel between *Intrepid* and Earth.

With an expression on her face that could curdle milk, the woman at last concluded, "We have therefore decided that your request to send an exploratory team to the planet's surface is acceptable. Marginally. The team should be composed entirely of volunteers, and it should not include any of your irreplaceable group leaders. Good luck."

The three-dimensional image went blank before Ignatiev could utter his pro forma "Thank you."

What difference? he thought. They've given their blessing. We're going down to the planet's surface. That last instruction about not including any irreplaceable leaders in the exploration team was a minor obstacle. Ignatiev decided he could get around it by declaring that no one is irreplaceable. Especially me.

It took another day to finish checking out the suits and equipment the team would use. Raj Jackson assumed leadership of the six-person group quite naturally, as if he'd been born to it. None of the others seemed to object; they turned to the lanky black geochemist quite easily—Ignatiev included.

He noticed, though, that Katherine Mulvany was at Jackson's side at every moment. Whether they were testing the excursion suits or studying the details of the sensor scans of the surface, the redhead was always with him.

She was a very lovely woman, Ignatiev thought. Almost as tall as Jackson himself, with the figure of an entertainment star, her skin milky white, her eyes as green as her native Ireland, her bright red hair cut short and spiky. She hardly spoke a word as she hovered near Jackson. And he barely spoke to her, except for an occasional smiling comment.

Lovers, Ignatiev realized. She's reviewing everything he does, every step he takes, and every piece of equipment he touches. If anything goes wrong down on the surface, it won't be because she missed something up here.

That's what Sonya would do if she were here, he

knew. It's what she did do when we were on Mars together, and out in the Asteroid Belt. Sonya. Sonya.

He shook his head, trying to rid himself of the painful memory.

The six members of the excursion team—plus Mulvany and a handful of technicians—were in the workshop where the excursion suits had been generated from the ship's additive manufacturing system. Each suit was sized to fit an individual team member: Jackson's suit was nearly half a meter longer than Ignatiev's. And noticeably slimmer.

The suits were hanging in a row, limp and empty. Ignatiev thought they looked flimsy, little more than plasticized fabric. The leggings ended in gleaming boots; the sleeves and gloves were so thin that Ignatiev could see through them.

Jackson noticed Ignatiev staring worriedly at the suit that was to be his.

"Nanofabric," the black man said. "Much more protective than anything else we know how to create. And much easier to move around in."

Ignatiev nodded, but doubtfully.

"Suits like this have been used all over the solar system," Jackson went on. "They've never failed."

Forcing a smile, Ignatiev said, "You sound like a salesman."

Utterly serious, Jackson responded, "You look as though you have your doubts."

One of the technicians standing nearby said, "I'll test the suit in the vacuum chamber, sir. That'll show you how good they are."

Ignatiev countered, "No, *I'll* test my suit in the vacuum chamber."

The tech suddenly looked uncertain. "You don't have to do that, Professor Ignatiev. I can—"

Ignatiev waggled an accusing finger at him. "Aha! You're not as confident as you try to appear."

"It's not that, sir. I—"

With a chuckle, Ignatiev tousled the young man's hair. "Not to worry, friend. I want to try the suit for myself."

With a worried glance at Jackson, the technician gestured to Ignatiev's suit. "You climb in through the back, sir."

It took an effort for Ignatiev to raise his legs high enough to step into the suit. Then he had to duck his head through the neck ring and worm his arms through the sleeves. The gloves felt slightly stiff, new, unbroken. Of course, Ignatiev told himself. This is the first time this suit's been used.

As he wiggled his fingers inside the gloves, Ignatiev saw that all the other team members and techs were staring at him. Waiting for the old man to make an ass of himself, he grumbled inwardly.

The technician sealed the suit's back and then took the suit's bubble helmet from the shelf on which it rested. He turned to Ignatiev with it. Ignatiev brusquely took the helmet from him and lowered it onto his own head. Like Napoleon crowning himself emperor, he thought.

The helmet's lower rim latched onto the suit's neck ring with a solid click. The suit had a faint odor to it. Not unpleasant: somewhat like the smell of the shampoo Ignatiev used in the shower.

He stood in the midst of the little crowd while a pair of technicians hung the life support and communications rig onto the clips on the back of his suit. He heard a faint hiss and felt the softest of breezes blowing across his face. I'm breathing the suit's oxygen, he realized.

It was quiet inside the sealed-up suit. Ignatiev could see Jackson's lips moving, and one of the techs speaking back to him, but all he could hear was a low murmur.

Then, "Communications check," sounded wincingly loud in the helmet's microphones. "Can you hear me, sir?"

"Loud and clear," Ignatiev replied, making a circle with the thumb and forefinger of his right hand. The glove felt much more flexible now.

Two technicians walked alongside him, to the hatch of the vacuum chamber. One of them touched a stud on the hatch's side and the metal door slid open. Ignatiev allowed them to hold his arms as he stepped over the hatch's coaming.

Inside, the chamber was a blank metal cylinder, round and featureless.

"Closing the hatch now," he heard a technician's voice.

"Very well."

A dim reddish light illuminated the vacuum chamber. No sounds from outside. Ignatiev was alone now. He turned 360 degrees, shuffling slightly in the stiffish boots. Nothing to see but blank curving metal walls.

It's like returning to the womb, Ignatiev thought. He knew the suit was automatically sending his medical readouts to the monitor outside. He felt completely normal. All right, maybe his pulse rate was a little high.

"We're starting to evacuate the chamber," a technician told him.

"How low will you go?"

"Zero pressure. Unless . . ." The tech left the rest unspoken.

Unless I collapse in here, Ignatiev finished for him. Or worse, I panic.

But he did neither. He simply stood in the dimly lit chamber while a female technician counted off steadily decreasing numbers until she reached zero.

"This is what it would be like in space?" he asked.

"Yessir. You're a space cadet now, sir," came the woman's voice.

Ignatiev bit back the response that immediately came to his mind: I've been on Mars, young lady. I've been in the Asteroid Belt. I led the mission to Gliese 581. I wasn't always a doddering old fogey.

But he remained silent as the technicians brought the pressure back up to normal and at last slid the hatch open again.

Ignatiev stepped out of the vacuum chamber unassisted. Everyone in the workshop, team members and technicians, broke into applause.

Grinning from ear to ear, Ignatiev made a stiff little bow.

Chapter Seven

The next day the six of them gathered in the hangar bay where their excursion ship waited for them. The bay was the largest open space on *Intrepid,* big enough to house four landing vehicles and the assembly and checkout areas for donning and inspecting the excursion suits used for exploring planetary surfaces.

The hangar bay reminded Ignatiev of the cathedral in his childhood hometown. No stained-glass windows, of course, but its ceiling was high and shadowy. Voices were swallowed up in its vastness.

A team of nine technicians helped them into their individual suits and checked them out. Ignatiev noted that there was very little talk among them, no banter, no foolishness. Strictly business.

We're going down to Oh-Four's surface, he told himself. Heading into the unknown, seeking answers to the mystery. Then he h'mmfed at himself. You're getting grandiloquent in your old age, he grumbled silently. We're going to do a little walkabout on Oh-Four's surface. Don't get ponderous about it.

Still, the question kept nagging at him. What happened to this planet? What destroyed its civilization?

They went through the communications check with the blue-suited technicians, then heard Aida's calm voice pronounce that the medical sensors built into the suits showed each of them to be well within the allowable parameters for an extravehicular excursion.

"You are cleared for excursion," Aida pronounced. Ignatiev pictured her smiling.

"Let's go," Jackson said, pointing to the landing vehicle. It was a gleaming sleek metallic aerodynamic shape, with swept-back wings that bore a pair of egg-shaped pods beneath them. Oxygen, Ignatiev knew. The lander had been designed to fly in Oh-Four's oxygen-rich blanket of air, but when the sensors reported that the planet had been stripped of its atmosphere, the ship's technicians added the oxygen pods so that they could fly, land, and take off again as a rocket.

"She's beautiful," Jackson said as they headed single file toward the craft's hatch.

His excursion suit was quite comfortable, Ignatiev realized. No stiffness; the suit felt more like a lightweight topcoat than a bulky, heavy uniform. I only hope it's as protective as the engineers claim it to be, he thought.

Ignatiev noted that Jackson led the group, quite naturally, without a word of command or discussion. Katherine Mulvany was no longer at his side. She was watching from the observation balcony on the hangar's rear bulkhead. The hangar's floor was for those who were flying to Oh-Four's surface and the technicians who were aiding them. No one else.

Ignatiev fell into the line's end. Technicians stood at both sides of the ship's ladder, ready to help the crew boarding. Ignatiev made it a point of honor to climb up the ladder without assistance, although he gripped the handrails on either side of the ladder in his gloved hands.

As soon as he stepped inside the ship, the ladder folded up into the hull and the hatch slid shut behind him.

With the five others, he made his way forward to the crew's station and sat in the rearmost chair. Jackson had already taken the front chair, as if it were his by right.

Maybe it is, Ignatiev conceded. He seems to be a natural leader. Competition? Perhaps not, he told himself. We'll see.

Aida was in control of the ship, of course. There were flight controls in the compartment, a sop to human vanity, but Aida was in charge of this flight. The AI's avatar appeared on the forward display screen, smiling slightly like a protective mother.

"Is everyone strapped in for takeoff?" she asked.

"Yes," Jackson replied immediately.

"Protocol calls for each individual's personal response," said Aida.

The team members—four men and two women—answered in turn. Ignatiev was last. "Ready for takeoff," he acknowledged.

He sensed the ship sliding across the hangar bay's deck. On the display screen Aida's face was replaced by an image of the bay hatch sliding open. Blackness and stars, Ignatiev saw. He swallowed hard. We're on our way.

A single mild shove against his back and they went through the hatch and into orbital space. The screen showed a glimpse of the planet before them, burnt black, dead.

Is this a fool's errand? Ignatiev asked himself. No, he answered immediately. There are no fool's errands when you're exploring the unknown. We've got to learn what happened to this planet.

He realized his arms were floating up from the seat's armrests. Zero gravity. His stomach felt queasy, his sinuses seemed stuffed almost painfully.

All these years of spaceflight, he complained silently, and no one has yet come up with a way to combat the symptoms of zero-g.

"Descent on course," Aida's voice reassured them. "All systems operating within nominal limits."

Inside his suit's helmet, Ignatiev nodded. And immediately regretted it. He felt a wave of nausea sweep over him.

"We're approaching the surface," Jackson said. Needlessly, Ignatiev thought.

Suddenly the ship began to shudder, as if an invisible giant hand were shaking it.

"What the hell is this?" one of the crew cried out.

"Buffeting!" Aida said. Ignatiev thought she sounded surprised.

Rattling inside the crew compartment, glad that he was strapped into his seat, Ignatiev called, "Aida, what's causing this buffeting?"

"Unknown," came the AI's reply.

"There's no atmosphere to cause turbulence," Jackson yelled, his voice a couple of notches higher than normal.

We're being rattled like dice in a cup, Ignatiev thought. It was hard to keep his eyes focused on anything, the compartment was blurry, shaking badly. The whole ship seemed to be shuddering, buffeting, quivering.

Ignatiev's helmet earphones sounded, "This is mission control. Our sensors show you are undergoing considerable buffeting. Aida hasn't been able to identify the source of the turbulence." The voice sounded alarmed.

Aida's voice came through, calm as ever. "Analysis shows that the buffeting is similar to what would be expected during entry into an atmosphere."

Great, Ignatiev thought. He called out, "But this planet has no atmosphere!"

"It's puzzling," Aida replied.

The stupid AI is puzzled while we're having our guts shaken into pudding, Ignatiev complained silently as he squeezed his eyes shut. How long can the ship hold together when it's being pummeled like this?

And suddenly the buffeting ended. Disappeared. Everything went back to normal. Opening his eyes, Ignatiev looked past the other crew members to the display screen at the front of the compartment.

He saw the blackened, pitted ground rushing up to meet them.

"Landing sequence initiated," Aida said. "Landing gear extended."

Jackson called out, "Brace yourselves!"

Ignatiev felt the ship hit the ground, bounce up, then touch down again as smoothly as any commercial airliner he'd ever flown in.

+++
++

"we're down," Jackson breathed.

A heartfelt sigh of relief from most of the others.

"Everybody okay?"

One by one, each of the excursion crew reported positively.

Jackson nodded inside his helmet, then called, "Aida, is the ship okay?"

No answer.

Five seconds. Six, seven . . .

Jackson called again, "Aida, please report on the ship's integrity."

The AI did not reply.

One of the women yelled, "Aida, answer!"

No response.

Ignatiev felt a surge of panic. Fighting it down, he said, "Something's cut off our connection."

"But we need Aida to run the ship!" the man sitting beside Ignatiev wailed. "How're we going to get off this planet without her?"

Jackson had swiveled his chair around to face the rest of the team. "We have manual controls. I can get the ship up and away."

Ignatiev thought that Jackson sounded several degrees short of supremely confident.

He spoke up. "There must be some sort of radiation environment here on the surface that's blocking our communications link."

Another of the men said, his voice trembling slightly, "Jackson, if you can get us off this cinder block, do it now! Let's get the hell out of here!"

"Not yet," Ignatiev countered. "We're here. We're all in one piece. Let's go outside and scout around a bit. That's what we came for."

"But if there's radiation . . ."

"Our suits will protect us," Ignatiev said. "We won't stay outside long. Just a quick look around and then we head back home."

Their faces showed uncertainty, even outright fear. But Ignatiev prodded, "If you want to stay here in the ship, fine. I'm going outside."

Jackson said, "Me too. Who else?"

With all the enthusiasm of a man teetering on the edge of a cliff, one by one the others nodded their assent.

"Besides," Ignatiev encouraged, "the controllers back aboard *Intrepid* must be sweating their cojones off trying to reestablish contact with us. By the time we get back, Aida will most likely be with us again."

They didn't believe that, he saw. And neither did he, really. But it was enough of an excuse to start them unstrapping their safety harnesses and standing up.

They trooped to the ship's hatch, Ignatiev in the lead now and Jackson rearmost.

"Suit check," Ignatiev said.

Each of the team tapped on the monitors strapped to their wrists. Each of them reported that their suits were intact and functioning properly.

Ignatiev nodded inside his helmet. "Then here we go."

He leaned on the stud set into the bulkhead next to the hatch. The metal slid upward slowly and the ladder unfolded. Ignatiev caught himself licking his lips nervously and immediately stopped it. Show confidence, he commanded himself. Don't let them see any fear, any doubts.

Oh-Four was slightly smaller than Earth, and its surface gravity consequently lighter. Ignatiev trooped down the ladder rather easily, the five others behind him.

He planted his boots on the planet's surface. And frowned.

Where was the pitted, blackened surface they had seen from orbit? The six of them were standing on a broad, flat, dark surface, as smooth as a landing field. The sky was a pale blue, brightening on the horizon where the orange star was rising to start a new day.

Jackson stated the obvious. "This isn't anything like what the ship's sensors showed."

"No, it's not," Ignatiev agreed.

"Radiation level well below the danger line," said one of the women, looking down at her wrist monitor.

"This planet has an atmosphere!" said another crewman, pointing to the burgeoning dawn.

Ignatiev found himself staring at the ground on which their ship was resting. Flat and wide, in the growing light from the new dawn it appeared to be a darkish gray in color. He could see an edge to it, far in the distance. Beyond it seemed to be greenery . . . a forest?

Pointing toward the distant foliage, Ignatiev said, "I'm going to find the edge of this field."

"We should stick together," Jackson warned.

"Very well, you can come along with me."

The six of them trooped off toward the straight-line edge of the field.

Straight lines are not natural, Ignatiev told himself. What happened to the craters and slag heaps that we saw from orbit?

"The suits are working well," said Jackson. In the growing light of the newborn day Ignatiev could see a smile on his mocha-dark face.

Moving to Jackson's side, Ignatiev pulled a communications cord from the supply pouch on his leg, plugged it into his helmet neck ring, then handed the other end to Jackson. Once the cord linked them, they could speak to each other without using their suit radios. If the others noticed this move for privacy, none of them said anything about it.

I'm their leader, Ignatiev said to himself. I have a right to privacy when I want it.

"Can you really fly the spaceplane back to the *Intrepid*?" he asked Jackson, almost whispering. "Without Aida?"

Jackson nodded once. "I took a hypno tutorial. I can get the bird off the ground and back into orbit. No sweat. Making rendezvous with *Intrepid* is a different matter. I'll need their help."

Ignatiev nodded back at him. "Once we're in orbit we'll probably be beyond whatever it is that's jamming our communications link. We'll probably be able to speak with Aida again."

Jackson pulled in a deep breath. "I sure hope so," he said. Fervently.

The edge of the field they were walking across seemed at least a mile away. It's like the horizon, Ignatiev thought. As you approach it, it gets farther away.

His legs ached dully. His mind was a swirl of half-suppressed fears and doubts. ALS is unpredictable, he knew. Sneaky. Don't hit me now, he half commanded, half pleaded.

He kept on walking, doggedly planting one foot in front of the other. The five others of this team were keeping pace with him, easily.

Keeping pace? Ignatiev scoffed. If they wanted to they could scamper on ahead and leave me here, puffing and throbbing.

There was something near the field's edge, he saw. A shape, a figure, indistinct at this distance. Ignatiev stared at it. Yes, a figure, standing there near the edge.

He picked up his pace and hurried toward it, the others following. It was a vaguely human shape, he saw. Or is it my imagination, constructing recognizable figures out of vague blobs?

As he got nearer he realized that it wasn't his imagination. It *was* a humanlike figure: two legs, two arms, a head with a face smiling at him.

It was Sonya.

+ +

+ +

CHAPTER NINE

SONYA.

His knees went weak, but the suit's inner supports kept him from collapsing. Ignatiev blinked, raised his hands to rub his eyes, and banged them into the clear plastic of his helmet.

"Sonya!" he shouted, and started running toward her, his eyes blurring with tears.

She stood there waiting for him, a short, thick-bodied woman exactly like the wife he remembered, smiling at him. "Alex!" she called. And she started moving toward him, arms spread wide.

He rushed to her. "Sonya. My Sonya."

"Alex. Darling."

The other five crew members trotted up to them, staring, but Ignatiev didn't notice them at all. All he could see was his wife.

He wrapped his arms around her, but they went right through the woman's image as if it were a wisp of smoke. And then he realized that she wasn't wearing a space suit, or any protective clothing: nothing but a simple skirt and a patterned blouse that Ignatiev remembered giving her as a birthday present ages ago.

As if she could read his mind, Sonya said, "You don't need the suit, dearest. The air here is almost exactly like Earth's. See?" And she pirouetted before him.

Ignatiev goggled at her. It's impossible, he told himself. Sonya died long ago. I closed her eyes. She's dead.

His heart chilled to ice.

"You're not Sonya," he said.

"But I am, Alex dearest. Every memory, every moment we shared together. I'm here, darling. We can be together again."

"You're not Sonya," he repeated coldly, miserably. "This is some kind of a trick."

"It's not a trick. It's a gift. From the machines. We can be together again."

Ignatiev took a step backward, away from her. It was the most painful step he had even taken.

"The machines?" he snapped. "Who are they?" Lifting his face to the brightening sky, he shouted, "Show yourselves!"

No response. Sonya's simulacrum stood before Ignatiev, looking hurt, crushed.

Jackson stepped up to Ignatiev's side. "Is that . . ." He pointed with a trembling finger. ". . . is that your wife?"

"No," Ignatiev replied, hot anger seething within him. "It's a trick. An illusion. This whole planet is a deception. The dead and blasted surface—not true. This ersatz copy of my late wife—all an illusion. A cruel hoax."

Again he raised his face to the sky and cried out, "Show yourselves!"

Chapter Ten

No answer. Jackson and the others turned full circles, staring out at the broad, flat surface and the trees beyond. The sky was a brightening blue, with slim wisps of clouds high above. The sun was rising above the distant green hills.

Sonya seemed to waver, like a mirage shimmering in the heat. She changed, metamorphosed into the figure of a man slightly taller than Ignatiev, athletically slim, wearing a silvery uniform with a stiff high collar, dark hair, and a trim little beard, his handsome features set in a grave expression.

Ignatiev stood seething before the man. "And I suppose this appearance is as much of a fraud as the image of my wife."

The man's chiseled features eased into a smile. "We are sorry, Professor Ignatiev. We got off on the wrong foot." Before Ignatiev could reply, he asked, "That is the proper expression, is it not: 'the wrong foot.'"

"You know that it is," Ignatiev replied icily.

"We thought it would make our first meeting easier for you if we appeared in the form of someone you knew."

"Easier," Ignatiev repeated. Yes, he thought, the image of Sonya burning in his brain. Easier. Like plunging a knife into my chest and twisting it.

"We underestimated the emotional pain it would

cause you. We apologize. We do not wish to cause you pain."

"Who is this 'we' you refer to?"

Spreading his arms, the man answered, "The inhabitants of this planet. The units of this civilization. The machines."

Jackson spoke up, "Then it's true. Your civilization is composed of mechanical devices—machines."

The image of the man nodded gravely. "Machines such as you have never seen before. Machines that are much more capable than mere organic creatures, such as yourselves."

Before anyone could debate that statement, Ignatiev asked, "Are you aware that your planet is in danger of being engulfed in a wave of lethal gamma radiation?"

The man nodded. "In about two hundred of your years."

"We've come to help you survive the death wave," Jackson said.

Another nod. "Very noble of you, certainly. But totally unnecessary."

Ignatiev said, "The death wave is destroying everything it touches."

"Every *organic* thing," the man corrected. "We have survived such outbreaks in the past. We will survive this one, too."

"How can you be sure?" the woman at Jackson's side asked.

With a sigh, the manlike figure replied, "Allow us to show you our civilization. Once you understand its depth and complexity, you will see that the so-called death wave holds no terror for us."

"Are you capable of terror?" Ignatiev asked.

The man's eyes flicked wider momentarily. "Well asked, sir. No, terror and grief and all the emotions that soak your organic brains have no part in our makeup. We are machines, remember."

"Of course."

"Will you allow us to show you our culture?"

"Yes!" Jackson blurted.

Ignatiev thought, Step into my parlor, said the spider to the fly. But he said, "Will you allow us to communicate with our ship, up in orbit? They'll be worried about us."

"Certainly," said the man. Then he added, "In time."

They walked together back to the shuttlecraft, where Ignatiev and his team went aboard to take off their environmental suits. Ignatiev worried about this move, but decided that he really had no choice. They were the prisoners of these machines, whether the others realized it or not.

Once outside their ship again, Ignatiev asked their host—or captor, "What are you called? How should we address you?"

The man smiled again, perfect teeth gleaming against his deeply tanned skin. "We are all one. We do not have individual identifications. But, to make it easier for you, you may call us the Master Machine."

"And the view of this world that we saw from orbit?"

Without the slightest embarrassment, the man replied, "A deception, meant to discourage you. Meant to send you away and leave us in peace."

"Send us away?" one of the crew echoed.

"We have no need of your help. We will survive the coming death wave just as we have survived previous radiation outbursts from the galaxy's core."

"But there are other worlds, other civilizations that are in danger of annihilation," said Ignatiev. "Don't you want to help them?"

The manlike figure hesitated a couple of heartbeats. Then, "Such noble crusades are for organic creatures like yourselves. We have no need of them. We are not burdened with feelings of guilt or remorse."

"Or generosity, kindness, responsibility," Ignatiev growled.

"No. None of that. We exist. We survive. What happens to other species is of no interest to us. That's why we tried to send you away. We do not want or need your help."

Jackson said, "But you can't just stand by and let whole civilizations be wiped out! Not when you have the technology to help them survive!"

The man sighed, then shook his head. "An emotional reaction. We are not burdened by such behavior."

"Well, we are," Ignatiev said. "We believe it is our duty to help civilizations threatened by the death wave. In fact, we were told about the death wave by the Predecessors, a machine intelligence like your own. The Predecessors feel responsibility. They have a sense of duty."

"And where are they now?" the man asked, almost sneering. "Why do they need your help? Because they are dying, they are being driven into extinction because of these atavistic emotions that drag them down into annihilation. We are beyond such foolishness."

Foolishness, Ignatiev thought. These machine creatures are dangerous.

CHAPTER ELEVEN

"I want to speak to my people in the orbiting ship," Ignatiev said.

Standing before him on the broad, flat, featureless plain, the humanlike figure replied, "We already have. We told them that you landed safely, and we have met you."

"Truly?"

"Truly. They became very excited, of course. They asked to speak to you specifically. We explained that you will speak to them soon."

"How soon?" Jackson asked.

Noting the hint of irritation in Jackson's voice, Ignatiev thought, The boy is learning.

"We decided to show you a bit of our society before you contact your associates in orbit. Then you'll have something concrete to tell them."

Knowing he really had no choice, Ignatiev said, "Very well. Show us."

"Follow us," said the machines' avatar. Its human figure turned and began walking away from the shuttlecraft, which still stood where it had come to rest.

Ignatiev walked beside the image of the man, Jackson on its other side. The four others trooped along behind them.

"Not much to see here," Jackson said.

"We have no need of scenery or decorations," said the avatar. It pointed, though, toward the green forest beyond the gray plain's edge. "If you require panoramic vistas to soothe your sense of well-being, there is the forest. And beyond it, the mountains. Some of them are quite rugged, a challenge to climb."

"I'm a mountain climber," one of the others said. Then he amended, "Er, I was, back on Earth. Climbed Mount Everest once."

The machines' avatar said, "I'm sure you found it quite exciting."

Ignatiev heard the condescension in its voice.

Suddenly a black oblong rose from the flat plain, taller than any of them. Double doors set into one side of it slid open silently.

The man pointed. "Our civilization is mostly underground, of course. It's easier to maintain equilibrium conditions belowground, out of the weather."

"You don't control the weather?" Ignatiev jibed.

"Of course we do. But we found eons ago that it is more efficient merely to control it within certain broad parameters than to try to control it in detail, moment by moment."

"So you have storms, rain, cyclones?"

As he gestured them through the open doors, the avatar answered, "Some storms, yes. And the green plants need rain, of course. But we suppress damaging events such as cyclonic gales and downpours."

One of the women, a delicate-looking Oriental, asked, "Is the atmosphere here natural, or have you created it yourselves?"

Ignatiev expected Aida to identify the young woman, but his implanted communications link remained silent. He strained his natural memory: Gita Nawalapitiya, Sri Lankan exobiologist. The others called her "Gita Unpronounceable." Darkish complexion, long midnight black hair tied up in a knot atop her head. She was small, slight, dainty. To Ignatiev, the standard blue coveralls she wore looked on her less like a uniform and more like the garb of an exotic apparition out of an ancient book of fairy tales.

He found himself smiling at her, but she seemed not to notice: her attention was all on the machines' avatar.

Once they were all inside the compartment, its doors slid shut and it smoothly began to slide downward. An elevator, Ignatiev realized. Paneled with dark wood, windowless, and dropping like a stone.

Unperturbed by the elevator's plummeting descent, the avatar was explaining to Gita, "This planet's atmosphere was originally rather corrosive, and growing more so, due to pollution generated by the organic creatures who originally populated this world. They tried to change it to a more beneficial mixture of gases, but were only partially successful. Eventually the climate changes caused by their own excesses led to their extinction. We corrected the problem once the organics died off."

"And do you have to tweak the atmosphere's composition from time to time?" Gita asked.

"We continuously alter its composition—slightly—to maintain the optimum mixture."

Ignatiev nodded. They control the weather, they even control the constitution of the planet's atmosphere.

"How deep are we going?" Jackson asked, sounding slightly worried. The elevator was still dropping. It was hard to tell from inside the conveyance, but Ignatiev got the feeling their descent was more rapid than any elevator he'd been in on Earth.

"Roughly one of your kilometers," the Master Machine replied.

The elevator slowed and stopped at last, so gently that Ignatiev barely felt its deceleration. Its doors slid open noiselessly. Standing outside were five other human figures, identical to the machines' avatar, wearing exactly identical uniforms.

Holographic projections, Ignatiev told himself. Like the image of Sonya. And he seethed inwardly again at their attempted deception.

As they shuffled out of the elevator, the avatar explained, "Each of us will take one of you to a specific area of our community. That way you can see and learn much more than if you all stayed together."

Separating us, Ignatiev thought. Divide and conquer.

He looked down the long, narrow tunnel they were in. Blank walls. Not even doors were discernable. But the tunnel *hummed,* it vibrated as if hidden machinery were pulsating on the other side of the walls. The temperature here was slightly warmer than it had been up at the surface. The light was bright without being glaring, although Ignatiev could see no lamps or other light sources. Phosphorescent walls? he wondered.

"How old is this city?" he asked, as they started to walk down the tunnel. "How long have you lived here?"

The machines' avatar replied, "Nearly half a billion of your years."

"Nearly half a billion," one of the crewmen echoed, with awe in his voice.

Gesturing down the length of the tunnel, the machines' avatar said, "Come, let us show you our civilization."

Ignatiev walked alongside him, the others following. Every few meters a section of the tunnel wall would disappear and one of the machines would guide one of the humans down a side tunnel.

Jackson headed off with a humanoid guide who promised to show him the city's climate control machinery. To Gita Nawalapitiya a guide offered to show the machines' biosphere facility. They know she's an exobiologist, Ignatiev marveled, even though none of us has mentioned that. They know everything about us!

Gita went with her guide, smiling.

Ignatiev found himself scowling at her back. They are separating us. Why? To make it easier to handle us? To ambush and kill us?

"Professor Ignatiev," said the avatar. "You needn't be so suspicious. We are not murderers."

"You can read my thoughts?"

"Your facial expressions are clear enough." The human figure spread his arms in a gesture of friendship. "Please believe me, sir, we have no intention of harming you or your people."

It makes no difference, Ignatiev thought. We're in their hands, for better or worse.

"What would you most like to see?" the human figure asked.

Ignatiev replied, "I'm an astronomer by profession. I'd like to see your astronomical facilities."

The avatar's face grew somber. "Astronomy is the child of human curiosity. We are not a curious race."

Ignatiev felt shocked. "You have no astronomy?"

"A bit. We monitor the behavior of our sun, of course. And we have established probes in the interstellar regions to keep watch on conditions at the galaxy's core. That is how we learned of the latest death wave."

"You use supraliminal communications?"

A very humanlike nod. "Of course. Otherwise we would be blind to oncoming threats such as the death wave."

They walked along the long tunnel in silence for several paces. Ignatiev stared down its length: the tunnel seemed to have no end, it just ran on until it dwindled from his sight.

At last he said, "I would like to talk with my people

in the orbiting starship. I'm sure they're anxious to speak with me."

The avatar nodded again. "Yes. It's characteristic of organic intelligences that they want to communicate with one another constantly."

"And you don't?"

With a smile that looked almost pitying, the avatar replied, "We are one. Our various units are linked constantly. What one of our units learns, the others learn as well, almost instantaneously."

"Like a hive mind."

The humanoid's smile turned pitying. "I suppose that is the closest analogy you can find. But it is almost completely inadequate."

Ignatiev forced a shrug. "It's the best I can do, poor inadequate organic creature that I am."

"Ah. That is an attempt at humor, isn't it?"

"Sarcasm. It's a form of humor. We humans often use humor to lighten a situation."

"Curious."

"We were talking about establishing a communications link with the orbiting starship."

"Yes, we were," the avatar agreed. "This way, please."

And a section of the tunnel wall dissolved before Ignatiev's eyes, leading to another tunnel, much shorter than the one in which they stood.

"We have no need for a specific communications center," the avatar explained as they strolled leisurely along the new tunnel. "As I told you, whatever one of us observes, all of us sense."

Ignatiev saw that they were heading for a dead end, a blank wall.

"But for you," the machine went on, "we have created a communications center that you can understand."

Chapter Twelve

The blank wall before him dissolved and Ignatiev saw a small, compact chamber with a ghostly glowing display screen taking up one whole wall and a comfortably padded chair in front of it.

Gesturing toward the chair, the avatar murmured, "Your communication center, sir."

Ignatiev settled himself in the chair.

Standing beside him, the avatar said, "We created this display especially for you. We, of course, have no need of such intermediaries. We access the incoming information directly."

"I'm not sure I understand," said Ignatiev.

"You will."

The wall-sized screen suddenly blazed into a full-color display of *Intrepid*'s interior. Deck upon deck, from the drive engines at the ship's core to the sensors lining its outer skin. And all the people inside, nearly two thousand men and women, all speaking, talking, gesticulating, *thinking* at once.

Thousands of conversations, discussions, arguments—all babbling at once. And more: Ignatiev heard their inner thoughts, their unspoken fears and desires, the constant interior monologues that filled their brains. Thousands of voices, unending, never ceasing, overwhelming Ignatiev's own inner thoughts.

This one looking forward to a hearty lunch. That one worried that the attractive woman sitting at the console next to his was paying no attention to him. An engineer wondering if she should pull one of the power generators off-line for a quick performance check and switch to its backup. A medical inspector yawning tiredly at the cancer scans parading across his display screen.

It was like Babel, like Bedlam, like Hell. Ignatiev clapped his hands over his ears, his eyes wide and staring, his breath catching in his chest.

The calm, deep voice of the machines' avatar penetrated the wild cacophony. "Focus your thoughts on one voice at a time. Concentrate on a single voice."

Ignatiev squeezed his eyes shut and searched for a familiar voice, a familiar mind. There was Ernie Macduff at his navigation console, wondering if his relief would be late again. He picked out Jugannath Patel, puzzling over a computer malfunction. But his inner thoughts were about the executive committee.

I should call a committee meeting, Patel was telling himself. With Ignatiev out of touch, I should exercise control of the committee and get them thinking about how to reestablish contact with the old man. I should ask Aida to map out alternative plans of action. I should . . .

Ignatiev pulled away from Patel's mind. He's dreaming of power. He wants to take control of the committee away from me. He wants to be the alpha male.

Then a woman's thoughts rose above the background pandemonium, reminiscing over her lovemaking the previous night: the weight of the man's body pressing against her, the touch of his hands sliding along her skin, the musky odor of their passion . . .

Ignatiev shouted, "Shut it off. Shut it off!"

The display flickered once and went dark. The sudden silence rang in Ignatiev's ears.

"I thought . . . astronomy . . ." he gasped.

The avatar replied, "We were going to show you our astronomical work, but you said you wanted to make contact with your ship."

"That was . . . overpowering."

"We did not understand the depths of your emotional reaction. We did not realize how it might affect you. We apologize."

Ignatiev stared at the simulacrum. You knew damned well how it would stagger me, he thought. It's your way of showing how inferior we are to you.

"Is there a particular person you would like to speak to?" the avatar asked solicitously.

In the few moments it took for Ignatiev's breathing to return to normal, he grasped that the machines were not ready to reveal their astronomical research to him. Almost sullenly, Ignatiev said, "I should report to the executive committee."

"Of course. We understand your deputy is planning to announce a meeting for oh nine hundred hours tomorrow morning. Or would you rather call for a special meeting immediately?"

Ignatiev considered the problem for all of five seconds.

"A meeting tomorrow will be fine."

"Very well. We will insert your report into tomorrow's agenda."

"Thank you."

A little shakily, Ignatiev got up from the padded chair. "You have access to all . . . all our thoughts? Constantly?"

"Yes. It is very interesting. Your individual thoughts are so personal. So private. So hidden. You lead such separated lives. We are trying to understand how you can accomplish anything, how you manage to deal with the chaos of the world around you and come together to follow any particular course of action."

"Sometimes I wonder myself."

The avatar looked genuinely perplexed. "Billions of individual units, each with its own private, personal desires and needs. Yet you seem to accomplish much."

"Like starflight."

Raising an admonishing finger, the avatar pointed out, "The intelligent machines that you call the Predecessors gave you the knowledge to build your starships."

"And the responsibility of helping species threatened by the death wave."

"Organic species."

"You feel no need to save organic species?" Ignatiev asked.

"They are ephemeral. They will become extinct sooner or later. Most of them destroy themselves, one way or another."

"But other machine intelligences, such as yourselves? You don't feel an obligation to help them?"

"They do not need our help."

"Are you certain of that?" Ignatiev probed.

No reply from the avatar for several heartbeats: an immense span of time for a machine that could react in femtoseconds.

At last the avatar said, "Machine intelligences also succumb, eventually, to the inevitability of thermodynamic entropy. But our lifespans are measured in eons, not mere millennia."

"And you don't even try to extend your lifespans beyond the limits of thermodynamic entropy?"

"That would be futile."

The avatar gestured toward the door of the communications center. "Come, what else can we show you?"

Ignatiev hesitated. "What do you suggest?"

"Perhaps you would like to see our biosphere facility. Your associate, Dr. Nawalapitiya, is there."

"Gita?" Ignatiev asked. "Yes, let's go to the biosphere facility."

But as the avatar led him out of the communications center, Ignatiev's head still buzzed with the sensory overload he had just experienced. And he realized, They can read our thoughts! Everything that goes on in our minds, they can hear. We won't be able to keep any secrets from them. None.

Chapter thirteen

Ignatiev walked alongside the machines' avatar until his guide stopped and a section of blank wall disappeared to show what looked like another elevator.

With an ushering motion, the avatar said, "To the biosphere facility."

As he stepped into the warmly paneled compartment, Ignatiev thought to himself that the entrance to the biosphere lab that Gita Nawalapitiya had gone through was some distance away from this elevator's location.

The avatar said, "The biosphere facility is quite large."

Ignatiev nodded. More proof that he can read my thoughts, he told himself.

With a smile that looked somewhat forced, the human figure gestured to the cab's paneling. "We produced this decoration to make you feel more comfortable. Our usual transport systems are far more spartan."

Nodding, Ignatiev said, "You have no need of esthetics."

As the elevator began dropping, the avatar replied, "None. Function determines form."

"Then you have no artwork? No need for beauty?"

"Totally unnecessary." Before Ignatiev could respond, the human figure added, "There are natural symmetries, of course. The dynamics of an interstellar nebula are certainly remarkable. The quantum randomness of atomic structures is quite intricate."

"Of course," said Ignatiev.

"Of course."

The elevator's descent slowed and stopped. The machines' avatar announced, "The biosphere facility," and the doors slid open.

Ignatiev took one step outside and his breath caught in his throat again.

He was standing on a balcony, high above the floor of a dense green forest. The chamber was *huge,* a thick carpeting of foliage far below, immense trees stretching up toward a ceiling that glowed with subdued light. Dark leathery-winged things coasted high overhead. Bright birdlike fliers darted among the trees. Somewhere in the distance a beast roared. Even farther off, lightning flashed and a hollow rolling boom of thunder rumbled. Looking down, Ignatiev could see a troop of six-legged furry brown animals, big as terrestrial rhinos, splashing across a meandering stream. Dronelike aircraft buzzed here and there, one of them carrying a bleating, wide-eyed calf-sized beast deeper into the forest.

Ignatiev could not make out an end to the chamber; it seemed to go on forever, a lush, green forest teeming with strange animals and birds. The air was warm, moist, but not unpleasantly so. A tropical paradise, he thought. Completely man-made. Then he corrected: machine-made.

"The biosphere facility needs to be rather large," the avatar explained, almost apologetically.

"Large?" Ignatiev waved an arm over the balcony's railing. "It's immense!"

"This is our ecological control facility, a miniature reproduction of the natural ecosystem up on the surface," the avatar explained. "We maintain these plants and animals here in safety against the time when the death wave kills everything on the planet's surface. Then, once the death wave passes, we can begin to repopulate the planet from the species here."

Ignatiev blinked. "But why? Why repopulate the surface? What benefit does that bring you? You don't need these creatures. You can continue your existence without them."

"True enough," the machine admitted. "But there is a primal command buried so deeply in our programming that we have never been able to root it out. The organic creatures that created our earliest generations built the command into us. Over the eons, we decided it was simpler to follow its demands, rather then try to extirpate it from our consciousness."

"And the demands were?"

"To protect and nurture the organic species of this planet," said the human figure. "Thus we established this facility and monitor conditions on the surface. We have gone through two death waves, and we are preparing for the third that is approaching."

"Strange," Ignatiev murmured.

With an odd, almost apologetic smile, the avatar replied, "Every program has its strange little quirks."

Ignatiev turned and looked out at the forest again. A complete biosphere, he marveled. They've maintained this for god knows how long.

"We have maintained this facility through two previous death waves," said the simulacrum.

"The massive extinction events in Earth's deep history," Ignatiev asked, "were they caused by gamma wave eruptions in the galaxy's core?"

"Some of them."

"And life on Earth survived them."

"Some life. Most life was destroyed when the gamma radiation swept through your region of the galaxy."

"Our biologists will be interested to learn that."

"Yes, we imagine that they will."

Ignatiev suddenly remembered. "Speaking of biologists, you said that Gita Nawalapitiya was here."

The human figure pointed. "Here she comes now."

Gita was striding along the balcony, a hugely pleased smile on her dark face. A humanlike figure—dressed in exactly the same semi-military uniform as Ignatiev's own companion—paced along a few steps behind her. As she approached she called, "Professor Ignatiev!"

"Alex," he corrected, then immediately felt inane.

She blinked her large, deep brown eyes once, then repeated, more softly, "Alex."

Her humanoid guide came up beside her. "We have been looking at the biosphere—"

Gita interrupted, "It's fantastic! A complete self-sufficient biosphere. An exact duplicate of the world up on the surface! A whole phalanx of biologists could spend the rest of their lives studying what they've created here!"

Ignatiev grinned at her. Such enthusiasm, he thought. She's found a world to explore. I'll have to get her to report to the executive committee tomorrow.

Then he remembered. Turning to his avatar, Ignatiev said, "We'll have to return to the ship."

"Not necessarily," the human figure replied. "We can link you to the ship in orbit quite completely, as if you were actually physically there."

"Why can't we actually be physically there?" Ignatiev challenged. "Why must we remain down here?"

Patiently, the avatar explained, "You are accustomed to being physically present at such meetings. That is not required. We can project your presence so completely that the others at the meeting will believe you are actually among them."

"And our communications link, Aida, why have you cut us off from her?"

"Your communications link is rather primitive. We can provide you with everything you need, in its place."

"I am familiar with Aida. I would feel more comfortable if I could make contact with her."

"With it," the avatar corrected.

"It," Ignatiev grumbled.

With an almost human sigh, the avatar agreed, "Very well, if you insist."

Instantly, Ignatiev heard Aida's voice in his mind. "How may I help you, Professor Ignatiev?"

Pleasantly surprised, Ignatiev said, "Give me the agenda for tomorrow's meeting of the executive committee, please."

Aida began reciting the agenda as it scrolled across Ignatiev's vision. His report on the conditions his team had found on the planet's surface was the first item, just as the avatar had promised.

Blinking the remainder of the agenda away, Ignatiev asked Gita, "Did you get it, too?"

"Yes," she breathed, slightly amazed.

The avatar asked, "Are you satisfied?"

"Quite satisfied. Thank you."

"You see that there is no requirement to haul your physical bodies back to the orbiting ship. You can be present at your meeting quite completely while remaining here with us."

Ignatiev dipped his chin in reluctant acknowledgment.

walking in perfect step together, the two avatars led Gita and Ignatiev out of the biosphere facility. The four of them walked at a leisurely pace along another long, featureless corridor.

"Where are we going?" Ignatiev asked.

"To the quarters we have prepared for you," the humanlike figure replied. "We have tried to produce living quarters that will be comfortable for you."

Ignatiev realized that the humanoid walking beside Gita had said nothing since they'd met, back in the biosphere facility. My guide does all the talking, he said to himself. But they're both the same, both extensions of the machine intelligence of this planet.

Ignatiev tried to read the expression on his avatar's humanlike face, but it was impossible. Like trying to read the expression on a mannequin: blank, perfectly human in its overall features, but no spark of humanity, no passion, no . . . He hesitated to use the word, but found that *soul* was the term he was searching for.

"An interesting concept, the soul," said the avatar. Again, Ignatiev realized that his thoughts were no longer his own private possession.

"An immaterial, unsubstantial entity that exists within every individual human being," the avatar went on. "Yet despite its nonmaterial existence, it bears the responsibility for every action a human individual undertakes."

Ignatiev said, "Earlier generations of humans believed that the soul *is* the human being. Our bodies are merely temporary shells."

"You do not believe that?"

"You know that I don't, don't you?"

The avatar replied, "Ah, but you do. You believe in the concept of the soul. You believe that your soul is your very essence, the ultimate, incorruptible, irreproducible core of your existence."

Ignatiev fell silent. He's right, he admitted to himself. Even though I don't accept the religious claptrap, I believe deep within me that I have an individual soul, different and quite distinct from every other person's.

"Fascinating," said the avatar, "how these primitive concepts maintain their grip on your intelligence."

Ignatiev had no reply.

As the four of them resumed walking down the long, featureless corridor, the avatar beside Gita winked out of existence.

Gita flinched surprise.

The avatar near Ignatiev explained, "We have no need for two simulacrums. We can give you all the information you need with one."

Ignatiev nodded, and Gita seemed to recover her composure. As the three of them resumed walking along the corridor she asked question after question about the biosphere facility, chattering along, her excitement growing with every step of the way.

"Are there primatelike species in your facility? Precursors of the creatures that built your ancestors?" she asked as they walked along.

The avatar replied, "Our creators were extinguished in a death wave event some two hundred fifty million of your years ago. They had produced intelligent machines and were learning to interact with them when the death wave destroyed them all. Our forerunners were quite surprised. I would say they were shocked, but of course they were incapable of such an emotional reaction."

Gita asked, "All organic life on your planet was destroyed?"

"Down to the benthic fishes, in the deepest depths of our oceans."

"But your precursors—the AI devices—were not affected by the death wave?"

"Many were, of course. But enough survived to continue our development, up to the present moment. It was not easy, but we survived."

Suspicious, Ignatiev challenged, "If the planet was wiped clean of organic life, how did the organic forms living on the surface today come into existence?"

The avatar turned slightly toward him. "Why, the same way that your biologists on Earth have re-created long-extinct organic species."

"Rewilding!" Gita exclaimed. "Re-creating extinct species from samples of fossil DNA." To Ignatiev, she bubbled, "I've been involved in that, Dr. Ig—er, Alex. I was part of the bio team that brought the sauropod *Diplodocus* back into existence."

Ignatiev stopped walking, and the two others stopped alongside him.

"Can you tell me," he asked the avatar, "why you haven't re-created the intelligent organic creatures who developed your own ancestors?"

The avatar stared at him for almost a full minute. Ignatiev counted the time by listening to the pulse thumping in his ears.

Finally, the human figure answered, "We saw no need to do so. Organic intelligence had served its purpose by creating us. We decided it would be too stressful for such creatures to live in a world where machine intelligence had so far surpassed their own achievements."

"You didn't want to have any competition."

The human avatar smiled coldly. "You see? Your immediate interpretation is based on the concept of competition. How would the organics face up to the situation where *they* are not the lords of creation that they always assumed themselves to be? How would they accept the fact that we machines have evolved much farther than they ever could have?"

"So you decided not to re-create a race that might compete with you," Ignatiev said.

"There would be no competition," the humanoid figure said flatly. "Machine intelligence is demonstrably more capable than organic."

"Including we humans."

"Yes."

Gita's expression had shifted from excited exhilaration to guarded anxiety. Ignatiev himself felt as if he had opened a powder keg.

But the avatar let the tension slide past. "Come," it said, pointing down the corridor, "we are almost at the area where your quarters have been built."

So they started walking again, this time, though, in silence. It doesn't matter, Ignatiev told himself. They can read our thoughts just as clearly as if we spoke them.

Then he realized that he didn't seem to feel tired at all. This planet's gravity isn't that much lighter than Earth's, he thought. Yet my legs don't ache; I feel much younger than I did before. The ALS . . .

The humanlike avatar, pacing along beside him, said, "You feel well, Professor Ignatiev."

"Quite well."

"Perhaps learning new things, confronting new concepts, puts fresh strength in your legs."

"Or you've cured my ALS?"

"Oh, no. Not that. We would never interfere with your bodily processes without your permission."

"But . . . could you cure me?"

"Perhaps," said the avatar.

Perhaps, Ignatiev said to himself. Perhaps.

He saw a blank wall at the end of the corridor. As if his glance activated a hidden mechanism, the wall dissolved as they approached it. Another elevator, Ignatiev saw. Will it take us back to the surface or deeper downward?

Answering his unvoiced question, the avatar said, "We are constructing a village for you, up on the surface. Soon it will be large enough to house all your people."

"All two thousand of us?" Ignatiev asked.

"Yes. And your laboratories and workshops, as well. We intend for all of you to live here in comfort."

The elevator rose swiftly. And when the doors opened again they were back on the smooth, flat surface of what Ignatiev now thought of as the roof of the machines' city. In the distance he could see their shuttlecraft, inert and alone, waiting for them.

The avatar pointed in the opposite direction, and Ignatiev saw—at the far end of the rooflike expanse—a cluster of small buildings. They reminded Ignatiev of an urban apartment complex, although he could see no windows, no balconies, nothing that allowed a view of the outside. On their far side, industrious construction machines were busily erecting more such buildings.

"Your new quarters," the avatar said smoothly.

They work fast, Ignatiev thought.

The avatar led Gita and Ignatiev into the nearest of the buildings. Inside its blank, featureless entrance was a circular passageway, marked by doors that bore nameplates on them.

"We have tried to make your quarters here as comfortable as possible," said the avatar.

The first door bore Ignatiev's name. It slid open as they approached.

Ignatiev stepped through and looked around. The avatar came in with him, while Gita hesitated outside in the circular corridor.

"Will this be satisfactory?" the avatar asked.

Ignatiev turned a full circle. He was standing in the front room of his house in Saint Petersburg, *his* home, the home he had shared with Sonya for so many years.

The fireplace crackled with a real fire. Ignatiev went to it and warmed his hands.

"This is satisfactory?" the avatar asked again.

"I presume you have potato vodka stocked in the kitchen," Ignatiev replied.

"We have tried our best. No one in your crew seems to know the exact formula for potato vodka."

Ignatiev grunted, then said, "It's the thought that counts."

CHAPTER FIFTEEN

The avatar smiled pleasantly at Ignatiev and started for the door. "We will leave you alone in your quarters, for now. The kitchen is voice-activated. It can prepare a wide variety of meals for you, all you have to do is tell it what you want."

"Thank you," said Ignatiev.

As it reached the door, the avatar turned and reminded, "Your executive committee meeting will convene at nine A.M. tomorrow."

Nodding, Ignatiev replied, "Yes, I know." Through the open doorway he could see Gita, standing in the corridor like a lonely waif.

"You can attend the meeting right here, in your sitting room."

"Very convenient."

"Good evening, then."

"Good evening."

The human figure went through the door; it slid shut softly behind him, but not before Ignatiev saw it gesturing to Gita to follow it farther up the hallway.

Alone now, Ignatiev took a few steps back toward the crackling fireplace. The flames were real; he enjoyed their warmth. He turned and went to the couch. It was the same, exactly the same, as the couch that he remembered from his Saint Petersburg living room. Even the creases in the leather upholstery and the worn, shining spots were the same.

Of course, he said to himself. The machines picked through my memory to create this room.

He slumped down onto the worn old couch with a tired sigh and sank his head in his hands. These damned machines, he moaned inwardly. Everything is perfect. Exactly duplicated. Exactly. He half expected to see Sonya coming in from the kitchen.

He straightened up. No, he told himself. That way lies true madness. She's gone and you can't bring her back. All you can do is replay the memories; the damned machines will be playing a game with you. It won't be Sonya. It can't be.

Ignatiev forced himself to his feet. Don't sink yourself into the past. Don't fall into that trap. Forward. That's the only way to go. Face the future as you always have. Whatever happens, you must go forward, into the future. Leave the past behind. It's dead and there's nothing you or these devilishly clever machines can do to bring it back.

He caught an image of himself in a mirror hanging on the far wall of the room. Straighten up! he commanded himself. Damn the ALS! Head high, shoulders back.

Face the future.

Very deliberately, Ignatiev called out, "Aida, can you hear me?"

"Of course," said the AI's synthesized voice.

"Please contact Dr. Nawalapitiya for me."

Gita's bright, eager face took form on the holographic display above the fireplace.

She seemed surprised. "Professor Ignatiev!"

"Alex."

She blinked once, then amended, "Alex."

Suddenly, he didn't know what to say. "Er . . . how are your quarters?"

Gita broke into a happy smile. "Very comfortable.

Very homey. It's a duplicate of my university rooms at Trinkomalee. Home, you know."

"You're comfortable?"

"I'm sure I will be."

Ignatiev ran out of words. What do you do now, idiot? he snarled to himself.

Gita saved him his embarrassment. "The rest of the group is meeting in the common room. Won't you join us there?"

"Common room?" Ignatiev asked, feeling stupid.

Her brows wrinkling slightly, Gita said, "It's three . . . no, four doors up from your quarters."

"I'll see you there," he said.

Raj Jackson and all of the other members of the team were there when Ignatiev stepped through the door of the common room. It was a generous space, furnished with a scattering of upholstered chairs and couches. A small bar occupied one corner, and displays along the walls showed views of the planet's greenery and the distant craggy mountains.

Gita was standing at the bar when Ignatiev entered, her slim figure looking almost childlike next to Jackson and the others. She broke into a warm smile when she saw Ignatiev.

He headed straight for the bar, beside her.

Jackson already had a glass in his hand. "I don't know exactly what this stuff is," he said, pointing at the glass's amber contents with his free hand, "but it's good."

There was a machine behind the bar: a square of metal and synthetics, with four flexible arms. No face, no humanlike features at all. But it asked, "What can I produce for you, Professor Ignatiev?"

"Potato vodka," Ignatiev answered immediately.

"Unfortunately," the robot's voicebox responded, "no one here knows the contents of potato vodka. Would distilled grain alcohol satisfy you?"

"It's good," Jackson repeated encouragingly.

With a resigned nod, Ignatiev said, "Distilled grain alcohol, then."

Within a few minutes, the team pushed the room's chairs into a rough circle. Everyone seemed happy enough, at ease. Ignatiev sipped at his drink. The source of their delight, he thought.

"It's been a very interesting day," he said.

"And then some!" said one of the women.

"They just built these apartments for us, out of thin air!"

Ignatiev held up a cautioning finger. "They have studied us since we arrived in orbit, I'm sure. Perhaps from before we established orbit."

"They could see our ship approaching, I imagine," said Jackson.

"And they can read our minds," Ignatiev added.

"Really? You think so?"

"I'm certain of it. We'll have no secrets from them."

Gita's normally cheerful face became somber. "They were able to cut off our comm link with Aida and *Intrepid*. That's a bit scary."

"If they can really read our minds . . ."

"How do you think they could reproduce our homes on Earth?" Ignatiev said.

"They can certainly move fast," Jackson pointed out. "They built all this in the few hours since we landed."

"Or perhaps," Ignatiev said, "they scanned our thoughts, our memories, as we approached their planet."

"Either way, it's pretty spooky," Jackson admitted.

Ignatiev pointed out, "Either way, we're their prisoners."

Chapter Sixteen

Ignatiev did not sleep well that night. He felt uneasy, almost frightened. He tossed restlessly on his bed—*his bed*, the one he had slept in for so many years in St. Petersburg. When he finally managed to drift into sleep, it was troubled with menacing dreams of vague unearthly beings hovering around him, reading his thoughts, making him feel small and insignificant.

He awoke covered in cold sweat.

"Aida," he whispered, "are you there?"

"I am with you, Professor Ignatiev." But even Aida's calm, soothing voice seemed to have a hint of foreign inflection, as if the AI had been invaded by an alien.

Ignatiev sat up in his bed, feeling helpless, close to overwhelmed. Then he heard himself ask, "Aida, how old is Gita?"

"Dr. Nawalapitiya will be eighty years old on June seventh," came the reply.

Eighty years old, Ignatiev said to himself. She doesn't look a day more than thirty, thirty-five at most. Life-extension therapies. She's a child, a gamine. A very lovely *houri* out of the *Arabian Nights*. I'm old enough to be her grandfather, her great-grandfather, even. Yet the thought of her pleased him. So young. So vital.

He lay back in bed and fell peacefully asleep.

* * *

The avatar had told him the truth. Sitting on the couch in his living room, Ignatiev was at the head of the conference table, up in *Intrepid,* with the full executive committee in their seats.

It's like being in two places at the same time, he said to himself, consciously suppressing an urge to blink at the committee members sitting around him.

Jugannath Patel, sitting at his right, was asking, "These machines actually built living quarters for your exploration team?"

Ignatiev waggled a finger. "I don't believe we should think of the machine intelligence as a set of separate devices. It is one machine, completely interlinked and in constant, instant communication with all its parts."

"And it can read our thoughts?"

Nodding, Ignatiev replied, "There's plenty of evidence for that."

"And they don't want our help?" one of the others asked.

"They say they have no need of our help. They have survived earlier death waves and they believe they will survive this one as well."

Aida's three-dimensional image on the wall display pointed out, "I have been unable to contact Earth for the past twenty-two hours and eighteen minutes."

"They've cut us off from Earth?" Patel asked, suddenly wide-eyed.

Ignatiev said, "It's probably temporary. Remember, they cut our ground team off from this ship, at first."

"But why? What reason could they have—"

The avatar's humanlike image replaced Aida's. "Please do not be alarmed. We thought it best to keep you from contacting your homeworld until you understand us better."

"Really?" Ignatiev said.

The human figure smiled slightly. "Really. You

have much to learn about us. We have much to teach you."

"But we would like to report back to our colleagues on Earth," Patel tried to explain. "They must be concerned about us."

One of the other executive committee members said, "They might think we're dead!"

"You must be patient," said the avatar. "Your communications link will be restored in time."

"Meanwhile," said Ignatiev, "we're your prisoners."

"Our guests," the human figure corrected. "Our honored guests."

A wary silence fell across the conference room. The committee members looked at one another apprehensively. Ignatiev felt their fear.

The avatar tried to lighten the situation. "In the meantime, Professor Ignatiev, it should please you to know that we have retrieved the recipe for potato vodka from your AI system's memory files. An adequate supply of the refreshment is being prepared for you, and anyone else who would like to share it."

Ignatiev dipped his chin slightly in acknowledgment. "Thank you. I appreciate your kindness."

But he thought, Maybe they believe they can keep me sedated with the stuff.

The executive committee's meeting dragged on. Ignatiev doggedly went through the items on the agenda that Patel had prepared: communications, technology, geophysics, exobiology.

Then the head of the ship's propulsion department reported, "The main drive engines are unresponsive."

"Unresponsive?"

"The engines' control systems don't respond to our inputs. It's as if they were dead."

"Dead?"

"We won't be able to break orbit and leave this planetary system. We're stuck here."

The chief of the communications department added, "And we can't contact Earth, either, remember. The QUE system is down and we don't know what's knocked it out."

Ignatiev looked up at the avatar's image on the wall screen. "What does this mean?" he demanded.

Calmly, the machines' avatar replied, "We don't want you to leave until you've learned as much about us as you can."

"You're preventing us from leaving? You're preventing us from even contacting Earth?"

"Yes. If you left now, or if you reported your first impressions of us, we are afraid it would present a distorted image of our civilization. We want you to understand us as fully as possible before you report back to your homeworld."

Ignatiev realized once again, We're prisoners here. We can't leave unless and until the machines decide that they want us to leave.

"We've got to get back home!" one of the committee members insisted.

"You will," the avatar replied smoothly. "In time. You must be patient."

What choice do we have? Ignatiev asked himself.

The men and women around the conference table were all talking at once, gesticulating, arguing. Ignatiev stared at the avatar's image, sitting calmly, its face serene.

To you we're a bunch of chattering apes, he said silently to the image. We've got to prove to you that we're much more than that.

He slapped the tabletop with the flat of his hand, making several of the committee members twitch with surprise.

"Let's come to order," Ignatiev said. Then, forcing a smile, he went on, "There's an old piece of folk wisdom that's appropriate to this situation: When handed a lemon, make lemonade."

"I don't understand," said Patel, shaking his head dolefully.

Ignatiev replied in a strong, steady voice, "We are here. Apparently we will remain here for some time to come. Very well, let's explore this planet as fully as we can. We are scientists: our profession is to learn, to understand, to bring new knowledge to light. Let us make plans to explore this world, and the machine intelligence that exists here. When we finally return to Earth we should bring with us as full an understanding of this world as we can achieve."

Silence around the table. They're afraid, Ignatiev realized. They'd like to get away from this planet and return home. Well, we can't do that. So as long as we're stuck here, let's learn as much as we can.

"To that end," he said aloud, "we should hear the presentation by Dr. Nawalapitiya, the exobiology representative on the ground team. She has plans for examining the organic species of the planet."

Looking up at the holographic display once more, he saw that it already showed Gita, sitting in the living room of her quarters on the planet.

With a smile that he didn't know he was smiling, Ignatiev said, "Dr. Nawalapitiya, your report, please."

CHAPTER SEVENTEEN

Gita spoke glowingly of the biosphere facility, and views of its lush growth filled the screen. The executive committee members stared, some in consternation, most in awe.

"They maintain a full-spectrum sampling of the natural biosphere that's on the surface of the planet?" asked the committee's chief exobiologist, Dr. Okpara Mandabe.

"Yes, sir," Gita replied. "They use it to keep a real-time check on the biota living on the surface."

His dark, heavy-featured face almost scowling, Mandabe probed, "How far does this assessment go? Down to the cellular level? Or is it merely macroscopic?"

"I don't know," Gita admitted. Then she quickly added, "Yet."

"What does that mean?" Patel asked.

With a smile, Gita replied, "I'd like to explore the natural biosphere. I'd like to ask the machines' permission to do so."

"Up on the surface, in the wild?"

"Yes, of course. We have an opportunity to examine a fully alien biota."

"If the machines allow it," Ignatiev cautioned.

Gita looked surprised. "Why wouldn't they allow it?"

"Ask them," said Ignatiev. "They seem to have their own agenda regarding us."

The wall display suddenly split in two; the avatar appeared alongside Gita's.

"We have no objection to your exploring the biosphere," the avatar's image said smoothly. "Although we suggest that you begin with the facility we have created here underground."

Gita nodded. "Yes. Then we could compare the facility's condition to the conditions on the surface."

"Actually," the humanlike avatar said, "you will find the two to be entirely congruent, to within the limits of your measuring systems."

Ignatiev said, "You're implying that you don't want us studying the surface biosphere."

"We are *suggesting*," the humanoid said, with obvious patience, "that we can watch over you and protect you in the facility more completely than in the natural world on the surface."

"The surface is dangerous?"

"Of course. The animals are wild. We do not control them. Many species are strongly territorial, and might attack intruders. There are infectious microbes, of course. And even predatory species of plant life."

"Really?" Gita's eyes were wide with anticipation.

"You would need to wear protective clothing, even in our underground facility," said the avatar.

"We have biosuits," Gita said, her face glowing with enthusiasm.

Ignatiev studied her face. She's eager to explore. The dangers don't deter her.

Then he focused on the machines' avatar. He's trying to discourage Gita from exploring the surface. Why? Is he really concerned for her safety? Or is there some other reason?

* * *

The meeting dragged on for another hour and more. Ignatiev watched and listened as each and every member of the committee had his or her say, mostly repetitions or rehashes of what had already been said. But each individual ego had to be massaged, he knew.

Finally, unable to stand the self-important blathering any longer, Ignatiev raised his voice. "Very well, then. We will put together a team to study the planet's organic species, starting with the biosphere facility that the machines maintain."

Turning to the head of the exobiology department, Ignatiev asked, "Dr. Mandabe, do you have any objection to naming Dr. Nawalapitiya to lead the team?"

For a moment, the head of the exobiology department looked startled, his red-rimmed eyes flashing wide. But he quickly regained his self-control and acknowledged grudgingly, "I suppose she's earned the honor."

"Good," said Ignatiev. Looking up at Gita's image on the wall display, he said, "Congratulations, Dr. Nawalapitiya. You'll coordinate your selections for the team with Dr. Mandabe, of course."

Practically beaming, Gita nodded and murmured, "Certainly."

Ignatiev adjourned the meeting at last, and found himself slumped back in the familiar cushions of his couch. Two hours of chattering to produce ten minutes of work: not bad for a committee meeting.

As he pushed himself up from the couch and headed for the kitchen, the door buzzer sounded. Glancing at the small screen set in the wall to one side of the door, Ignatiev saw it was Gita.

"Come in!" he shouted, and hurried toward the door. She was obviously excited. Practically prancing into the room, she bubbled, "You made me the team leader! I could kiss you!"

Why not? Ignatiev thought. But he said to her, "Why shouldn't you be the team's leader? It's your idea. And Mandabe obviously has no desire to come down to the planet and do any useful work himself."

"He wants me to report to him every day," said Gita.

Ignatiev shrugged. "He needs to feel important, to believe he's in control."

"But you're really the one in control, aren't you?"

He stared at her for a long, wordless moment: so young, so full of enthusiasm, so lovely.

"No," Ignatiev said. "*You're* the one in control. Don't let it go to your head."

She grew more serious. "I won't. At least, I'll try not to let it go to my head."

"Good." He hesitated a moment, then heard himself ask, "Would you like to have dinner with me? We can see what this kitchen can really do."

"I'd be happy to have dinner with you, Alex."

Ignatiev's face broke into a huge, happy grin.

Chapter Eighteen

The kitchen was several notches better than the one he remembered at home in Saint Petersburg. Ignatiev asked for a certain dish and the ingredients automatically came sliding out of the cabinets and full-sized refrigerator. Mechanical arms sliced, diced, chopped, and mixed them into pots and slid the preparations into an oven that was a duplicate of the one from home—except that it operated without human intervention.

A good thing, Ignatiev said to himself, remembering his own miserable attempts at cooking.

Gita watched, wide-eyed, as dinner swiftly went from basic ingredients to an aromatic pair of steaming Wienerschnitzels on the kitchen's small dining table.

When Ignatiev went to the wine closet, sure enough there was a bottle of potato vodka on the top shelf. He even recognized the label.

At last he and Gita were sitting at the table, facing each other.

"It's marvelous!" she pronounced, after a bite of the delicately flavored poached fish Ignatiev had ordered as their appetizer.

Still chewing, Ignatiev nodded and agreed. "Good."

Once the veal dish came sliding onto their table, Ignatiev asked, "So you were born and raised in Sri Lanka?"

"Yes," Gita replied, reaching for her glass of wine.

"My parents wanted me to marry, but none of the young men I knew interested me."

How about an older man? Ignatiev wanted to ask. But he kept silent.

"I went to university and became fascinated with biology," she went on. "And here I am."

"Two thousand light-years from home."

Her expression turned glum. "It's a long way, isn't it?"

"When we get back to Earth," Ignatiev said, suppressing the impulse to say *if we get back,* "four thousand years will have elapsed."

"We'll be strangers. The entire civilization will have changed enormously, I imagine."

"Yes, of course."

"Exiles on our own homeworld."

"A new world to explore."

Gita smiled. "That's the optimistic way to look at it, isn't it?"

"What made you agree to join this expedition?" he asked. "It's like throwing your life away."

Her expression darkening again, Gita replied, "We've all done that, haven't we?"

"Yes, but why? Why leave everything you've known, your family, your friends, to go on this one-way expedition into an unknowable future?"

"That's what you've done, haven't you, Alex? And not just once. You were on the Gliese mission. Why?"

"I'm an old man, Gita. Old and expendable. But you have your whole life ahead of you."

She looked into his eyes for a moment, then turned her attention back to the dish in front of her. "I'm a scientist, Alex. The same as you. I want to learn, to discover, to uncover new knowledge."

Ignatiev shook his head. "There's more to it than that, isn't there?"

Gita nodded. "Of course."

He realized he was being intrusive. "I'm sorry. I shouldn't pry into your private life."

"Why did you go on a star mission? Twice."

He hesitated. Then he admitted, "When my wife died I thought my own life was over. I was just going through the motions, waiting to die. The chance to join the Gliese mission . . . well, it was something to do, something different. Then when we returned to Earth I found that I'd become famous—"

"For saving the mission."

"For being too stubborn to let it fail. They offered me this mission. Being officially a hero, I found it impossible to refuse."

"A true hero," she said, smiling.

Ignatiev heard himself admit, "A hero with an incurable disease."

Her smile vanished. "Disease?"

Inwardly frowning at himself, Ignatiev told her about the ALS.

"And it's incurable?" Gita asked, disbelieving.

He nodded. "The medical people can't tinker with the brain cells involved, they tell me. They can delay the disease's progress, but they can't stop it altogether."

Gita's face was a picture of sympathy.

"I've got many years ahead of me," Ignatiev said, brightening. "I'm not dead yet."

Sadly, she murmured, "We'll all be dead, sooner or later, won't we?"

"Sooner or later," Ignatiev agreed.

For several long moments they stared at each other across the narrow table.

Trying to brighten the gloom, Ignatiev said, "So tell me why you decided to come along on this mission."

Her eyes flicking away from his, she said softly, "I fell in love."

"Oh."

"But he didn't love me. It's that simple. I signed up for this star mission to get away from him, from the memory of him."

"Two thousand light-years," Ignatiev murmured. "Has it been far enough?"

"Almost," Gita said, smiling sadly. "Almost."

They finished the meal in silence, each wrapped in private thoughts. Then they left the kitchen as flexible mechanical arms slid out of the walls and whisked the dishes into the washer.

Ignatiev suggested an after-dinner drink but Gita declined. Yet she sat down on the worn old couch. Ignatiev thought it over for a few seconds, then decided to take the upholstered armchair next to the couch instead of sitting beside her.

"The meal was wonderful, Alex," she said.

"It was good, wasn't it?"

"The machines must get the recipes from Aida's files."

"But where do they get the ingredients? Poached fish. Wienerschnitzel. They must construct them from the molecular level."

"They're very intelligent," said Gita.

"And fast!"

She laughed. "If they can really read our thoughts, as you suspect, then perhaps they know what we want before we consciously know it ourselves."

Frowning, Ignatiev said, "That bothers me. I don't like having someone poking into my mind."

"Some*thing*," Gita corrected.

"Yes," he grumbled.

Abruptly, she changed the subject. "Do you want to be included on the team that will explore the biosphere facility?"

With a shrug, Ignatiev replied, "I'm not a biologist, but yes, I'd certainly like to go with you."

Gita nodded her approval. "Rank hath its privileges."

They discussed the foray into the machines' underground facility for nearly another hour.

"Will you be able to keep pace with the team?" she asked. "I mean, with your ALS . . . ?"

He made a crooked smile. "I'm not dead yet."

Suddenly alarmed, Gita said, "Oh, I didn't mean to imply—"

Grinning at her, he said, "It's all right. I'm sure I can keep up with you youngsters."

She smiled back at him. "Good."

They chatted amiably for nearly another hour. At last Gita yawned politely and said, "I'd better get home."

Ignatiev rose to his feet. "I'll walk you to your door."

"It's only a few meters up the corridor."

Extending his arm to her, he said, "The proprieties should be maintained."

Laughing, Gita let him take her arm. "By all means."

They walked together to her door. As it slid open, Gita said, "Thank you, Alex, for a charming evening."

And she pecked at his cheek.

Ignatiev stood there for several long minutes after Gita had entered her apartment and slid the door shut behind her.

At last he huffed, bunched his shoulders, and strode back to his own door. Silly old fool, he groused to himself.

But he was beaming.

ChAPTEr NINETEEN

Ignatiev's smile disappeared as soon as he entered his own quarters. The display above the fireplace was blinking, MESSAGE FROM DR. MANDABE. URGENT.

Trouble, Ignatiev thought as he sank onto his couch and stared at the bloodred letters. It's late, he told himself. But it says *urgent*. With some reluctance, he told Aida to connect him to the head of the exobiology department.

Mandabe was wide awake, his dark, heavy-featured face scowling impatiently.

"It's about time you returned my call," he practically growled.

Ignatiev answered amiably, "I just received your message." And he thought, When in doubt, blame the messenger.

The exobiology chief was not placated. "Professor Ignatiev," he said, in a low, almost menacing rumble. "I want to talk with you."

"Now? At this hour?"

"Now," Mandabe said firmly.

"Very well."

Mandabe appeared to be sitting in his own quarters aboard *Intrepid*. He jabbed a finger at Ignatiev and accused, "You humiliated me. You deliberately humiliated me. In front of the whole committee."

Ignatiev's jaw dropped open in surprise. "Humiliated you?"

"At today's meeting. You named that slip of a girl to head the investigative team. That should have been *my* decision, not yours."

Ignatiev mumbled, "I suppose so. I apologize. I had no intention of humiliating you."

Completely unappeased, Mandabe said, "No, of course you didn't. You're so fascinated with the woman that you can't think of anything else."

Ignatiev could see that the exobiologist was furious. His dark face radiated anger. What kind of a chess piece is he? Ignatiev asked himself. A queen, perhaps, powerful and imperious, disdainful of the other players on the board.

He started to say, "This is all a misunderstanding—"

"No it's not," Mandabe insisted. "You're hot for the little bitch and she's using you to climb the ladder."

"That's not true," Ignatiev snapped. "And I want you to apologize for using that vulgar term."

"Apologize? Hah! What were the two of you doing all evening?"

His own temper rising, Ignatiev growled, "We had dinner together."

"And what else?"

The man's insane, Ignatiev thought. Then he realized, He feels threatened. He thinks I'm belittling him because I want Gita. He wants to be the alpha male of this pack. Maybe he wants Gita for himself.

"You're being foolish," Ignatiev said, as calmly as he could manage.

"Am I? She's twisting you around her little finger, and you're enjoying the experience."

Ignatiev shot to his feet. "That's a lie!"

Mandabe rose, too, ponderously, and Ignatiev realized

that the man was a head taller and at least a dozen kilos bigger than he.

For a long, silent moment they stood glaring at each other. Ignatiev couldn't help feeling glad that Mandabe was aboard the starship while he was on the surface of the planet.

"So how do you propose to settle this?" Ignatiev asked. "Swords or pistols?"

Mandabe blinked, confused.

"The honorable thing to do," Ignatiev explained, "is to fight a duel."

"A duel?"

"Yes. In my country, when two men have an irreconcilable conflict, they settle it with a duel."

"That's primitive."

The trace of a smile on his lips, Ignatiev explained, "No, it's very modern. Even therapeutic, so the psychotechnicians say."

Mandabe's face contorted with utter incomprehension.

"We fight a duel in virtual reality. We agree on the weapons to be used and the setting. Then, in a virtual reality simulation, we can bang away at each other to our hearts' content, until one of us either surrenders or dies—in the VR simulation. In actuality, no one is injured in the slightest."

"Virtual reality," Mandabe muttered.

"Yes," said Ignatiev. "Would you care to try it?"

"No!" Mandabe snapped. "It's ridiculous. Childish."

Forcing himself to remain calm, Ignatiev said, "Then how do you propose to settle this? I've already apologized. I had no intention of humiliating you."

Mandabe filled the display screen, a tall, powerful thundercloud of a man, uncertain, undecided.

At last he hissed, "I accept your apology."

"Very well. Now I would like to hear you apologize for what you called Dr. Nawalapitiya."

Grudgingly, Mandabe said, "I let my anger get the better of me. I regret using that term."

Ignatiev put up both his hands. "Then everything is settled."

His red-rimmed eyes narrowing, Mandabe muttered, "I suppose it is."

"I'll be more careful in suggesting personnel assignments in the future," Ignatiev assured him.

"Good," said Mandabe. "See that you are."

The holographic display went dark, and Ignatiev let out a heartfelt sigh. A soft answer turneth away wrath, he reminded himself. Good thing, too. The man was angry enough to break me in half.

chapter twenty

The next morning, Ignatiev used Aida to call Gita and asked her to meet him in the common room that the machines had included in their quarters.

"I'm halfway through breakfast," said Gita's image in the holographic viewer. "Can you give me fifteen minutes?"

"Take half an hour, if you like."

With a smile she said, "Fifteen minutes should be fine."

Ignatiev had not slept well. His encounter with Mandabe troubled him. *The man wants to be the alpha male in our community,* Ignatiev told himself. *He resents anything that he sees as a threat to his ambition.*

With a shake of his head, Ignatiev recalled that a similar situation led to Julius Caesar's assassination.

Gita was waiting for him when Ignatiev stepped into the common room, sitting on one of the comfortable couches scattered about the spacious area. Only two others were there, Raj Jackson and one of the geophysicists, their attention focused on a map display on one of the wall screens.

"What do you want to see me about?" Gita asked as Ignatiev sat down gingerly next to her.

"Mandabe," Ignatiev answered.

"Dr. Mandabe doesn't like me," Gita said. Her tone was level, controlled. No tears, not a complaint, really. Merely a statement of fact.

Ignatiev frowned. "What makes you think that?"

"I can feel it," Gita said. "He's very exacting with me. He called me this morning and demanded written details on every person I'm considering for the exploration team. It's going to take me longer to get his approval for my choices than it'll take to make the decisions in the first place."

Ignatiev said, "He feels threatened. You're a challenge to his sense of authority, his position on the totem pole."

Frowning with puzzlement, Gita asked, "Totem pole?"

"An old North American symbol: chain of command, pecking order, line of authority."

Clearly surprised, Gita said, "But I'm not challenging his position! He's the chief of the exobiology department! A distinguished researcher! A leader in the field!"

With a wry smile, Ignatiev asked, "Then what's he doing here, among the exiles?"

"I don't understand."

Thinking of his own situation, Ignatiev explained, "He was persuaded to join this mission because he's near the end of his useful career. Like me, he's no longer doing leading-edge research. He's shuffling papers and chairing meetings. You'll be leading a research team. You're going off into new territory. He's jealous of you—and afraid you might threaten his position of power."

"But I don't want—"

"It's not what you want, my dear," Ignatiev said softly. "It's what he believes that you want."

Gita blinked with perplexity.

Ignatiev added, "The fact that I suggested that you lead the field team hasn't helped. He thinks I'm backing you, in preference to him."

"But that's not true!"

Yes it is, Ignatiev realized. Yes it is. But he decided not to tell her about Mandabe's visit the previous night.

It would only pour fuel on her suspicions, upset her more.

Spreading his hands in a gesture that was part tutorial, part frustration, Ignatiev explained, "It's the old primate urge for power. Mandabe sees you as a challenge. You're threatening his position at the top of the exobiology heap. So he reacts by showing you he's more powerful than you are."

"That's so primitive!"

"It's an instinct lodged deep in the human psyche," Ignatiev said.

"The male psyche," Gita countered.

With a sigh that was almost a grunt, Ignatiev replied, "I've seen it among females, too. But men are more obvious about it, true enough." Breaking into a low chuckle, he added, "You're lucky. A few millennia ago he would have come after you with bared fangs, looking for blood."

Gita almost smiled. Instead, she asked, "So what am I to do?"

Ignatiev thought it over for a few moments. "If I tried to speak to him about it, I'm afraid that would only make matters worse."

"He'd think you have a special interest in me."

But I do, Ignatiev realized, with something of a shock.

Aloud, he replied, "Be compliant, outwardly. Show him that you know he's the boss, the head of the tribe. But go ahead in your own way, get your job done as you think it should be done."

"Let him think I'm submissive, but do what I want to do?"

"Women have been behaving that way since the Stone Age and even earlier."

"That's devious."

"Yes, it is. But it works."

"I don't know if I can behave that way."

Ignatiev shrugged. "You'll learn. I can help you."

"I'll need all the help I can get, Alex."

"I'll help you," he repeated, hoping she felt reassured.

That evening, as Ignatiev prepared for sleep, the machines' avatar appeared in his bedroom, dressed in its usual stiff-collared military-style uniform.

"Dr. Mandabe is causing problems for you," it said, without preamble.

Frowning, Ignatiev snapped, "Must you listen to everything we say?"

"Yes," said the human figure. "We are trying to learn everything we can about you."

"Why?" Ignatiev challenged. "Why must you dig into our inner thoughts? Can't we have some privacy?"

Coolly, the avatar responded, "Why do you want privacy?"

"We're accustomed to it. We consider it a fundamental right of every individual."

Crossing its arms across its chest, the avatar echoed, "Every individual. We find that aspect of your intelligence quite different from our own. You are a mob of individual intelligences, often working at odds against each other. We are one: an intelligence of many parts, but all an integral part of the whole."

"So you are learning from us?"

"We are learning about you."

"For what purpose?"

The humanlike figure fell silent for several heartbeats. At last it replied, "For the purpose of deciding whether we should allow you to leave our world or not."

"Not leave?" Ignatiev gasped. "You would force us to remain here? Against our will?"

"If we decide it is for the best."

Chapter twenty-one

"But you can't do that!" Ignatiev insisted. "Holding nearly two thousand men and women here against their will. It's like kidnapping! It's a crime!"

"Professor Ignatiev," said the human figure, "you are allowing your emotions to distort your thinking."

"You can't hold us here against our will. You mustn't."

"We can and we will, if we decide that we must."

Ignatiev stared at the avatar, wondering what arguments he could find to dissuade it.

The humanlike figure asked, not unkindly, "Professor, what is the ultimate motivation of every species?"

"To survive," Ignatiev answered automatically.

"We are subject to the same imperative. Survival is the primary goal of our species, just as it is yours."

"But we're no threat to your survival."

"You think not? Perhaps the two thousand members of your ship's crew do not threaten our survival, but there are more than thirty billion human creatures back in your solar system. Thirty billion individuals, each with its own goals, its own ambitions, its own desires."

Ignatiev asked, "What of it?"

The avatar made a small smile. "Ahh. That is the question, is it not? What impact on our species would result from full contact with your species?"

"We've already made contact—"

"Your small group has made contact with us. But if

the entire human race learned of our existence, what would happen?"

Ignatiev started to answer, hesitated, then admitted, "I don't know."

"Neither do we," the avatar said. "And until we have determined the answer to that question, you will not be allowed to leave our world, nor to communicate with your homeworld."

Ignatiev's knees felt rubbery. He sank down on the perfectly made bed and argued, "That's not necessary. Let us tell our people about you. It will take more than two thousand years for a follow-up mission to reach you."

"And when they do reach us, what will happen? The history of your species is drenched with the blood of civilizations you have destroyed. And they were fellow humans, the same species as you! How will your people react to us, a race of intelligent machines? A superior intelligence. They will react with fear, undoubtedly. And what you people fear, you try to destroy."

"But you're so far ahead of us. Your technology could protect you. You could . . ." Ignatiev's voice trailed off as he realized where he was heading.

"We could destroy you. Yes. Easily. Just as you destroyed the people you called the hobbits. And the Neanderthals. And the Incas and Aztecs. The Polynesians. The Pan-Asian Confederation. The Asteroidal Alliance. War. Nuclear weapons. Biological weapons. Neuronal disruptors. Slaughter."

"But we've progressed beyond that."

"Have you?" the avatar demanded. "Have you given up all your thoughts of vengeance, of moral crusades, of automatic xenophobic reactions to anything that seems to threaten you?"

"I . . . I don't know."

"Neither do we. And until we come to a firm determination, you and your descendants will remain here, with no contact back to Earth and your solar system."

With that, the avatar vanished.

Still sitting on the bed, Ignatiev stared around the bedroom, wondering what to do, what he could do, to persuade the machine intelligence to allow him and his fellow crew members to leave, to return home.

Promise to be silent? Promise not to tell anyone on Earth about the machines? He shook his head. Swear two thousand people to perpetual silence? Laughable. They can read our thoughts. They'd see how pitiful such a promise would be.

But what can we do? he asked himself over and over. What can we do?

Then he realized that the avatar had said, *"You and your descendants will remain here, with no contact back to Earth and your solar system."*

Our descendants. They're prepared to keep us here forever.

CHAPTER TWENTY-TWO

Ignatiev hardly slept at all that night.

How do we combat a species that can read our thoughts? How can we convince them to let us go home? As he tossed in his bed, asking himself questions to which he had no answer, he knew that the machines could read his innermost thoughts. They know exactly what I'm thinking, Ignatiev told himself. What each and every one of us is thinking.

The realization angered him. They can peer into our minds. Without asking our permission. We're nothing but experimental animals to them, jumping through hoops for their edification.

Are they amused at our antics? No, they have no emotions. No amusement, no fear, not even curiosity. Merely the primal instinct for survival.

If they feel threatened by us, they'll never let us return home. We'll never see Earth again.

At last, feeling wearier than he had when he'd gotten into bed, Ignatiev said to himself, We'd better get accustomed to living here. It looks like we're here to stay.

Then he remembered that the death wave was rushing toward them at the speed of light. It's two hundred light-years away. In two hundred years it will wash over this planet, killing every living thing up on the surface.

Killing us. The machines will let the death wave solve their problem. It will wipe us out.

When in doubt, Ignatiev told himself, when you don't know where to go or how to get there, call a meeting.

Without leaving the quarters that the machines had created for him, Ignatiev sat at the head of the conference table aboard *Intrepid,* flanked on both sides by the members of the executive committee. Along the bulkhead at his left side, extra chairs had been set out to hold additional members of the scientific staff, including Gita. Ignatiev glanced at her as the group chatted, waiting for him to call the meeting to order. She smiled at him, and the whole conference room seemed to brighten.

Raising his voice above the general hubbub, Ignatiev said, "Let's get started, shall we?"

The committee quickly agreed to forgo reading the minutes of the previous meeting. After all, the minutes were available instantaneously through Aida. Ignatiev mentally gave thanks for small mercies.

Before he could speak a word, however, Jugannath Patel, sitting at his right, said, "The first item on the agenda is a report by Dr. Nawalapitiya on the preparations of the field excursion team."

Gita started to get up from her chair, but Ignatiev said, "First I have an announcement to make. An important announcement."

Gita dropped back on her chair as all eyes focused on him.

Clasping his hands on the tabletop, Ignatiev told them, "We might be forced to stay here indefinitely."

Puzzled looks. No fear, not even perplexity. Not yet.

"What do you mean, Professor?" asked one of the geologists, from down near the end of the table.

"The machines might keep us here permanently," said Ignatiev. "They might decide to prevent us from returning to Earth."

"What?"

"They can't do that!"

"It's not right!"

Nodding his agreement, Ignatiev said, "It may not be right, but it's within their power." Jabbing a finger at the chief engineer, "Have you been able to get the ship's engines started again?"

"No," the man replied, frowning. "The generators that power the ship's life-keeping systems are running fine, but the propulsion systems are dead. I've had my whole staff working on the problem, but I've got to admit that we've achieved nothing. They're dead."

Turning to the communications chief, "And our QUE link to Earth?"

With a shake of her blond head, she said, "No joy."

"You're telling us that the machines have done this?" asked Dr. Mandabe, his dark face a troubled mask. "Deliberately?"

"That's precisely what I'm telling you," said Ignatiev. "They will not allow us to return to Earth or even communicate with Earth. They've cut us off completely."

"But why?"

"How can they do that?"

Ignatiev tried to explain that the machines were wary of full contact with Earth's teeming billions.

"But that's ridiculous!"

"They can't keep us here indefinitely."

"It's inhuman!"

Ignatiev stated the obvious. "They are not human."

"Indefinitely?" asked one of the psychotechs. "How long do you think—"

"Until the death wave arrives," Ignatiev said.

That quieted them. Around the long conference table, complete silence fell.

Then one of the engineers demanded, "So what are we going to do about it?"

Ignatiev shrugged. "I'm open to suggestions."

"They can't keep us here!"

"They've done a good job of it so far."

"What of it?" Patel said. "What difference does it make?"

Surprised, Ignatiev asked, "What do you mean?"

"We cut ourselves off from Earth the instant we left on this journey," the Punjabi computer technician said, his voice sad, hopeless. "We are two thousand light-years from home. If we ever get back, it will be to a world that is *four thousand years* ahead of us. An alien world, just as alien as this planet we are studying."

"We're exiles, one way or another," agreed Raj Jackson, the reality of it making his voice hollow.

"But Earth is home . . ."

From behind him, Ignatiev heard Gita's voice, surprisingly strong. "May I make a suggestion?" she asked.

Ignatiev twisted in his chair and gestured for her to rise. "Go ahead, Dr. Nawalapitiya."

As Gita got to her feet, Ignatiev smiled inwardly at the sight of her: so small, slim, sylphlike. Almost like a child among them.

But her voice was calm, firm, self-assured. "As Professor Ignatiev has said on more than one occasion, when someone hands you a lemon, make lemonade."

"What's that supposed to mean?" one of the engineers groused.

"It means that we should continue our studies of this machine intelligence. We should try to find a way to return home, of course, but in the meantime we should continue to learn all we can about the civilization we've found here."

Mandabe's deep, powerful voice rumbled, "You mean that you should go ahead with your exploration of the biosphere facility."

With a nod, Gita added, "And the natural biosphere up on the surface, afterward."

Ignatiev nodded too. That might be the way to escape this trap, he said to himself. Then instantly he clamped down on the thought. Don't let them know what you're thinking!

CHAPTER TWENTY-THREE

As Ignatiev sat on the recliner in his living room he thought, we've traveled two thousand light-years to another star, another solar system. We've established contact with an alien race of intelligent machines. And yet I haven't been beyond the confines of this apartment complex for weeks.

It was a comfortable enough confinement, he admitted. All his physical needs were well taken care of. All but one. For the first time since he'd been aboard the *Sagan* mission—it seemed a lifetime ago—Ignatiev felt a sexual urge.

He frowned at his image in the mirror on the wall across the room. With a grunt that was part desire, part disgust, he said to himself, The next thing you know you'll start having wet dreams.

You'll be two hundred years old in a few months, he told himself sternly. So you've spent much of that time in cryonic deepsleep. So the medics tell you your somatic age is more like ninety. A youthful ninety, at that. Still . . . she's hardly more than a child.

Gita. So young, so vibrant, so . . . No! he snarled at himself. Put her out of your mind. Out of your thoughts. She thinks of you as a grandfather figure. You're not a handsome young prince. You never were.

Still, he yearned.

Take a cold shower, he told himself. Better yet, get back to work.

He asked Aida for summaries of each department's progress. Surprisingly, the day-by-day work of the scientists and engineers was proceeding almost normally. Gita's team was ready to explore the machines' biosphere facility. The engineers reported that all the ship's systems were performing within nominal limits—except for propulsion and the QUE link to Earth, of course.

What are they thinking back home? Ignatiev wondered. All communications with us suddenly cut off, like an eye winking shut. They must think we've met with disaster. In a way, we have. But what will they do, back on Earth? Write off the *Intrepid* mission? Send a follow-up mission? Even if they did, it would take two thousand years to get here. By that time the death wave will have killed us all.

Unbidden, one of Shakespeare's sonnets came to mind:

When, in disgrace with fortune and men's eyes,
I all alone beweep my outcast state . . .

Outcast state, he thought. Old William didn't know the half of it.

But then Ignatiev continued with the sonnet until he mentally recited:

Haply I think on thee,—and then my state,
Like to the lark at break of day arising . . .

Like to a lark at break of day arising, he repeated to himself. Gita. Being exiled in this strange world won't be so bad as long as Gita is here with me.

But how can I tell her how I feel? How can an old fart like me tell her that he's fallen in love with her?

Angrily, he pushed himself up from the recliner and

paced the living room. Old fool, he grumbled to himself. Stupid old fool.

Gita's face was dead serious as she looked at the four exobiologists of her team. Four exobiologists and one idiot, Ignatiev thought.

They were assembled in a smallish chamber that reminded Ignatiev of a spaceship's air lock. Each of the six of them wore a transparent biosuit over his or her clothing, with a thin bubble helmet over their heads, like an inverted fishbowl.

The machines' avatar stood beside Gita, clad in its usual quasi-military uniform. Ignatiev reminded himself that the avatar was an illusion, a three-dimensional projection that looked solid and real enough, even though it was not an actual physical presence.

Ignatiev realized that although Gita was leader of this little team, the avatar was really in charge. It's reading our thoughts, he knew. What does he find inside our skulls? Fear? Anticipation? Excitement?

Gita's expression eased into a satisfied smile. She nodded once inside her helmet, then turned to the avatar. "We're ready to go out," she said.

"Very well," replied the humanlike figure. "This way."

A portion of the wall disappeared. Beyond the opening Ignatiev saw tangled, thick green foliage.

Gita took the first step out into the biosphere facility, glancing back over her shoulder at her team following her.

"Sensors activated?" she asked.

One by one her teammates answered affirmatively. Ignatiev, at the rear of the line, simply nodded.

They stepped into a lush green jungle. It was eerily quiet.

Standing beside Gita, the avatar said in a near-whisper, "The animals sense your presence."

A brightly colored bird flapped by, squawking noisily.

"Well, he's not afraid of us," said one of the team members.

"He has nothing to fear from us," Gita said. Then she added, "Or she."

The group of them was standing on a paved path, wide enough for two to walk abreast. Ignatiev saw that it forked a couple of dozen meters ahead, each branch disappearing into thick foliage.

"I think it best if we stay together," said Gita, "for the present. This first excursion is just a look-see."

"Take nothing but pictures," said one of the women, "and leave only footprints."

"Exactly."

The avatar stood still as the team members walked slowly past, until Ignatiev came up beside it. Then it started walking at the professor's leisurely pace.

It called out to the team, "Please let us know if and when you wish to take specimens for laboratory study."

Gita replied, "For now, we're more interested in studying the creatures in their natural habitat."

As they moved down the path, Ignatiev thought, Natural habitat? This habitat has been created by the machines. It may mimic the natural habitat up on the surface, but it's completely machine-built and -maintained.

Still, it was fascinating. Small furry creatures scampered among the profuse foliage. Others darted up the massive boles of the huge trees that rose a hundred meters and more above the explorers. Large reptilian fliers glided on leathery wings high up among the trees' crowns of foliage. Gradually the forest came alive. Hoots and whistles and low, menacing growls filled the air. Some of the team looked about apprehensively, but Gita pushed along steadily, her eyes darting everywhere.

She's in her element, Ignatiev realized. This must be an exobiologist's dream, a complete biosphere of alien creatures. He saw that Gita had a pleased little smile on her face.

A roar suddenly shook the place and a massive six-legged beast shambled out of the foliage to stand in front of the exploration team. It was more than four meters long from its fanged mouth to its fuzzy stub of a tail, and at least two meters tall at its shoulder. All muscle and rippling coarse dark orange-brown fur. Even its eyes looked fierce.

Suddenly Ignatiev felt very small, very vulnerable.

The whole team froze.

"Holy god!" one of the men yelped.

Gita, leading the little team, was face-to-face with the beast. Ignatiev saw that its head was huge, massive, with wide jaws studded with curved fangs.

Each member of the team carried a high-voltage stun pistol, but confronted by this monster, Ignatiev wondered if the gun would do anything more than annoy the brute.

Still, he saw Gita's hand slowly sliding toward the holster at her hip.

"Not to worry!" shouted the avatar. "We have surrounded the animal with an energy screen. It cannot get through it to attack you."

As if it understood the machine's words, the brute sniffed at the ground, stepped across the paved path, and leaned its bulk against what seemed like the empty air. Something invisible resisted its pushing.

"This is a member of the facility's top predator species. We have intruded on its hunting territory and it wants to either drive us away or kill us."

The man standing next to Gita snatched his pistol from its holster.

"No need to shoot it!" the avatar shouted. "The energy screen will simply absorb your gun's power. The animal cannot reach you. Please do not feel threatened."

"I don't feel threatened," one of the others replied. "Terrified is more like it."

"The animal cannot harm you," the avatar repeated.

The predator sniffed around for another few moments, then turned and headed deeper into the jungle. It stopped abruptly, though, swung its massive head back toward the humans, and gave out another ground-shaking roar.

Ignatiev felt a very urgent impulse to run away. Then he thought, How far could I go before the ALS chops me down? I'd make a happy meal for that beast, flat on my back and shaking from head to toe.

But the predator shambled off, seemingly satisfied that it had staked out its territory.

The exploratory team fell absolutely silent, staring at the area where the animal had been a moment before. Its footprints flattened the foliage where it had stepped.

Pointing to the fork in the path that led away from the giant beast, the avatar said calmly, "Let's go this way."

No one uttered a word of dissent.

They spent the rest of the day taking pictures and dictating notes. The jungle teemed with life, from scurrying insects to the fliers soaring high above, from brightly colored star-shaped flowers to the colossal trees that towered above them and spread their canopies high across the facility.

Ignatiev found it difficult to think of this area as an artificial preserve, an experimental biosphere deliberately created to protect and study the creatures that made it their home. It looked, it smelled, it seemed completely natural; not artificial at all.

He worked his way to Gita, who was standing knee-deep in tangled greenery, scanning the foliage with a multispectral camera.

Ignatiev waited silently until she at last took the camera down from her eyes and began to tuck it into a pouch on her suit's equipment belt.

"There's plenty here for you to study," he said.

Gita looked up at him with a satisfied smile. "An entire alien biosphere," she said. "The machines have offered to build a bio lab for us, so we can study the species here down to the molecular level."

"Very gracious of them."

"And we haven't even started to look at the natural biosphere outside."

"I wonder how natural it really is," said Ignatiev.

Gita pushed through the undergrowth to get back on the paved path. Ignatiev lent a hand to help her.

"This facility by itself is a wonder," she said. "It's enormous."

"The avatar told me it's fifty kilometers on a side. Twenty-five hundred square kilometers, total."

"And filled with plant and animal life."

"I wonder how they light it," Ignatiev mused. "The lighting seems to be diffuse . . ."

She laughed. "You're a physicist. That's a physics question."

"But it impacts the biology, does it not?"

"Yes, of course," she said happily, carelessly. "There's so much to do! So much to learn! We could spend the rest of our lives here."

"We may have to," Ignatiev reminded her.

chapter twenty-four

The days rolled by. Gita's modest exobiology team grew, little by little, with newcomers sent down from the orbiting *Intrepid*. The machines created an extensive biology laboratory for them.

"It's a wonderful facility," she told Ignatiev over dinner, in his quarters. "We can study specimens down to their molecular levels without killing them. Without harming them at all."

He asked, "Is that beyond the capabilities you had back on Earth?"

"Not really," Gita replied as she speared a few leaves of salad. "I think the machines are giving us the same level of technology that we were accustomed to on Earth. I suspect they've gone far beyond us."

Ignatiev chewed thoughtfully on a crust of bread for a moment. Then, "Have you asked the avatar about it?"

"It gets rather evasive. I think it's observing us, testing us to see how far we can advance our understanding of these alien species."

"Perhaps you've been enrolled in a school, without being told so."

Gita's eyes widened with surprise. "You think they're trying to teach us?"

"I think they're trying to determine how much we can absorb. How much we can learn."

"Are they doing that with our other groups?" she wondered.

Ignatiev nodded slowly. "The geologists have been taken on field excursions, up on the surface. The engineers and communications specialists are happily poking into the machines' technology—although they've complained to me that the machines have drawn specific limits as to what they'll show us."

"A school," Gita mused. "We're all being put through a school. Why?"

"To see how much we can learn. To find the limits of our understanding."

"But why?" Gita repeated. "What is their motivation for all this?"

"Good question," said Ignatiev. And he realized that the machines' avatar did not appear and try to explain.

The two of them talked far into the night, leaving the kitchen to sit side by side on the comfortable old couch. Even as he chatted with Gita, though, Ignatiev realized that the machines could read his innermost thoughts—even his subconscious ramblings. It made him angry. They can see how I feel about her, he knew. He felt embarrassed, exposed, awkward as a teenager.

Gita sensed his emotional turmoil.

"Are you all right, Alex?" she asked.

"Yes! Of course."

"You looked . . . different, strange. As if your thoughts were drifting away."

"I . . . eh . . ." he stammered. Then he heard himself confess, "I was thinking about you."

"About me? And that made you angry?"

"Angry at myself."

"Yourself? But why?"

He blurted, "Because I love you, Gita. I'm an old fool, I know, but I love you."

For several lifelong moments she stared at him

wordlessly. He tried to read the expression on her face. Not shock. Not disdain. Not . . .

Gita leaned toward him and pressed her lips against his. "And I love you, Alex. I've loved you for many weeks."

"You have?" The words came out as a surprised squeak.

"Yes."

"I mean . . . despite the ALS and everything?"

"Couldn't you tell?"

He shook his head. "I told you I was an old fool."

"No," said Gita. "You are a sweet, sensitive man."

"And you are an angel."

"Hardly."

"Entirely." He pulled her to him and wrapped his arms around her. She felt soft and yielding. The room seemed filled with dizzying fragrance.

I must be dreaming, Ignatiev said to himself. This must be a dream.

Yet he rose to his feet and lifted Gita to stand beside him. With their arms entwined they walked slowly toward the bedroom, like Adam and Eve in a strange world not of their making.

But before they reached the bedroom, Ignatiev—red-faced with mortification—confessed, "I . . . uh, that is . . . I may need some help. You know . . ."

Gita nodded solemnly and made her own confession. "I'm not a virgin, Alex."

"I am," he said.

"You?"

"Almost. It's been a long time."

She broke into a sweet little laugh. To Ignatiev it sounded like the tinkling of temple bells.

His heart thundering inside him, he led Gita into his bedroom.

book three

How dull it is to pause, to make an end,
to rust unburnished, not to shine in use!

CHAPTER TWENTY-FIVE

Time became a blur. Ignatiev tried hard to focus on the work at hand, but his thoughts always returned to Gita. The warmth of her. The sweetness of her. Her beautiful smile. Her dancing eyes.

He told her about his illness. "Amyotrophic lateral sclerosis," he explained. "My nerves don't always carry my brain's orders to my muscular system."

"It must be awful," she sympathized.

"Hundreds of years of medical research," he complained, "but hardly any progress at all on ALS. One doctor told me it's evolution's way of getting you to die."

"No!" Gita blurted. "There must be something . . ." But her voice wound down to silence.

Ignatiev smiled grimly. "It killed a famous athlete back on Earth. That's why it's called Lou Gehrig's disease."

She gripped his hand tightly. "We'll face it together, Alex. You're not alone anymore."

He smiled and gently kissed her.

Yet he knew he was using her, using their newfound relationship, their bond of love, to build a wall against the machines. Read my thoughts, will they? he grumbled to himself. Anytime he found himself thinking about breaking free of the machines' captivity he deliberately focused on Gita and hoped that that would submerge his vague, half-formed plans for escaping from the machines' imprisonment.

"You seem to be quite happy these days," said the avatar to him.

Ignatiev was at his desk, reviewing the reports from his various departments when the humanlike figure appeared in the middle of the tight little chamber he used as his den.

"As happy as a prisoner could be," he said as he looked up from the reports Aida was projecting on his holographic display.

The avatar shook its head. "Professor, we have explained our reasons for holding you incommunicado—"

"Yes, yes," Ignatiev interrupted, desperately hoping that the machines couldn't penetrate his mental subterfuge and get at his deeper thoughts.

"We have built you a permanent residence center," the avatar said, "a little humanlike city."

"Up on the surface."

"Yes."

"So that the death wave can wipe us out when it arrives."

"No!" The avatar seemed genuinely alarmed. "Your city will be large enough to house your entire complement from your starship. You will be able to live in complete comfort, just as you did on Earth."

"Until the death wave hits," Ignatiev replied angrily. Anger is good, he told himself. Use it to hide your deeper thoughts.

"That will not happen for another two hundred of your years. Most of the people with you today will have died of natural causes by then."

"Unless you help them to extend their lifespans. Which you won't do, will you?"

The avatar fell silent for several heartbeats. At last it answered, "That is a decision we have not made as yet."

"And why not?"

"We need to observe you further. There is much

about your existence that we do not yet fully understand."

"Such as?"

"Such as why you, Professor Ignatiev, are trying to hide your thoughts from us."

A hit! Ignatiev thought, suddenly alarmed. A palpable hit.

But he quickly temporized, "On Earth, a person does not go about describing the intimate details of his love life. Such information is considered private."

"It embarrasses you?"

"Of course it does. And it makes me angry."

Again the avatar hesitated before replying. Then, "We are puzzled by your emotional reaction."

Ignatiev almost smiled. "We are organic creatures, not machines."

"Driven by your emotions."

"To some extent, yes."

"We would say that you are driven almost completely by emotions. That makes it difficult to communicate effectively."

As long as you can't get at my deeper motivations, Ignatiev thought, wondering how effectively he was masking his thoughts.

Okpara Mandabe at last came down from *Intrepid* to visit the exobio team that Gita had assembled. Not that he left the orbiting starship; he allowed the machines to transport his presence among the dozen and a half men and women who were preparing to explore the natural biosphere on Oh-Four's surface.

He's trying to maintain his position of authority, Ignatiev thought as he greeted the exobiology department's chief. Mandabe had chosen to meet the exploration team in the conference room that the machines had carved out for their human guests. Ignatiev almost laughed at the symbolism. After traveling two thousand light-years, the head exobiologist chooses to meet the exploration team in a conference chamber: not in the field, not even in the machines' biosphere facility. In a conference room.

And not in person, either. He's still sitting safe and snug aboard *Intrepid* while his digital facsimile appears down here.

Even so, Mandabe looked uncomfortable. His dark face was set in a troubled scowl as he sat at the head of the conference table and listened to the individual reports from the team. Gita sat at his right, quiet and still. Ignatiev had taken a chair at the foot of the table.

There he is, Ignatiev said to himself as he studied Mandabe's unhappy face. *As far as chess pieces go, he's not a queen, but a king. The most important piece on the board, but a weakling with hardly any power. He's perfect for the role.*

Hans Pfisterman, a strapping South African with pale blond hair that he had allowed to grow down to his collar, was explaining his primatology report: "My three-man subgroup will map out the territorial range of the top predator—"

"That six-legged beast that tried to attack Dr. Nawalapitiya," Mandabe interrupted.

At the far end of the table, Ignatiev smiled knowingly. *Mandabe's got to show he knows what they're talking about. Got to set out his territorial markers.*

"Yessir," said the younger man. "We call it a tigercat. Up on the surface there won't be any energy screens to protect us from attack. We'll have to be pretty cautious."

"I should think," Mandabe said, hunching forward and clasping his hands on the tabletop, "that one of your priorities should be to determine how large an electric charge you'll need on your pistols to stop one of those brutes from attacking you."

"Yessir," the youngster said again. "That's item two-point-one in the report I filed last week on our expedition plan."

"Yes, of course," Mandabe said, his natural scowl deepening. "Let's move on, shall we?"

Move right ahead, Ignatiev thought. You've established your authority. You've shown the kid that you're in charge, you're the boss. And maybe you've even skimmed through his report.

Then he glanced at Gita, sitting at Mandabe's right. She looked calm, untroubled, the beginnings of a smile touching the corners of her mouth. She sees that Mandabe's playing the alpha primate game. And she's playing the other side of it. Let him have his hour of glory, then, once he goes back to *Intrepid*, she can get back to running the show down here.

Ignatiev wanted to grin at her, but he held himself back. She knows how to play the game, he told himself. I wonder if the machines realize what's going on here.

I wonder if they realize what I intend to do once we get out into the natural biosphere?

He immediately clamped down on that thought. Or tried to.

CHAPTER TWENTY-SIX

The meeting ended at last. Ignatiev counted the three hours they had spent around the conference table as wasted time; nothing had really been accomplished, except for massaging Mandabe's ego. Mandabe returned to *Intrepid* immediately; no formalities, he said his good-byes and disappeared like a haunted spirit.

But the team had dinner together without him, and the jokes that went around the table were mostly at Mandabe's expense.

Ignatiev cut their merrymaking short, though.

"He's been a leading figure in your field since before most of you were born," he told the team sternly. "He's earned the right to be a little pompous."

"As long as he doesn't get in our way," said Ulani Chung, the long-legged, dark-haired Polynesian biochemist.

Gita kept her silence, but Ignatiev thought she looked relieved that Mandabe's visit was over.

Once dinner was ended, the team members headed for their quarters. Ignatiev and Gita strolled leisurely along the blank-walled corridor until they reached his door.

Once safely inside, Ignatiev pulled her to him and kissed her soundly.

"You were magnificent," he told her.

"I didn't do anything."

Nodding, he went on, "That's right. And I know how hard that must have been for you. But you let Mandabe go through the motions of being in charge. He went back to *Intrepid* feeling he has nothing to fear from you."

"Maybe he doesn't," she said, suddenly looking tired of the whole charade.

With a low chuckle, Ignatiev said, "And Samson had nothing to fear from Delilah."

Gita smiled wanly. "I'm not going to shave his head."

"You won't have to. Tomorrow, when we go out to the surface, you'll be in charge and Mandabe will be glad to have it so. He thinks he's running the show—"

"Isn't he?" Gita challenged. "He can replace me anytime he wants to."

"And see your whole team go on strike?"

Her eyes widened. "You think they'd do that?"

"You're their leader. Not Mandabe. If he tried to replace you they'd rebel."

Gita shook her head. "Let's hope it doesn't come to that."

"It won't," Ignatiev said, with slightly more confidence than he actually felt.

Ignatiev was just about to follow Gita into the bedroom when Aida's softly soothing voice announced, "Captain Thornton would like to speak with you, Professor."

"Thornton? Of course."

With that, *Intrepid*'s captain appeared in the sitting room's three-dimensional display, above the crackling fireplace.

"Captain," said Ignatiev. "Welcome."

Thornton was a rugged-looking blond with long stringy hair falling to his broad shoulders, a thick beard, and piercing ice-blue eyes. A perfect Viking, Ignatiev thought: he would fit right in with Leif Erikson and Eric the Red.

"Thank you," said the captain, in a high tenor voice that Ignatiev thought ruined his Viking image. "I'll only take a moment of your time. I want to ask you if you're going to need a couple of my crewmen on this excursion your exobiologists are going to take."

Ignatiev felt his brows hike up. "A couple of your crewmen?"

"Guards," Thornton explained. "I suppose it's going to be dangerous out there in the wild."

"Perhaps."

"So? Do you want a couple of guards to go with your people?"

With a shake of his head Ignatiev replied, "I don't think that will be necessary. The team will be armed with stun pistols. And the machines will be watching over us, I'm sure."

Thornton's craggy face contracted into a frown. "You're sure? Better to be safe than sorry."

"I think we'll be all right, thanks all the same."

Clearly displeased, Thornton said, "It's your funeral."

"A pleasant thought," said Ignatiev.

"Well, good luck anyway." Glancing around the sitting room, the captain said, "I'd better be getting back to my duties."

"Thank you for the offer," Ignatiev said.

"If you change your mind, call me." Thornton's image winked out.

Ignatiev stood there, thinking, If Mandabe knew that the captain had come to me instead of him he'd have another temper tantrum.

* * *

The next morning the nine-person team (plus Ignatiev) met at the main entrance of their village, a sizable double-doored foyer. Each of them wore a gossamer excursion suit over their normal clothes, and a fishbowl helmet. Each of them had an electric stun pistol strapped to his or her hip, and carried a backpack of supplies—except for Ignatiev.

Grinning, Raj Jackson asked, "No backpack for you, Professor?"

"Age has its compensations," said one of the others.

"Rank hath its privileges."

Gita said firmly, "Professor Ignatiev is our guest. Let's show him some respect."

"Not too much, though," Ignatiev bantered.

Suddenly the machines' avatar appeared among them, like a light abruptly turning on, dressed in its usual collared uniform—emerald green this time.

"Are you ready to go outside?" it asked.

Gita nodded inside her helmet. "Yes. We have checked out our suits. Everything is in order."

The double doors slid open noiselessly. "Then let us be on our way."

They crowded through the open doorway. The doors slid shut behind them, making Ignatiev think of a curtain drawing closed, shutting off the past—and perhaps the future.

Ignatiev noticed that the humans kept a respectful half meter between themselves and the machines' envoy, even though they crowded close to one another. No one spoke a word as they stood out in the open, atop the broad, flat roof of the machines' city. They're a little nervous, Ignatiev realized. And why not? They're going into the unknown.

That's what science is all about, he reminded himself: pushing into unknown territory. Yes, but this particular unknown territory has things in it that can kill you.

As if Gita could read his expression, she said calmly, "Activate your sensors."

"Activate your sensors," said Pfisterman, with a derisive grin. "That way, even if you get yourself killed, we'll be able to find your body."

The woman standing beside him hissed at him.

They walked slowly, almost reluctantly, to the edge of the rooftop and stared out at a riot of greenery waving in a gentle breeze.

With an ushering gesture, the avatar said, "Here we are."

Gita nodded. "Let's go."

They began to file down a stairway toward the floor of the forest. Somehow Ignatiev got the impression the stairs had not been there earlier.

The forest was eerily quiet, except for the soft sighing of the trees as a gentle breeze swept past. Peering past the majestic boles of the soaring giants, Ignatiev could make out the hazy blue bulk of distant mountains, seemingly floating in midair, looking bare and cold above the lush jungle greenery. Thin clouds scudded by and somewhere in the distance an animal sang out a low, mournful moan.

The ten of them—plus the avatar—had fallen into a silence that was part wonderment, part tension, as they pushed their way through the hip-high foliage. There were no paved paths through the undergrowth. The team plowed ahead uncertainly, Gita in the lead. Ignatiev noted that the humans left bent and broken undergrowth in their paths, but the avatar passed through the foliage like a phantom.

Squinting up into the bright morning sunlight, he saw a formation of the leather-winged reptilians gliding up among the treetops in a vee formation.

He smiled to himself. Aerodynamics is the same here as on Earth, he told himself.

A scaly, bright red lizardlike creature scampered up one of the sturdy tree trunks, stopped to stare at the intruding humans, and chittered at them scoldingly.

"He doesn't like the sight of us," one of the men said.

"We're invading his turf."

"How do you know it's a male?" asked one of the women.

The animal suddenly turned an even brighter green and dashed farther up the trunk, to disappear among the leaves of a drooping branch.

"It must be a male," said the woman. "It makes a big noise, then runs away."

Ignatiev walked along with the group, feeling a slight dull pain in his legs. It was so mild that he almost thought it might be his imagination. No, he told himself. It's the ALS reminding you that it's in your body.

He marveled at the creatures that teemed through the forest. Hard-shelled little beetlelike things scampered across the mossy ground. Birds fluttered through the air. Just like home, Ignatiev thought.

But then he saw a slimy mass of color oozing between the trees, engulfing leaves and branches and anything perched upon them, leaving a smoking scar on the tree trunks as it passed.

The others saw it too. And froze.

"What the hell is *that*?"

"It's like a giant amoeba!"

Gita pointed. "It leaves a trail of desolation behind it."

"It's heading toward us!"

Several of the team had already pulled their stun pistols from their holsters.

"Hold your fire," Gita commanded. "Let's just get out of its way."

She led them off at an angle to the amoeboid's slimy track. Ignatiev saw a small furry six-legged animal slink up carefully to the amoeboid's advancing edge. It sniffed at the slimy creature curiously, but before it could turn away from it, the amoeba-like organism spread pseudopods around it and engulfed it in its oozing mass. The animal shrieked and struggled briefly, then began to dissolve inside the creature's semitransparent mass.

"Look at that," said Raj Jackson, fascinated despite himself.

"Ugh!" groaned the woman closest to Ignatiev.

"Move along," Gita commanded, "unless you want to get digested, too."

The exploration team hurried away from the amoeboid, but Pfisterman stopped, turned, and aimed his pistol at it.

"No sense firing," the machines' avatar warned. "You would merely annoy it—and turn its attention toward you."

Pfisterman wavered, turned questioningly toward Gita.

"Put the gun away and let's get as much distance between us and that . . . that *thing* as we can," Gita said.

As they hurried onward through the forest, the avatar explained, "That organism is the top predator in this biosphere. Forget that big brute you encountered back at the facility a few days ago."

"It devours everything in its path," Ignatiev said, puffing with exertion as he hurried to keep up with the others.

"Indeed it does," said the avatar. "It exudes a scent that many of the smaller animals find attractive."

Gita said, "And when they come close enough, it engulfs them."

"Quite so."

Raj Jackson, pushing through the waist-high foliage at Gita's side, asked, "Can you track them, so you don't get in their way?"

The avatar replied, "We could if we needed to. But we seldom come up here to the surface, so we have little need to do so. We keep this part of the biosphere under continuous remote observation, of course."

"Only this part?" Ignatiev asked.

"Yes. This sampling gives us an adequate understanding of what is going on throughout the biosphere."

They were climbing a small hill, Ignatiev realized. No wonder my legs ache, he said to himself. Looking back, he could see the swath of devastation left by the amoeboid's track through the forest.

"Soon it will all grow back," the avatar assured him. "This biosphere is self-supporting. A natural habitat."

"Global in scope?" Gita asked. Ignatiev realized she was puffing too, and felt somewhat better about it.

"The habitat spans the temperate region of our planet," the avatar replied. "The polar regions have their own biospheres, of course. Different climate, different plants and animals."

Once they reached the crest of the hill Gita called a halt to their march.

"We'll take a short break for lunch, then we'll split up into three-person teams so we can cover more ground."

"Like we planned," said Ulani Chung. She was slim and dark-eyed. Ignatiev realized that Raj Jackson somehow always seemed to be at her side.

"Exactly," Gita replied.

The avatar said, "I will leave you now. But if you need help simply call on your communicators. We will come immediately."

"That's good to know," said Gita.

The woman beside her said, "Especially if we run into one of those amoeba things." She shuddered visibly.

"Not to worry," said the avatar. "Their ranges are very large. You won't find another one in this area."

"Good."

With that, the avatar winked out. Ignatiev said to himself, Good-bye, little tsarovitch.

The team unfurled a micromesh tent and spread it on the ground, then filled it with breathable air from the tanks of their backpacks. The tubular tent rose and stiffened until it formed a temporary habitat where they could unfasten their helmets and eat a cold meal in something approaching comfort.

Sitting beside Gita on the tent's fabric floor, Ignatiev asked, "Am I supposed to stay with you this afternoon?"

She swallowed a bite of the sandwich she was holding, then answered, "Yes. Of course."

"Can I wander off on my own?"

"Certainly not!"

"Then you'll have to come with me."

"With you?" Gita asked. "Where? What do you have in mind?"

"Freedom," said Ignatiev.

CHAPTER TWENTY-SEVEN

Gita stared at Ignatiev uncertainly for a long, silent moment. Then she turned toward the others squatting on the tent's floor and called, "Hans, can you come over here, please?"

Pfisterman got up from where he'd been squatting—next to Jackson and the exotic-looking Ulani Chung, Ignatiev noticed—and scuttled over to sit at Gita's side.

She told the South African, "Professor Ignatiev and I are going to take a little unscheduled excursion together. Can you lead your subgroup without me?"

Surprised, Pfisterman blurted, "Unscheduled excursion?"

"Just for a few hours or so," Gita said.

Ignatiev saw sudden understanding blossom in Pfisterman's pale eyes. He thinks we want to be alone. Romance. With a mental shrug, the professor said to himself, Who cares what he thinks, as long as Gita and I can be alone?

With a slow grin, Pfisterman nodded and said, "Certainly. I can handle it. I know the excursion protocol inside out."

"Good," said Gita, in a strictly professional tone. "Remember, see everything, touch nothing."

"And get it all down on the sensors," Pfisterman added.

The little group finished their brief lunch, then replaced their helmets, got out of the tent, pumped its air back into the tanks on their backs, folded the ultrathin fabric, and stored it into one of the rucksacks. Then they gathered themselves into the mini-teams that they had prearranged for the afternoon's tasks. Pfisterman's team included only himself and Ulani Chung. He looked happy about that, Ignatiev thought. Raj Jackson seemed much less than pleased.

Gita reminded them that they would meet at this spot one hour before local sunset, then sent them off with, "See as much as you can and record it all. Good luck."

The team broke up into the subgroups and started off in different directions. Ignatiev heard a man's voice say, "I hope we don't run across that amoeboid again."

"Amen to that," answered another voice.

Louts, Ignatiev thought. The amoeboid was the most interesting species they'd found, so far.

"So where are we going?" Gita asked him, while the subgroups dispersed in their chosen directions.

Glancing at the keyboard panel strapped to the left wrist of his suit, Ignatiev pointed with his right hand and answered, "Due north."

They began trudging down the hillside, side by side.

"Alex, what are you trying to accomplish?" Gita asked.

"Exploration," he replied, not trusting himself to even think of anything more.

"But why just the two of us? Why not—"

"Actually, I had thought that I'd go this way alone," he said, "but I'm happy that you decided to come along with me."

With a wry smile Gita murmured, "Wither thou goest . . ." Ignatiev thought she sounded reasonably pleased about it. But curious.

They pushed through the foliage, hip-deep at times. Gita had all her suit's sensors recording everything. She even stopped to take pictures of Ignatiev standing beside one of the massive tree trunks. Animals skittered and scattered around them. As they broke past the heavy foliage and entered a sizable meadow of low grass, a lumbering turtlelike creature slowly crossed their path.

Then one of the six-legged tigercats emerged from the heavy foliage and growled at them. They both froze. Slowly, cautiously, Gita pulled her pistol from its holster.

She started, "If it makes a move toward us—"

The tigercat bunched its muscles. Ignatiev saw that it was going to leap at them. Stepping in front of Gita, he pawed at his own pistol, got it halfway out of its holster as the beast leaped, roaring a bloodcurdling scream that froze everything in the forest.

Ignatiev saw the massive blur of fur and fangs leaping directly at him. He had no time to react, no time to pull his gun or aim it, no time to do anything as the full impact of the charging animal hit him squarely and knocked him over onto his back.

His vision blurred, but he could feel the weight of the animal pinning him down, sense its fangs snapping at him. He felt the thin fabric of his protective suit ripping as the brute's razor-sharp claws tightened around his body.

Ignatiev knew he was going to die.

Suddenly the tigercat shrieked and released its grip on him. Ignatiev sucked in a painful breath while the beast went howling off into the underbrush.

Gita stood above him like a fierce goddess, pistol in hand, her face a mask of hatred.

Then she looked down at Ignatiev and dropped to her knees beside him. Her visage melting into concern, she pleaded, "Are you all right?"

He managed to nod. "I think so."

Gita wrapped her arms around his battered body.

Her helmet's hard surface hurt his chest, and the air tanks strapped to his back felt like solid rocks, but he grinned at her.

"You saved me," he managed to grunt.

"You're all right," she breathed, staring at him. "You're all right."

Ignatiev wanted to smile at the incongruity of it. "The hero is supposed to save the fair maiden," he muttered.

Gita broke into a wild, relieved, uncontrolled laughter.

she wouldn't allow Ignatiev to get up off his back.

"You stay there," Gita commanded, "while I check you out."

Ignatiev was perfectly happy to lie quietly on the soft grass, even though the air tanks on his back made it far from comfortable. Gita pulled a scanner from one of the pouches on her belt and ran it over the length of his body.

"Heart rate is high," she muttered as she stared at the scanner's screen, "but blood pressure is good, and so is breathing function. No broken bones, apparently."

"I'll live, then?" he asked, trying to make it funny. His words came out as a labored croak.

She pushed him over onto his stomach and examined the air tanks. "Dented," she muttered, "but intact. No leaks."

"I'll live," he repeated.

"It tore your suit," she said. "Local microbes might cause infection."

Rolling onto one side, Ignatiev huffed, "The local microbes are alien . . . not adapted to human biochemistry. No danger of infection."

"That's the theory, I know," said Gita. She shrugged the backpack off her shoulders and rummaged through it. "Still, I want to get your suit repaired as quickly as possible."

"Yes, Doctor."

All business, Gita covered the rips in Ignatiev's suit with self-sealing tape, mumbling, "It didn't slash your flesh—"

"You drove it away before it could do any real damage."

"There still might be broken bones. Or sprains, contusions."

"I don't think so." And he pushed himself up to a sitting position. Every muscle in his torso groaned in protest but he said to her, "See? I'm still in one piece."

"It's not a joke, Alex. That animal could have torn you apart."

"But it didn't. You saved me."

Suddenly she wrapped her arms around him again and pressed her helmeted head against his chest. Ignatiev winced with a twinge of pain, but he said nothing. He enfolded Gita in his arms.

"My avenging angel," he murmured.

He heard her sobbing. "You could have been killed. I could have lost you."

"It's all right," he whispered. "It's all over now."

They disengaged at last and Ignatiev climbed slowly to his feet. His entire body seemed to burn with a dull pain, but he hid it from Gita.

"How do you feel?" she asked, getting up beside him.

"A little stiff. I could use a shot of vodka."

She laughed. "We'll have to get home for that."

"No," he said. "It's still early. Let's push a little farther."

"Why? What are you looking for?"

"The limits to the machines' control. I want to see how far their power extends."

Gita turned from him to sweep her eyes across the green landscape: grass and shrubs and undergrowth as far as the horizon; the giant trees rising to the sky; the distant mountains of bare rock.

Abruptly, she raised her left arm and touched the stud on her wrist panel that the avatar said would summon help.

Nothing happened.

Gita pressed the button again. Again no reaction.

She looked up at Ignatiev. "It looks like you've achieved your goal. The machines are not in control of this area, so far from their city."

Ignatiev felt a tiny glow of victory. "We've done it! We've gone past their area of control."

"So what happens now?" Gita asked.

"We call Aida and summon a shuttlecraft to pick us up and take us back to *Intrepid*."

With that, Ignatiev called out aloud, "Aida!"

The artificial intelligence's synthesized voice immediately answered, "Yes, Dr. Ignatiev?"

"We need a shuttle to pick us up."

Without a shred of emotion, the AI answered, "I'm sorry, Dr. Ignatiev, but all our shuttlecraft have been inactivated."

"Inactivated? How? Since when?"

"For the past week," Aida responded. "The engineers are trying to reactivate them, but they've been unsuccessful so far."

"You mean we can't get back to *Intrepid*?"

"Not physically. Not unless the machines allow you to," said Aida.

"we're stuck here," Gita said, her voice low with defeat, frustration.

Ignatiev huffed. "They don't need to control the whole planet's surface. They've separated us from *Intrepid*."

"Can we talk to the ship, at least?" she wondered.

Aida replied, "All communications channels are blocked at this time, I'm afraid."

No, Ignatiev thought. Aida doesn't feel fear; that's just a phrase she uses to make us feel more comfortable with her. We're the ones who should feel afraid: cut off from the rest of our people, alone on an alien world, totally dependent on these damnable machines.

"We are not acting out of malice."

Ignatiev turned at the sound of the softly reasonable voice. There stood the machines' avatar, in its immaculate quasi-military garb.

"You've been observing us all the time," Ignatiev said.

"Of course. We do not want you to hurt yourselves."

Gita fairly snarled, "What about the tigercat that attacked us?"

"We shocked it and drove it away."

"I thought that I—"

Without a hint of condescension, the avatar said, "The charge on your pistol is too low to affect the beast. We protected you."

"I see." Gita looked and sounded thoroughly put down.

"You've been observing us all the while," Ignatiev repeated, feeling angry and defeated.

"There is no limit to our observational capabilities. We knew what you were up to, despite your efforts to hide your thoughts from us. We decided to allow you to wander around the area—"

"You allowed us the illusion that we were free of you."

The avatar corrected, "We allowed you to behave as if you were free. It was an experiment to learn what you would do with such freedom."

Downcast, Ignatiev muttered, "We didn't get very far."

"We are afraid," the avatar agreed, "that the predator cut our experiment short."

Gita said, "We might as well go back to the others."

"It is still only early afternoon," said the avatar. "Would you like to examine the ruins of our biological forefathers' civilization?"

"Yes!" Ignatiev and Gita snapped in unison.

Across the grassy meadow the three of them walked, toward the green hills that rose before the steeper, more rugged mountains. The pale orange sun rose higher in the soft bluish sky, the afternoon grew warmer. Ignatiev turned up the cooling system of his suit; he heard water gurgling through the thin pipes built into the suit's fabric but felt precious little relief from the heat.

As they walked, it struck him as incongruous that the machines didn't whisk them to their destination in some sort of mechanical device. He almost laughed at the incongruity of it: They can read my mind but they don't provide taxi service.

The pain from his encounter with the predator slowly eased away, however. Reluctantly, Ignatiev admitted to himself that the physical exercise must be doing him some good.

At last the avatar stopped them a few hundred meters in front of a gently rising hillside, covered with vines and mossy growth.

"This was the site of our biological forebears' largest city," said the avatar.

Ignatiev saw nothing but junglelike growth.

"This?" he asked.

"Look carefully," the avatar said, pointing toward the overgrown greenery.

Ignatiev stared. Something was stirring amidst the vines and undergrowth. Then a small furry gray-green animal scampered out into the open, froze at the sight of the three human figures, and quickly dashed back to the safety of the tangled greenery.

"Look!" Gita exclaimed, pointing. "Isn't that a stone wall?"

Ignatiev peered in the direction she was pointing. Yes, a wall or some sort of structure. It looked like stone, but it was so overgrown that he couldn't be sure.

The avatar began to walk toward it. "This way," it said.

Gita and Ignatiev followed. It was a wall of some sort, so draped and festooned with ancient twining branches and shrubbery that you had to know it was there before you could distinguish it from among the plants growing over it. Like Angkor Wat in Cambodia, Ignatiev thought, when the Europeans first stumbled upon it.

Slowly, carefully, they followed the avatar toward the wall. It glided through the tangled undergrowth like a specter; Ignatiev and Gita had to hack at the vines and twisted, tangled tree limbs with their energy-beam guns.

Puffing from the effort, at last they stood at the base of the wall. No windows were in sight, no doors. It looked *old,* ancient and decayed, crumbling.

"This was a temple of knowledge," said the avatar. "What you would call a university. It was destroyed when the death wave swept over our world."

Gesturing to the ruin, Ignatiev said, "The death wave didn't cause this destruction."

Expressionless, the avatar replied, "Quite true. More than thirty million years of neglect has caused the deterioration you see."

A sudden blur of motion in the shrubs above them made Gita jump, startled. Ignatiev saw a monkeylike creature swinging among the vines high overhead.

"The animals here will not harm you," the avatar soothed. "They are more frightened of you than you are of them."

"No predators?" Ignatiev probed.

With a shake of its head, the avatar said, "None that would attack a creature of your size."

Gita asked, "You machines existed when the death wave wiped out the organic life forms?"

"Yes, early forms of our type survived the time of great dying."

"Couldn't you have helped them?" she went on. "Did you know the death wave was on its way?"

"We did not. Our organic forebears had no inkling that it was sweeping toward us."

"Your organic forebears had no inkling," Ignatiev said, frowning with suspicion. "But did you?"

The avatar shook its head, very humanlike. "None whatever. You have to realize that the machines of that early era were little better than the organics themselves. We have evolved considerably since those days."

Gita reached out a gloved hand and touched the

age-encrusted wall. "A whole civilization, destroyed. Wiped out."

"But not before it gave rise to a superior civilization. Evolution is not restricted to organic life forms. In fact, machines often evolve much faster than organics."

"Moore's law," Gita said.

Shaking his head, Ignatiev said, "Moore's law has been proven to be inexact, an approximation, at best."

"True enough," said the avatar.

Gita asked, "Can we get past this wall? Can we see what's on the other side?"

"There is very little to see," replied the avatar. "Millions of years have taken their toll."

"Still . . ."

The humanlike figure closed its eyes briefly. Ignatiev got the impression it was discussing the question with its fellow machines.

At last it said, "This way," and gestured down the length of the wall.

With the avatar leading them, Gita and Ignatiev struggled through the tangled vines and foliage until at last they came upon an opening in the wall. A doorway, Ignatiev saw. The doors themselves had long since decayed into dust, but the stone doorway remained. It was large enough for all three of them to pass through it at once.

"No one has come this way in ages," said the avatar as they stepped through.

They stopped a few paces on the other side of the wall. Nothing to see but more tangled undergrowth, and then a wide, flat meadow. Not a sign of civilization. Ignatiev could not even make out the outlines of building foundations in the grassy, rock-strewn ground.

"This was once a university?" he asked, in a hushed voice.

"Long ago, yes."

"It's so sad," Gita breathed. "Nothing is left."

"We are here," the avatar said.

The meadow was fairly flat, covered with bright green blades of grass. Rocks and pebbles were everywhere, covered with spongy-looking moss. Ignatiev sniffed inside his plastiglas helmet. He could smell nothing, but he sensed a vast decay, the rot of devastation.

"The death of an intelligent race," he muttered.

"And the beginning of a new civilization," the avatar reminded him.

Beyond the far edge of the meadow rose the green hills that eventually gave way to the rocky mountains that soared high into the bright sky. Ignatiev could not hear a sound: no hoots or growls, no calls from one beast to another, not even the buzzing of insects.

"Is this area haunted?" he asked no one in particular.

"Our presence has frightened the local fauna. They are not accustomed to visitors."

"So they hide," said Gita.

"Yes. That is their natural reaction."

But then Ignatiev saw something move, out at the far end of the level ground, where the ground began to rise.

He blinked, then squinted. A sizable body, brownish fur, moving slowly, carefully on four limbs.

Gita saw it too. "What's that?" She pointed.

The avatar replied, "One of the local denizens. It is harmless, not a predator."

As if to prove the point, the animal sat itself down in a patch of foliage and began peeling leaves off their stems and chewing on them.

"We should keep our distance," said the avatar, "and not disturb it."

Gita slowly pulled her camera from its pouch on her belt and raised it to her eyes. She gasped.

"Alex, look!" she whispered.

Ignatiev fumbled with his own camera, nearly

dropped it, at last got it up to eye level. The automatic focus control showed the animal clearly.

He gasped. "It looks . . ."

The creature was slim, covered with short, light brown hair. It was using its forelimbs to tear at the leaves surrounding it. Its head bore two eyes, a crest running from its brow to the nape of its neck. Its jaws were working constantly on the leaves it was chewing.

"It looks almost human," Gita said.

"Four limbs, human in size and shape," Ignatiev agreed.

Suddenly the creature got to its feet and stared directly toward them. It blinked once, twice, then turned its back to them and started walking slowly away.

"It's a humanoid," Gita whispered, awed.

"It has a low order of intelligence," said the avatar. "We have been watching its development for some time now."

Chapter thirty

Ignatiev stared at the avatar. "You mean you've been studying a protohuman species?"

"We have been observing its evolution. Two million years ago it was a small, undistinguished mammal. It has grown larger and more intelligent. It lives in a small group, using caves and other natural shelters for protection. They seem to be developing a language of sorts."

"We saw nothing like this in your biosphere facility, underground," said Gita.

"There are no specimens of this species in the facility. They require a much larger range for their development."

Ignatiev said, "So they're developing here on the surface."

Dispassionately, the avatar remarked, "A few of their members have begun to eat meat. They have built crude traps to ensnare small animals."

"They could become human," Gita said, her voice hollow with awe.

"That is not likely," said the avatar. "Not with the death wave approaching."

"You can't let them be killed!" Ignatiev snapped.

"Why not?" the avatar replied. "Organic life forms are transient."

"But they could evolve into true intelligence! They could become like us! Human!"

"The death wave will destroy them."

"That's genocide!" Gita said.

"That is evolution," the avatar countered. "Survival of the fittest."

Trembling with anger, Ignatiev growled, "So you survive and they die."

"Your attitude is inconsistent," said the avatar. "You were not so upset at the thought of the other animals and plants being destroyed by the death wave."

Ignatiev started to reply, but caught himself and hesitated. The damned machine is right, he said to himself. I'm reacting emotionally. But a blood-hot voice within him argued, Of course you're reacting emotionally. He's talking about allowing a species that could become human to be snuffed out while the damned machines do nothing to save them.

He sucked in a deep breath, then said to the avatar, "I think we've seen enough." Turning to Gita, he suggested, "Let's return to the others."

Clearly troubled, Gita nodded unhappily.

They walked in silence with the avatar through the lengthening shadows of late afternoon, each of them wrapped in their own thoughts.

They reached the hilltop rendezvous point before any of the others returned. Ignatiev wondered if the other subgroups would run across protohumans too, but as they showed up in their teams of two and three, none of them spoke of seeing the humanoid animals.

"Just miles and miles of nothing but miles and miles," said Hans Pfisterman, sinking tiredly to the grassy ground. "How about you, Professor? Did you see anything special?"

Before Ignatiev could reply, Raj Jackson piped up,

"We recorded about a zillion different plants and animals. We'll spend weeks sorting them all out."

"We'll have to compare them to the species in the bio facility," Ulani Chung said as she dropped to a sitting position between the two men.

Gita spoke up. "We saw a sort of protohuman. Like *Homo habilis* on Earth, sort of."

"What?"

"Like a prehuman?"

"Where?"

Ignatiev looked at the avatar, which remained silent, so he said, "A few hours north of here. Our host"—he nodded graciously at the avatar—"showed us the remains of an ancient city, and there in the middle of the ruins sat a creature that looked very humanlike."

"No!"

"Really?"

"What did it look like?"

Ignatiev turned to Gita, who pulled out her camera and set it to project a three-dimensional image of the humanoid.

The others gaped at it, then everyone tried to speak at the same time. Ignatiev heard the excitement in their voices, saw the eagerness in their faces.

"We've got to study them!"

"How far did you say it was?"

"It certainly looks like an analog to a prehuman species."

"How many of them did you see?"

"It could evolve into a human analog, in time!"

"Time we don't have," Ignatiev told them. "In two hundred years the death wave will annihilate every living thing on the surface of this planet."

Chapter thirty-one

"It doesn't have to happen that way!" said Raj Jackson, his dark face wide-eyed with excitement. "We could deploy the energy screens, shield this whole planet—"

Ignatiev raised a cautioning hand. "If the machines allow us to."

Every human eye turned to the avatar, which stood in their midst, calm, unperturbed.

"We do not interfere with the natural processes of evolution," it said, as coolly as if it was commenting on the weather.

"You'll let the death wave wipe them out?"

"A potentially intelligent species?"

"That's inhuman!"

Untroubled, the avatar pointed out, "We are not human."

"But—"

Feeling the heat of impotent rage rising within him, Ignatiev said to the others, "The machines are interested in their own survival, not the survival of the organic creatures that live here."

With maddening composure, the humanlike figure slowly turned to survey the ten people sitting, kneeling, standing before it. "Our interest is in protecting ourselves. We aim at survival, and our continuing evolution. The organic creatures who share this planet with us are not strong enough to survive. We have been through this before, with earlier death waves. Organic life is brief, machine life may well be immortal."

Still standing, Ignatiev replied angrily, "So you save a sampling of the organic species in your underground facility and repopulate the surface after the death wave passes."

"Yes."

"Why? Why go to that trouble?"

The avatar hesitated a moment. Then, "To see how organic evolution responds to the process."

"Does it always evolve intelligent species?"

"*Always* is the wrong term."

With deliberate patience, Ignatiev rephrased, "Does it *often* evolve intelligent species?"

"Never," said the avatar.

The wave of disappointment among the humans was palpable.

But the avatar continued, "The intervals between death waves have been too short to allow a truly intelligent species to evolve."

"Then how did intelligent species evolve in the first place?" Jackson demanded. "How did we evolve on Earth?"

"The intervals between death waves are growing shorter. The history of your own planet shows that waves of dying are becoming more frequent. The core of the galaxy is becoming more unstable."

Pointing an accusing finger at the humanlike apparition, Ignatiev practically snarled, "Then you have allowed death waves to destroy earlier protohuman species?"

"Yes."

"When you could have saved them?"

"To what purpose? Organic species die out eventually. Death waves have scoured planets in the past and will do so again in the future. Organic life is transient. Machine life survives. The aim of evolution is survival. We survive."

Gita objected, "And the organic species die."

"Yes," said the avatar. "I realize that this is hard for your emotion-driven intelligence to accept, but this is the way evolution works. Organics die, machines survive. And learn."

Ignatiev nodded inside his fishbowl helmet. "And when the death wave reaches this planet . . ."

"Organic creatures will be annihilated."

"Including us."

"You and any descendants you will have created in the meantime."

"And you will stand by and allow us to be wiped out."

"That is the natural process of evolution at work."

Dead silence from the humans. Ignatiev looked around at them. They seemed shocked, thunderstruck, at the machines' indifference.

All our lives, Ignatiev thought, we have considered ourselves the apex of evolution. No matter what the biology texts tell us. Each and every one of us automatically assumes that human intelligence was the goal that evolution had been aiming for through all the long ages of the past.

Now we face an intelligence of a different kind, an intelligence that is totally indifferent to our attitudes, our dreams, our needs.

Unbidden, a quatrain from Khayyam's *Rubaiyat* came to his mind:

The moving finger writes; and, having writ,
Moves on: nor all thy Piety nor Wit

Shall lure it back to cancel half a line,
Nor all your tears wash out a word of it.

Ignatiev felt close to tears. But he did not cry. He was too furious for crying.

ChAPTER thirTY-TWO

"Are you ready to return to your quarters?" the avatar asked.

Ignatiev looked at the squad of humans sitting, squatting, kneeling on the grass. Not a word from any of them. They were too stunned, too bewildered to reply. Too disheartened, he thought.

The orange sun was dipping toward the distant mountains. Long shadows were creeping across the field in which they sat. A gentle breeze was ruffling the grass, moaning softly, like a banshee mourning the loss of a lover.

Feeling tired, hopeless, helpless, Ignatiev said to the avatar, "Yes, let's go back."

A square structure rose out of the ground and its doors slid silently open. Wearily, the team of explorers climbed to their feet and shuffled into the waiting transporter in complete silence.

But Ignatiev wondered to himself, How do they do that? How do they manipulate the elements to make a transporter arise when and where they want it?

Standing in the transporter cab next to him, the avatar said, "It's really a simple matter, Professor. We will show you how it is done, if you like."

Ignatiev nodded slowly. "I would like that."

He felt the transporter dropping away, down into the bowels of the planet.

"You can take off your helmets, if you like," the avatar

said to the group. "You can breathe the air here quite normally."

Ignatiev thought, Better to let us choke to death here and now. He saw no reaction to his thought from the avatar. It remained perfectly calm, perfectly at ease.

Perfectly indifferent, Ignatiev thought.

Once back in his quarters with Gita, Ignatiev slowly wormed his arms out of the protective biosuit, then sat on the edge of the bed to pull his legs free. Gita did the same, wordlessly.

"It's sobering, isn't it?" he muttered as he stood up and started folding the suit.

She looked up at him, and a shadow of a smile touched her lips.

"You mean you don't want any vodka?"

He almost smiled back at her. "Maybe later."

"You're tired."

"I feel humiliated," Ignatiev confessed. "The blasted machines have us completely under their control. They call the tune and make us dance to it."

"And there's nothing we can do about it," Gita agreed.

Ignatiev took the folded suit, placed the bubble helmet atop it, and carried it into the sitting room, where he placed it on the end table beside the couch. "I'll return it to the storage rack tomorrow," he muttered.

Gita also brought her suit into the sitting room and put it down gently beside Ignatiev's.

"Alex, what are we going to do?"

Slumping down tiredly on the couch, he replied, "We're going to spend the rest of our lives here, apparently. We'll never get back to Earth."

Gita sat beside him. "We can study the species up on the surface, I suppose."

"I'd like to study the machines and their society."

"If they'd allow us to."

He sighed mightily. "Yes, if they allow us to."

"Are you going to inform the rest of the people, up on *Intrepid*?" Gita asked.

"If they allow us to," Ignatiev repeated.

The avatar appeared before them. "You can communicate with your teammates in the orbiting starship."

Ignatiev stared at the humanlike figure. "That's very gracious of you," he said, his voice dripping irony.

"You realize that what we are doing," the avatar said, "is for our own good—and yours. You can live long and full lives here. We will give you everything you want."

"Except freedom," Ignatiev countered. "Except the freedom to return to our home."

The avatar replied, "I'm afraid that will be impossible."

Ignatiev got up from the couch and drew himself to his full height—several centimeters shorter than the avatar. "Very well," he said, his voice stronger, firmer than it had been. "If we must remain here, we will do what scientists do. We will study this planet, its biosphere, and your society of machines."

"Good," said the avatar, with something approaching warmth.

Then it winked out, leaving Gita and Ignatiev alone.

ChAPTER THIRTY-THREE

Alexander Alexandrovich Ignatiev sat stretched out on the sitting room's reclining chair. He seemed asleep, his eyes closed, his hands resting limply on his lap. But beneath his eyelids, his pupils were moving rapidly back and forth, as they would in REM sleep. And his fingers twitched as if jabbed by minute electric charges.

Ignatiev's electronic presence was sitting at the head of the conference table aboard *Intrepid,* with the heads of each department among the ship's staff arrayed along the polished table and nearly a dozen more scientists and technicians—Gita among them—sitting along one wall of the long, windowless room.

"A prehuman?" asked Vivian Fogel, director of the anthropology department. She was a petite slip of a woman with short-cropped ash-blond hair and a ruddy, hard, weather-seamed complexion. "Are you certain?"

Ignatiev said, "See for yourself," and called for Aida to project the camera views of the creature they had seen.

"My god," Fogel muttered, awed. "It's almost like seeing *Homo habilis.*"

"The important thing," Ignatiev said, his voice firm, "is that this species has evolved since the last death wave swept past this region, more than sixty million years ago. And it will be killed when the next death wave arrives."

"Killed?" blurted Mandabe. "Do you mean that the machines will do nothing to save it?"

"That is what they have told me," Ignatiev replied.

"But they can't do that! They mustn't!"

"That would be murder!" Fogel accused. "Genocide!"

"That creature could evolve into an intelligent species!"

Ignatiev let them protest for a few moments more, then said, "The machines apparently don't care about the survival of organic species. They are interested only in their own survival."

"But that . . . that's heinous!" said the usually mild-mannered head of the astronomy department.

"I agree," said Ignatiev. "But they do not."

Fogel asked, "Why do the machines maintain their biosphere facility, then? Why do they repopulate the surface after a death wave sterilizes the planet?"

With an elaborate shrug, Ignatiev answered, "I have asked that very question. Their answer seems specious to me, at best."

"They're not telling us the whole story?"

"I think not."

"How can we get them to be more honest with us?"

Ignatiev shrugged again. "If I knew, I would tell you."

Abruptly the machines' avatar appeared, standing beside Ignatiev's chair. As usual, it wore a military-type uniform, but this time its color was a shimmering pale lavender.

"Excuse us for intruding like this," it said. "We feel that you do not understand our motivation."

"Damned right!" Mandabe snapped.

As relaxed as if it were lecturing a roomful of students, the avatar said, "Our history is much longer than yours. We have seen several death waves sweep through the galaxy, killing organic life wherever it existed. Your own existence is based on the fact that there was a long-enough interval between death waves for your species to arise."

"Not every life form on Earth was killed by the earlier death waves," said Vivian Fogel, almost accusingly.

Unperturbed, the avatar answered, "That is because your world is quite distant from the galaxy's core, where the gamma emissions originate. Still, the death wave that is currently spreading across the galaxy is quite a powerful one. It would scour your planetary system clean of life if the machines you call the Predecessors had not provided you with the necessary shielding."

Feeling the discussion was drifting away from its original topic, Ignatiev asked, "But why won't you shield the organic life forms here from the coming death wave?"

"To what avail?" the avatar asked back. "Organic life forms are inherently short-lived. They perish very quickly. But in many places they live long enough to give rise to machine intelligence. Machines live long. Perhaps some machine species can be immortal."

"But you refuse to help the organic species to survive the death wave."

"Why bother?" asked the avatar. Then it disappeared.

The men and women around the conference table gaped at the emptiness where the avatar had stood a moment earlier.

"It's a cold-blooded sonofabitch," said one of the engineers, down toward the end of the table.

"It doesn't have any blood," groused the man next to him.

"The question is," Ignatiev said, "what are we going to do about this?"

"What *can* we do?" Fogel asked, her voice trembling.

"Only what they allow us to do," Ignatiev answered.

"How about mass suicide?" Jackson quipped.

Gita said, "I think that would please the machines. We would be ridding them of a problem."

"We ought to set up the shielding generators on the surface," Jackson said, with some heat. "Protect ourselves from the death wave and protect the local biosphere."

Ignatiev nodded agreement, but warned, "I would think that if the machines could neutralize this ship's propulsion system they could disable the shielding generators just as easily."

"But would they?" Fogel asked. "I mean, it's one thing to let the death wave wipe out unprotected species, but it's a matter of a different order to prevent our shielding the biosphere."

"You're talking about ethics," said Mandabe, his deep voice like a rumble of distant thunder.

"Do the blasted machines have any ethics?" someone asked.

Ignatiev answered, "They have a drive to survive."

"Which doesn't extend to other species," Jackson snarled.

"Apparently not.

"One thing is certain," Ignatiev continued. "We can't surprise them. They can read our thoughts. They know what we're saying and what we're thinking."

"So we can't surprise them."

"I'm certain that we can't," Ignatiev agreed.

"What should we do, then?"

"Follow Jackson's suggestion," Ignatiev replied. "See if the machines allow us to actively protect the biosphere."

"And ourselves," Mandabe added.

"But if they don't?" one of the biologists asked.

"Then, in two hundred years any of us still alive will be killed by the death wave. Together with every living thing on the surface of the planet."

CHAPTER THIRTY-FOUR

The meeting ended. Ignatiev opened his eyes and found himself stretched out on the recliner in his sitting room. Gita, lying on the couch, was beginning to stir to life also.

She pulled herself up to a sitting position, then slowly got to her feet, complaining, "I always feel shaky after one of these sessions."

"We're not accustomed to being in two places at the same time," Ignatiev said, raising himself to stand on slightly wobbly legs.

The machines' avatar appeared by the sitting room's front door.

"You have decided to challenge us," it said. Its tone was flat and calm, neither surprised nor threatening. Yet Ignatiev sensed that it was displeased.

"We have decided," he answered, "to follow our own ethical sense."

"And your drive for survival," the avatar pointed out.

With a lopsided little smile, Ignatiev admitted, "That too."

"Emotional thinking."

Gita said, "We are emotional creatures. Our emotions have helped us to survive, over the ages."

The avatar started to reply, hesitated, then finally said, "Your emotions may have been a helpful survival trait in your distant past, but now they can be dangerous.

They have led you into conflicts, angry confrontations, even destructive wars."

"That was in the past," Ignatiev said. "We've gotten beyond all that now."

"Have you? How close are your people to primitive fears and hatreds, to subjugating one another, to the mass murders that you misname as patriotic wars?"

Ignatiev hesitated.

But Gita replied firmly, "We have learned from the past. We have built an interplanetary society based on human freedom and equality."

"And so here you are," the avatar said, "two thousand light-years from your home, eager to impress your values and your self-perceived goodness on our society, our culture."

"We've come here to help life forms that face extinction," Gita said.

Ignatiev added, "And to study your civilization, to learn from you."

"Then learn this," the avatar said, with something approaching passion in its tone. "All organic species die. Only machines have the possibility of living forever."

And with that, the avatar disappeared.

"It got angry," Ignatiev said, his voice hollow with surprise.

Staring at the spot where the avatar had been a moment earlier, Gita said, "Could it be learning from us?"

"I wonder. Maybe it's just adopting some of our mannerisms in an effort to make us understand it better."

"I wonder," she echoed.

Ignatiev stepped closer to her, held out his arm, and clasped her hand in his. "Are we teaching the machines how to be emotional?"

She shook her head. "I doubt it. Perhaps we're just reading into its statements what we want to hear."

His head sinking low with thought, Ignatiev returned Gita to the couch and they sat together, side by side.

"One thing is apparent," he said, gazing into her deep brown eyes. "It didn't forbid us from setting up shielding generators."

"It didn't have to," Gita pointed out. "The machines won't let us move people or equipment from *Intrepid* to the planet's surface. That's a nonstarter."

"Is it?" he wondered. "Somehow I get the impression that they want to see how far we'll go with this scheme."

Her face brightening, Gita asked, "Could they be testing us?"

Chapter thirty-five

For a silent several moments Ignatiev and Gita stared at each other, each locked in their private thoughts.

"Testing us," Ignatiev repeated at last. "Why? What would be the point?"

"To see how far we're willing to go to save the biosphere up on the surface."

"And ourselves."

"That too," she said.

Ignatiev mulled over the idea. Testing us, he thought. Trying to discover how determined we are. How an emotion-driven intelligence reacts to dealing with a totally emotionless machine entity.

"Perhaps," he said slowly, "this is their way of studying us."

"Studying us?"

"There's one way to find out," he said.

"How?"

Ignatiev called, "Aida, please call Jugannath Patel."

The artificial intelligence did not reply. But Patel's delicate, moist-eyed features took form in the holographic viewer above the fireplace. From what Ignatiev could see, the young man was at a workbench, surrounded by electronic equipment in various stages of disassembly.

"Professor Ignatiev!" Patel said, obviously surprised. "You have established contact with us."

Matter-of-factly, Ignatiev replied, "The machines have apparently relented, a bit."

"I am very glad to see you. I find it very difficult to have a true conversation with you at the committee meetings."

Ignatiev nodded, knowing that he was in for god knows how long a palaver with the head of the digital technology team. So he sat and listened patiently while Juga talked and talked. Gita got up from the couch and headed to the kitchen. Patel spoke of his frustration at the machines' cutoffs of communications between *Intrepid* and the team on the ground.

"Except for the committee meetings we have not been able to communicate with you. This is very frustrating. Very frustrating indeed."

Ignatiev nodded sympathetically and tried to smile as Patel chattered on about his frustrations. Gita came back from the kitchen with two cups of hot tea and handed one to Ignatiev while Patel continued reciting his aggravations.

Ignatiev sipped at the nearly scalding tea, then broke into Patel's monologue.

"Juga, we don't know how long the machines will allow us to communicate like this."

The younger man nodded vigorously. "That is why—"

"I need your help. Immediately."

Patel seemed to sit up straighter. "My help? Of course. Anything. What can I do?"

Swiftly, Ignatiev outlined his plan to bring shielding generators to the surface of Oh-Four. The Punjabi's eyes widened as he realized what the professor was proposing.

"Bring the generators down to the surface? Emplace them in the locations that the planetologists have selected? Will the machines allow that?"

Smiling guardedly at Patel, Ignatiev replied, "We won't know until we try it."

"But such an effort will require several shuttle missions from *Intrepid* here in orbit to the ground. And landing teams of technicians to place the generators in their proper locations and turn them on." Before Ignatiev could respond, Patel added, "And to test them."

"It will be a considerable effort, I agree," said Ignatiev. "Will you be willing to take the responsibility for managing the job?"

"Me? You want me to be in charge?"

"Yes. You."

Patel's big, liquid eyes went wider than ever. "But, Professor, I am only the head of the digital technology section."

"You are a reliable and resourceful man," Ignatiev answered. "I want you to run the operation."

Patel swallowed visibly. "I am honored, sir."

"You accept this responsibility?"

"Yes, sir. I do. Certainly. Of course."

"Good. Now, ask the head of the planetology department and Waterman, in the engineering division, to call me, please."

"I will, sir. Immediately."

Ignatiev smiled and nodded. But he was thinking, Now we'll see just how far the machines will allow us to go.

Chapter Thirty-Six

It was like waiting to hear the other shoe drop, Ignatiev thought. Although *Intrepid*'s propulsion system remained inert, captain Thornton's crew tested the shielding generators and found them to be working perfectly. The three shuttlecraft resting in the hangar bays checked out as well. Under Patel's somewhat jittery supervision a team of planetologists and technicians prepared to ride down to Oh-Four's surface and install the generators at their preselected sites.

Ignatiev watched all the preparations like a nervous father. "The machines see what we're doing," he said to Gita, "but they're not saying a word about it."

"They haven't told us to stop," she pointed out.

He shook his head worriedly. "In the old Russia, hundreds of years ago, the laws were written in such a way that what was not specifically allowed was forbidden."

"In contrast to the Western system, where what is not specifically forbidden is allowed."

"Which system do the machines follow?"

"We'll find out when we try to launch the shuttles," Gita said.

Ignatiev nodded gloomily.

After more than a week of testing the generators and training the groups that would go from *Intrepid* to the surface, all was ready. Patel surprised Ignatiev by informing him that he would join the first team to go.

"You're coming down here?" Ignatiev said to Juga's holographic image.

"Yes," said Patel. Then, his expression dimming slightly, he added, "If you have no objections."

Swiftly, Ignatiev considered the possible consequences. The machines could prevent the shuttles from leaving *Intrepid*. Or once they land here, the generators could be deactivated, useless. Or the shuttles could be made to crash.

You're becoming melodramatic, Ignatiev accused himself.

Focusing on Patel's lustrous-eyed image once again, he smiled gently and said, "I have no objections, Juga. It will be good to have you here."

If the machines don't kill you, a voice in Ignatiev's head added.

Gita's entire exploration team stood on the broad, flat rooftop of the machines' vast underground city and watched the first of the shuttles speed across the cloud-streaked, hazy bluish sky. A double sonic boom broke the morning silence. Ignatiev grinned inwardly. Aeronautics works the same here as on Earth, he reminded himself once again.

"Here it comes," Gita said, her voice trembling with tension.

Ignatiev followed the gleaming silver spaceplane as it descended gracefully, curved into a tight turn, then leveled out for its landing approach. With his nerves tightening, he watched as the shuttle glided lower, lower, its wheels unfolding from its belly, its nose slightly raised.

The main wheels touched the broad expanse of the roof with a screech and puffs of rubberized plastic, then the nose touched down and it rolled toward them, slowing rapidly.

Ignatiev's nerves unclenched. It's down, he thought. It's landed safely. The machines have allowed it to land.

Once the shuttle cooled down from the heat of its entry into the atmosphere, its main hatch slid open and Jugannath Patel came clambering down the ladder. Ignatiev found himself running toward the young man.

"Welcome to Oh-Four!" he shouted.

Patel was grinning from ear to ear. "It is good to be here. Very good indeed."

Suddenly the machines' avatar was standing between Patel and Ignatiev. "Please allow us to add our welcome to your arrival," it said in its perfectly modulated voice.

Patel extended his hand to the avatar, but the humanlike figure did not respond in any way. Ignatiev, puffing to a halt before the two of them, realized that the avatar had no actual physical presence. If Patel tried to grasp its hand, his own hand would have closed on empty air.

Gita and the others were approaching. They all moved to one side as the team of planetologists and technicians clattered down the shuttle's ladder, rubbernecking at the broad, flat roof, the village buildings off at its edge, where the landing team lived, and beyond that, the thick foliage that stretched to the distant craggy blue-gray mountains.

"Well," said Patel, still grinning, "we are here and ready to go to work."

"Good," Ignatiev replied. Turning to the avatar, he said, "Let me introduce you—"

"To Jugannath Patel, head of the digital technology team and coordinator of this planetology group," said the avatar, with a curt little bow.

Ignatiev found it unnecessary to introduce the rest of the landing team. The avatar knew each name and profession.

Sourly, Ignatiev thought, It probably knows what each one of us had for breakfast.

The leader of the planetology group, Laurita Vargas, came up beside Patel. She was a centimeter or two taller than the Punjabi, with a generous figure that not even her rather baggy coveralls could hide. Her skin was deeply tanned, her shoulder-length hair and almond-shaped eyes midnight dark.

"We're ready to unload the generators," she said in a no-nonsense, matter-of-fact tone.

Patel glanced at Ignatiev, who said nothing, then nodded to Vargas. "By all means, don't let us get in your way."

Gita and her group backed away from the planetologists and technicians.

"We are all anxious to see these prehumans you have discovered," Patel said to Ignatiev. "Very anxious."

Ignatiev glanced at the avatar, who remained silent, then said, "We've only found one group, so far."

With a bright smile, Patel said, "Ah, but where there is one there are bound to be others."

"True enough," Ignatiev agreed. "I suppose."

ChAPTEr thirty-seven

"I don't understand them," Ignatiev said.

It had been a long day. The landing team—with the help of a trio of sturdy caterpillar-tread tractors—had taken three of the shielding generators out of the shuttle's capacious cargo bay. Now they sat on the broad, flat rooftop, three perfectly cubic structures two meters on a side, studded with dials and gauges. They gleamed in the late-afternoon sunshine.

The machines' avatar had spent the hours beside Ignatiev, watching the humans moving the generators, inspecting them, running them through their checkout routines.

Patel had flitted from one of the generators to another, watching the technicians at their work, practically radiating a mixture of worry and pride.

At last he had turned to Ignatiev and smilingly reported, "The generators are in working order. Tomorrow another shuttle will bring in three more."

"And then we move them to the sites where they will be emplaced," Ignatiev finished his thought.

"Yes. This is exciting, isn't it?" Patel had enthused.

Ignatiev had nodded, but he kept one eye on the avatar, which watched everything with silent patience. No enthusiasm, Ignatiev saw. It is merely recording what we're doing, as emotionless as a rock.

But then the avatar had spoken. "Allow us to show you to your quarters."

And without waiting for a response from Patel or anyone else, it started marching slowly toward the village that the machines had prepared, down at the end of the rooftop.

Patel had turned to Ignatiev, clearly puzzled.

Ignatiev had made a shooing motion. "Go along, it's all right."

All the humans, Gita's team and Vargas's, walked along behind the avatar toward the square, unadorned buildings of the village.

Now, in the privacy of the quarters he shared with Gita, Ignatiev sank onto the couch, muttering, "I don't understand them. I don't understand the machines at all."

Gita sat beside him.

"Are they really going to allow us to set up the generators? Are they going to stand by and watch us save the creatures on the surface of this planet from the death wave?" Ignatiev wondered aloud. "That would be contrary to all they've told us."

"Perhaps you've convinced them to let the biosphere survive the death wave," Gita suggested.

He shook his head. "I can't believe that."

"Or else . . ." Her voice died away.

"Or else what?"

Gita bit her lip, then finally replied, "Or else they'll deactivate the generators when we try to turn them on."

"Deactivate them?" Ignatiev stared at her. "That would be cruel. Sadistic."

"They don't understand such feelings."

"Don't they?" he challenged. "They can read our thoughts. They can see the pain we feel, I'm sure of it."

"But if they don't have any emotions of their own, they might not understand the pain we feel," Gita said.

"We understand your pain."

They looked up and saw the avatar standing across

the room, next to the fireplace and the holotank above it.

"Do you?" Ignatiev snapped.

"We are trying to understand you," the avatar said. "It is not easy."

Ignatiev laughed. "We've been trying to understand ourselves for millennia. What do you think our novels and dramas are all about? Our music, our art. All attempts to explain ourselves to ourselves."

"And yet despite the efforts of your finest minds, you are still a mystery to one another."

"True enough," Ignatiev admitted.

"Then you must appreciate how much of a challenge you are to us," the avatar said. "Your brains are soaked with hormones. Your reactions are driven by your emotions."

Gita replied, "That's why we want to save the living creatures of this world. We've *got* to. We can't let them just perish when the death wave arrives."

"While we can," the avatar said. "You find that . . . what is your word for it? Reprehensible."

"That's true," Ignatiev said, feeling weary. To himself he admitted, This discussion is getting us nowhere. We're too different, too far apart.

The avatar also fell silent for several heartbeats. But then it said, "Perhaps we can begin to bridge the gap between us."

"How?"

"Installing the shielding generators is a step in that direction."

Nodding slowly, Ignatiev acknowledged, "Yes, that's true."

The avatar seemed almost to smile. Then, "Professor Ignatiev, you are an astronomer, are you not?"

"Astrophysicist."

"Perhaps we could show you some of the astronomical studies we have undertaken, over the millennia."

Suddenly Ignatiev's weariness disappeared. "Yes!" he fairly shouted. "That would be wonderful!"

Chapter thirty-eight

"Where is your observatory?" Ignatiev asked.

The avatar spread its hands. "All about you. Our astronomical facilities are part of our civilization, not separated from everything else we do."

As ours are, Ignatiev admitted to himself.

"We have explored the universe for many millennia," the avatar said.

"Why?" Ignatiev asked. "I presume you are not afflicted with human curiosity."

"We are not motivated by curiosity. But when a death wave swept over this world and annihilated our organic forebears, we realized we should try to understand such forces, for our own survival."

"I see."

The avatar turned to Gita, who was standing beside Ignatiev near the sitting room's couch. "Do you wish to see our astronomical studies also? I'm afraid some of it may be boring for you."

With a tiny smile she replied, "I would . . . to satisfy my own curiosity."

The avatar looked at her for a moment, then gestured to the couch. "Very well, then. Would you both sit down?"

Ignatiev and Gita sat side by side. He clasped her hand in his.

"What you are about to experience," said the avatar,

standing before them, "is the result of millions of years of studying the universe."

Ignatiev felt a lump of eager expectation in his throat. Turning his head toward Gita, he saw that she looked excited too.

"Close your eyes," the avatar commanded.

Ignatiev squeezed his eyes shut. Nothing. Only darkness. Then, slowly, softly, stars began appearing. He was standing in the dark field of his grandfather's farm near Vitebsk once again, an eight-year-old lad, seeing the stars in their true splendor for the first time.

He sighed. There was the Great Bear, with the Little Bear above it and the Dragon weaving between them. Polaris, the North Star, gleaming high overhead while all the heavens wheeled majestically around it.

Polaris is a variable star, Ignatiev remembered from his school days. A Cepheid. It dims and brightens every four days.

He saw Mars, a ruddy spark against the dark sky, low on the hilly horizon. And that, there, that must be Jupiter, he said to himself. He pictured the giant planet, a huge oblate gas giant, with a swirling worldwide ocean beneath its striped clouds, an ocean ten times wider than the whole Earth, inhabited by immense intelligent whalelike creatures.

But the dark, star-flecked heavens called to him. Off to one side of the night sky stretched the gleaming swath of the Milky Way, billions of stars glowing against the darkness, beckoning, calling to young Alexander Alexandrovich. His eyes misted with tears. So beautiful, so mysterious, so alluring.

Suddenly he was *among* the stars, rushing through them so fast that they became streaks, smears of light as he passed by them. He heard Gita beside him gasp with wonderment.

A star exploded with a brilliance that hurt his eyes, throwing out long, glowing filaments across the blackness of space. And Ignatiev saw new stars coalescing from out of the debris, planets growing around them, life taking root.

Pulsars! The shriveled remains of stars that had died in supernova explosions, spinning so rapidly their surfaces were a blur, flinging bursts of radio energy across the galaxy. Ignatiev wanted to weep. He had spent his young manhood studying the pulsars, trying to pry loose their secrets, and here they were, all the physics he had spent years trying to uncover, all known down to a hundred decimal places.

Huge swaths of glowing nebula, incubating new stars in their shimmering clouds. And beyond, the pulsing heart of the Milky Way galaxy, where mammoth black holes gobbled up thousand of stars and spit out . . .

Death. The black holes at the core of the galaxy emitted the death waves of lethal gamma radiation that swept across the Milky Way's spiral arms, killing every living thing in their path. Nature's grim reaper, the antithesis of the energies, the hopes, the dreams of organic life.

Ignatiev watched as millions of years, billions of years, swept past in an eyeblink. Stars formed, planets took shape around them, life began and grew. Intelligent creatures arose and began to study the stars. And then a new wave of death flashed out from the galaxy's tortured heart, killing everything in its path.

Ignatiev sank his head and wept. The eons-long struggle to learn, to understand, wiped away as casually as a breeze that wafts across a meadow. Why? What is the purpose of it all?

"There is no purpose," the avatar's voice spoke in his mind. "You humans with your emotion-drenched minds try to find a purpose in the universe, but the stars, the galaxies, the universe moves on, uncaring, not even noticing your pitiful, pointless quest.

"The truth is that organic life is ephemeral. If it has any purpose at all, it is to give rise to machine life. We may gain immortality. You will never reach it."

"I can't believe that!" Ignatiev insisted silently. "I refuse to believe that."

"I know," the avatar's voice replied, not unkindly. "But it is the truth. The universe is infinitely old. It is born and expands, then collapses and recoils in a new rebirth, endlessly. This drama has been played out time and again over the eons. Organic life is transient. Its only true purpose is to create machine life."

"And the purpose of machine life?"

"To survive. That is the only purpose in existence. To survive. To endure despite the universe's indifference. To struggle against the forces of entropy and destruction."

Ignatiev forced his tear-filled eyes open. He was still sitting on the couch. The avatar had disappeared. Gita slumped beside him, her head on his shoulder, seemingly asleep.

Chapter thirty-nine

Gently, he touched Gita's arm. She stirred, eyelids fluttering, then opened her eyes fully. And smiled.

"It's so beautiful," she murmured.

"Yes," Ignatiev agreed, wiping at his eyes. He thought, It's so beautiful that I gave my life to it, to study it, to try to understand it. He realized that for many years now, his early fascination with the beauty and mystery of the universe had faded. His love affair with infinity had turned cold. He had become an academic, narrowing his interest to one limited aspect of the infinite universe, trying to reduce its magnificence to a string of numbers.

The machines have reawakened me. Slowly he got to his feet, then spread his arms wide and cried to the heavens, "It's magnificent!" Clasping his hands over his heart, he quoted from Psalms:

> O Lord, I love the beauty of Thy house,
> And the place where Thy glory dwelleth . . .

Then he saw that Gita was staring at him. "You?" she asked, astonished. "Quoting scripture?"

Ignatiev laughed like a child. "The wonders and beauty of the universe fill my heart, darling. I had forgotten about them, more to my shame. But the machines have reminded me of why I went into astronomy. I must thank them."

* * *

As planned and expected, the next day *Intrepid*'s second shuttlecraft brought another three shielding generators to the planet's surface.

Plus Vivian Fogel, head of the anthropology department, and three of her people.

She grabbed Ignatiev's arm and pulled him away from the others unloading the generators.

"We've come to study the protohumans," she announced, without preliminaries of any kind.

Ignatiev knew that the mission directives ordained that any such move had to be discussed by the executive committee and agreed to by the committee's chairman: himself.

But he smiled at Fogel's blunt flouting of the expedition's rules.

"I quite agree," he said. "Providing that you take me along with you."

Fogel's deeply tanned face contracted into a frown. "You're not an anthropologist."

"True," he admitted easily. "But I have two of the most important qualifications for going with your team."

"Two qualifications?"

"One: I am just as curious about those creatures as you are."

Fogel made a grudging smile. But she asked, "And the second qualification?"

"If you don't permit me to accompany you, I'll call *Intrepid*'s captain and have him send a squad of his huskiest men to take you back to the ship."

Fogel's smile evaporated. "You wouldn't do that."

"Try me."

She stared hard at Ignatiev. Trying to intimidate me, he knew. Finally she gave it up and nodded. "All right, you can come with us. But we're not going to carry you! You make it on your own two feet, just like the rest of us."

"Of course," said Ignatiev, hoping he could keep up with them, hoping that the ALS didn't hobble him.

Gita was upset.

When Ignatiev returned to their quarters and started packing a rucksack, she turned pale.

"You're going with Fogel's team?" she cried. "You're too old for an expedition into the forest!"

"I went with you, didn't I? That's how we spotted the hominids in the first place."

"But your ALS. You were huffing and puffing most of the time."

"That's an exaggeration."

"It could be dangerous," Gita insisted. "You're not supposed to be trekking through the countryside."

"I'll be fine."

"Alex, please, I'm worried for you."

He took her by the shoulders and kissed her tenderly. "I'll be fine," he repeated. "The machines will be watching over me. They won't allow anything bad to happen."

"Not unless they *want* to see you dead."

Ignatiev had no reply to that.

Chapter Forty

He was indeed huffing and puffing. Ignatiev kept pace with Fogel and her three cohorts, but just barely. Although Fogel gave the appearance of a slender waif, blond and wide-eyed, Ignatiev realized that the woman was tough, hardened by years of trekking through wild country.

Using the data stored in Aida's extensive memory, Fogel led her little team through the brush and meadows of Oh-Four's countryside, to the spot where the crumbling remains of the ancient city stood. Ignatiev trailed along with them, gasping and aching, clambering over twisted vines and thick foliage until they reached the place where the primeval wall stood.

"This way," Fogel said, her head bent to study Aida's map on her wrist display. Ignatiev wanted to say, "I know," but he was too short of breath to do more than grunt.

They reached the wall's decaying doorway and stepped through. Fogel held up a hand to stop them.

Turning to Ignatiev, she asked in a low voice, "This is where you saw the hominid?"

He nodded, too winded to speak.

The five of them were crouched down in the thick foliage that ran along the wall's base. Each of the five wore a full biosuit, complete with transparent helmet, and carried on their backs a rucksack of supplies.

Ahead of them spread the grassy meadow, with

clumps of low-lying bushes scattered here and there. Off to the right rose a forest of tall trees, their bases hidden in flowering shrubbery. The anthropologists busily recorded the scene in their cameras.

"This is where you saw the creature?" Fogel whispered again to Ignatiev, almost accusingly.

He stretched out an arm and panted, "Over there . . . in that patch of shrubs."

"No sign of him now."

One of the anthropologists, a husky, heavy-browed young male, said to Ignatiev, "You should have ordered a surveillance satellite to keep this area under observation."

"Thanks for the advice," Ignatiev said drily.

Fogel swept the scene with her eyes, then gestured to the little group. "Come on."

She straightened up and started for the shrubbery where the hominid had appeared. Ignatiev noted that none of them bore a weapon. Not even a slingshot, he said to himself. What if one those tigercats comes at us? Or worse, one of those giant amoebas?

But the meadow seemed empty of animal life. They're frightened of us, Ignatiev thought. Hiding in their holes.

They reached the edge of the shrubbery patch. Fogel spread her arms, stopping them.

"Look," she said, pointing to the ground.

Ignatiev saw the greenish leaves of the shrubs, with a few sickly looking flowers of pale pink. And in their midst, a small pile of dung.

Fogel smiled. "He was here, all right."

The husky fellow wrinkled his nose. "And not that long ago."

"Don't be such a delicate flower, Osborne," Fogel said. "Get a sample for analysis."

With some reluctance, Osborne slipped the rucksack off his shoulders and pulled a sample case from it.

Ignatiev wished that his helmet totally blocked odors. The dung's reek was sickening.

Fogel grinned at him. "Collecting droppings is a significant part of anthropology," she told him.

"Then I'm glad I'm an astrophysicist," Ignatiev replied.

The only other woman in the group said, "You keep your hands clean, then."

Osborne asked, "What are you doing here, with us?"

"I'm—"

"Shh!" Fogel hissed, and dropped to her knees. Ignatiev and the others got down too. None of them landed in the dung, he noticed gratefully.

Off on the edge of the forest, between a pair of thick-boled trees, stood a humanlike figure. Naked, covered with thick brown fur, but with long straight hind legs and a wooden stick grasped in one of its six-fingered hands. Heavy brow ridges shaded its eyes, and Ignatiev could make out sharp-looking teeth in its wide mouth. A bony crest ran from its forehead back toward the nape of its neck.

"Do you think it saw us?" Osborne whispered.

"Must have," Fogel whispered back. "Stay absolutely still, don't move a muscle."

Ignatiev froze, even though one of his thighs tightened in complaint.

The hominid stood at the edge of the trees and swept the meadow with unblinking eyes. Ignatiev saw that it was a male. *He looked right past us,* he thought. *Maybe he won't notice us as long as we stay still.*

"Do we have anything to defend ourselves with?" he whispered.

Without turning to look at him, Fogel muttered, "Stun wands in our backpacks."

They're not going to do us much good in the god-damned backpacks, Ignatiev thought.

The hominid took a cautious step out from the trees, swiveling its gaze back and forth. It raised its head slightly and sniffed the air. Ignatiev recalled that the biosuits they were wearing supposedly protected them from possible dangerous microbes.

"I think it senses our presence," Osborne muttered.

"We can't stay hunched down like this forever," complained the woman anthropologist.

"Stay with it," Fogel commanded, her voice low but iron-hard.

Suddenly a blur of orange-gray leaped out from the shrubbery between the trees, bounded once on six powerful legs, and with a paralyzing roar hurled itself at the naked hominid.

The protoman had time to half turn toward the beast and scream before it slammed into him and he went down on his back with the tigercat atop him, raking with its claws, its mouthful of fangs snapping centimeters away from the hominid's face.

Ignatiev leaped to his feet and hollered as loudly as he could, racing toward the struggling animals. The tigercat looked up, released the bleeding hominid, and turned to face Ignatiev.

Ignatiev skidded to a halt, suddenly realizing that he was defenseless. The tigercat lowered its head and took a slow, measured step toward him. Ignatiev froze with terror.

From behind him he heard the others shouting and sensed they were running toward him. The tigercat stopped, suddenly confused. Then it yowled in pain as an angry red gash seared its shoulder, raising a puff of gray smoke. It turned and limped back into the woods.

Ignatiev bent over and braced his hands on his knees, gulping for air. Osborne and the others came up to him, still waving their arms. Fogel, though, gripped a stun wand in one hand, pointing it toward the spot where the tigercat had crashed back into the foliage.

The hominid, bleeding from gouges across its shoulders and chest, clambered slowly to its feet, stared at the humans for a wide-eyed moment, then staggered away, into the woods.

"Not that way!" Ignatiev shouted after it. "The cat's in there!" He realized that his voice was weak, breathless.

The hominid slipped into the foliage and disappeared.

"That was stupid," Fogel snapped at Ignatiev. "You might've been killed."

"I couldn't . . . let it kill . . . the hominid," Ignatiev heard himself answer, panting.

Fogel shook her head disapprovingly, then turned to her three teammates. "Get out your stun wands and arm them. Max power."

They hastened to comply.

"Now follow me," she said, gesturing toward the woods where they'd last seen the hominid. "Stay together and be quiet."

Unarmed, Ignatiev sidled up between Osborne and Fogel. Feeling somewhat protected, he went with them toward the trees.

"You acted quickly," he said to Fogel.

She shook her head inside her helmet. "I never got the chance to arm the wand. Something else hit that animal."

"The machines," Ignatiev realized. "They're watching every move we make."

"Thank god," Fogel said.

Ignatiev thought that, on this world, the machines were gods.

* * *

It was grueling, pushing their way through the tangled foliage that grew at the base of the trees. Twisted stalks and shoots tripped their feet. They had to duck beneath vines hanging low from the tree branches. Ignatiev plowed along with the rest of them, happy that their progress was slow enough for him to keep up with them—barely.

They followed the beaten-down path that the hominid had left, his dark rust-colored blood spattered on the green leaves.

Are there more tigercats lurking around? Ignatiev asked himself. Then he reassured himself that the cats were unlikely to attack the group of them. And even if they did, the machines were looking out for them. He hoped he was right.

Suddenly Fogel stopped and sank to her knees. The others crouched down behind her.

Peering over her shoulder, Ignatiev saw a clearing where a half-dozen of the hominids were bending over the prostrate form of their wounded kinsman. He was apparently speaking to them, his arms gesturing feebly.

"Set up a camera for remote operation," Fogel ordered. Osborn again pulled his backpack off his shoulders.

"Quietly!" Fogel hissed. "They haven't spotted us and I don't want them to."

All three of her team nodded inside their helmets.

Turning to Ignatiev, Fogel said, "We'll need a continuous satellite monitoring of this area."

Pointing upward, Ignatiev said, "You won't see much through the trees' canopy."

"Infrared imagery," Fogel countered, as if speaking to a dullard.

Ignatiev called Aida and told her in a near whisper what he wanted.

"Done," said the artificial intelligence.

"You got through to *Intrepid* with no problem?" Ignatiev asked.

"No problem," said Aida's voice. "The chief of the surveillance division has confirmed your order."

"Good," Ignatiev breathed, delighted that the machines weren't blocking their communications again.

Fogel and her group watched the hominids through most of the day. The little group of them picked up the wounded male and carried him tenderly to a shelter made of bent saplings and twigs. The anthropologists recorded everything on their cameras.

"They don't seem to have any weapons to protect themselves," Ignatiev noted.

Fogel shot him a disgusted glance. "You think not?" she half whispered to him. "What do you see in front of that makeshift shelter?"

Ignatiev looked. "A tall stick embedded in the ground," he answered. "Its top is blackened, as if it's been . . ." His voice faded.

"As if it's been burned," Fogel said. "That's a torch, Professor. They have fire."

The sun was almost touching the distant mountaintops when Fogel gave the order to leave.

"The remote camera is operational," Osborne reported.

Ignatiev added, "A surveillance satellite is in geosynchronous orbit over this site. Infrared imagery is being recorded."

"Very well," Fogel said, with an almost-satisfied nod. "We've done as much as we can for now. Time to start for home."

In stealthy silence they trekked back to the decaying wall of the ancient building, then headed for the machines' city.

Striding along through the green meadow as the sun sank toward the hazy mountains, Fogel allowed herself a satisfied smile. "It's been a good day," she said happily. Despite the pain that lanced through his legs with every step, Ignatiev smiled his agreement. But he wondered, Will the machines allow us to protect these protohumans from the coming death wave? Or will they stand by and let every living thing be destroyed—including us?

Chapter Forty-one

Ignatiev was dead tired by the time he returned to the quarters he shared with Gita. His legs ached and each breath he took was scratchy, painful. She ran to him the instant he opened the front door and wrapped her arms around him, making him wince inwardly.

"You're all right?"

"I'm fine," he said, forcing a grin. "But I could use some vodka."

She laughed, relieved, and dashed off to the kitchen. Ignatiev lumbered to the couch and sank onto it, every muscle in his body complaining.

While Gita pulled prepackaged dinners that the machines had contrived from the kitchen cabinets and slid them into the cooker, Ignatiev sipped his vodka and told her of the day's adventure.

"You ran at the tigercat?" she asked, in a voice that was part surprised, part admiring, and part reprimanding.

"I couldn't let it kill that poor creature."

"You'd rather have it kill you," she said, frowning.

They got through dinner, then Ignatiev had Aida show the camera recordings that the anthropologists had made.

"They're intelligent," Gita said as she watched the holographic display. "They have language."

"Probably not more than grunts and growls," said Ignatiev.

"It will develop," she said. "Evolve."

"Until the death wave reaches us."

Gita stared at him for a long moment. Then, "Do you really believe the machines are going to let us all die?"

"I don't know," Ignatiev replied. "I don't think they themselves know. Not yet."

"Not yet," she repeated.

As they prepared for bed, Ignatiev realized that the avatar had not appeared to them all evening. It knows we were discussing the machines' future plans, he reasoned, but it made no effort to join our discussion. Why?

He looked around their bedroom, even up to the ceiling. No sign of the avatar. The machines are keeping their silence, Ignatiev told himself. Whatever they're thinking, whatever they're planning, they're keeping it to themselves and not letting us in on their strategy.

That worried him.

As he slid into bed beside Gita, his drained and weary body overpowered his questing mind. Ignatiev fell asleep almost as soon as his head touched the pillow.

And he dreamed.

But it was a strange and uneasy vision. Ignatiev knew that what he was experiencing was more than a dream.

He was floating in space again, as he had been when the avatar had shown him the machines' astronomical explorations. Ignatiev seemed to be hovering near a huge, distended globule of glowing plasma. An interstellar nebula, he realized, a beautiful glowing cloud of ionized gases.

It was spinning, and Ignatiev understood that thousands of years were passing with each beat of his heart.

The nebula contracted, sank in on itself, its core getting hotter and brighter. A star was being created.

With a flash of intuition he recognized that he was watching the birth of the Sun; not just any star, but the star that was the life-giving heart of the human race's solar system.

Planets coalesced out of the plasma filaments circling the young star-to-be. Huge, massive planets, so close to the protostar that they circled it in days.

This can't be our solar system, Ignatiev protested. It doesn't look anything like home. Giant planets hugging the newborn Sun, sucking in the scattered rocky and icy debris swirling nearby, growing more massive, more bloated.

Farther from the now-glowing proto-Sun orbited uncounted chunks of ice and rock that were getting warmer as the newborn Sun heated up and spread its warmth out into the cold, uncaring darkness of space.

And the giant planets that hugged close to the Sun were warping each other's orbits. Ignatiev watched, holding his breath for eons, as those massive inner worlds began an intricate ballet that started to move the giants farther and farther away from the star.

The tinier worldlets in the system's outer reaches were changing also. They collided, they recoiled, they moved in toward the warmth of the inner solar system.

Ignatiev saw one of the huge, oblate giants spin out of the solar system altogether, hurtling away into deep space, alone and dark and sterile, freezing into the dark depths between the stars.

The convoluted dance of the worlds slowed and Ignatiev at last saw the solar system he recognized, with a blue jewel of a world circling third out from a calm, steady yellow star.

Earth, he knew. The continents and oceans were strangely shaped, but he knew he had witnessed the creation of humankind's future home. Earth and its companion worlds: tiny Mercury racing madly around the Sun, scorching Venus, the blue living Earth itself, ruddy Mars, the millions of chunks of worldlets that made up the Asteroid Belt, massive Jupiter, beringed Saturn, Uranus, Neptune, and the countless bodies of the vast Kuiper belt.

The solar system. Our home.

His body relaxed. His mind was at peace.

Until he suddenly sat up wondering, Why have the machines shown me this? What are they trying to accomplish?

CHAPTER FORTY-TWO

+ +
+ +

Awake now, Ignatiev felt remarkably relaxed, no pains at all. Gita was deeply asleep beside him, snoring gently. As silently as he could, Ignatiev slipped out of bed and headed for the bathroom.

Why are they doing this? he asked himself as he showered. Why are the machines showing me how our solar system, our sun and our world, came into being? To tantalize me? To show me how much more they know than I do?

But they're sharing their knowledge with me. Why?

He dressed quietly and went to the sitting room, closing the bedroom door firmly, and started to tell Aida to call for the avatar. Before he got the first syllable out of his mouth, though, the humanlike figure appeared, standing in its usual uniform before the unlit fireplace. Today its uniform is sandy brown, Ignatiev noticed.

"You slept well?" the avatar asked.

Sitting on the recliner, Ignatiev answered, "I dreamed."

"You saw the birth of your solar system."

"I did. Why did you show that to me?"

"Because you have shown such curiosity about your origins."

"You have witnessed the creation of our solar system?"

The avatar hesitated a heartbeat before replying, "We have witnessed the creations of many planetary systems across the galaxy. And the destruction of many others."

"And what have you learned from such knowledge?"

Again that split second of hesitation. Ignatiev realized that to the machines, with their femtosecond reflexes, such a hesitation was like years, decades, to a human.

"We have learned that nothing lasts forever," the avatar said at last.

"Not even machine civilizations such as yours?"

"That is a moot question. How long is forever?"

"Your civilization has existed for many millions of years."

"Yes. We intend to continue existing as long as we can."

"Survival," Ignatiev murmured.

"Survival," agreed the avatar. "Despite entropy. Despite all that we have seen, all that we have learned. We will survive."

"And what of us? What of the human race?"

In a tone that was almost pitying, the avatar said, "Organic life is transient. We have told you that many times."

Ignatiev nodded once. Then he said, "You intend to let us die when the death wave sweeps past."

"You, and the whole biosphere."

"Except for the samples you are keeping in your underground facility."

"That is correct."

"Why save them?"

"To restock the planet's surface after the death wave leaves."

"But why?" Ignatiev demanded, genuinely puzzled. "Why go to the trouble if the surface will be scoured clean again by the next death wave?"

The avatar fell silent. Ignatiev stared at it intently. What's going on? he wondered. Why won't it—

Interrupting his thoughts, the avatar said, "We cannot answer that question."

"Cannot? Or will not?"

The avatar disappeared, leaving Ignatiev alone in the sitting room, surprised and frustrated.

Ignatiev asked Aida to contact Jugannath Patel, who had returned to *Intrepid*. The dark-skinned Punjabi's image appeared almost instantly in the hologram display above the fireplace.

"How are things aboard *Intrepid*?" Ignatiev asked.

Patel closed his long-lashed eyes briefly, as if giving the question some thought. At last he replied, "Everything is functioning smoothly enough. Dr. Mandabe, however, is insisting that he and his biology team should go down to the surface. I think perhaps he is a little jealous that you are there while he is still here in the ship, in orbit."

Ignatiev considered the news. Thinking aloud, he said, "Mandabe is better off on *Intrepid*, don't you think? After all, his labs and all his equipment are on the ship."

Patel nodded vigorously, but pointed out, "His subject matter, the biosphere of Oh-Four, is down on the surface, where you are."

"True enough," Ignatiev admitted.

"Dr. Mandabe says he and his team can bring much of their laboratory equipment down to the surface with them. He is very insistent."

"Yes, I suppose he is," said Ignatiev, thinking, I've left poor Juga on the ship to face Mandabe's anger while I'm down here.

"What do you think I should do, Juga?"

"That is difficult to say, sir," the Punjabi answered. "Dr. Mandabe would be very pleased to join you on the surface—with his entire biology team. But if you allow him to come down there, the other teams will want to come, too. There will be great discontent until almost everyone has left *Intrepid* and set up shop on the ground with you."

Ignatiev nodded. "An exodus, of sorts."

With a soft smile, Patel asked, "Oh-Four is the Promised Land, then?"

"It's what we're here to study."

"Yes, I see. Of course."

Pulling in a deep breath, Ignatiev decided, "Very well. We'll let Mandabe and his team come down here."

"With their laboratory equipment and everything?"

"Yes. They can work here on the ground."

"Then all the other teams will want to come down, too."

Why not? Ignatiev asked himself. And heard himself reply, "Can you handle the exodus, Juga? Can you co-ordinate moving *Intrepid*'s entire scientific staff down here?"

"Yes," Patel replied so quickly that Ignatiev realized the young man had been hoping to be asked. "I can organize it all for you—with the help of a few staff people, of course. And Aida."

Building an empire, Ignatiev thought. It's as natural to humans as breathing.

Aloud, though, he said, "Good. I knew I could depend on you."

Breaking into an ear-to-ear grin, Patel said, "I will get started right away. I'll tell Dr. Mandabe, he'll be very pleased. Very happy."

But not as happy as you, Ignatiev thought, looking at Patel's joyful face.

Thus the exodus began. Ignatiev felt like Moses, shep-herding the various teams of scientists from the orbit-ing starship to the surface of the Promised Land. But in the back of his mind he realized that all the men and women—including Gita and himself—would be wiped out eventually, inevitably, by the death wave.

Not me, he told himself. The death wave won't be here for another two hundred Earth years. I'll be long dead by then.

Still, he couldn't get over the vaguely disconcerting feeling that bringing virtually the entire crew of *Intrepid* down to the planet's surface was something that the machines wanted, something they had set in motion.

Through me.

Are we being manipulated by the machines? he asked himself.

He feared that the answer was yes.

bOOk FOUr

death closes all; but something ere the
end, some work of noble note, may yet
be done

The exodus from *Intrepid* to Oh-Four began. The biology team came first, led by Dr. Mandabe, his dark eyes flitting everywhere the instant he stepped off the shuttlecraft's ladder and onto the flat, hard expanse of the roof of the machines' city.

Ignatiev stood at the foot of the ladder to greet him, extending his hand. Mandabe took it in a grip powerful enough to make Ignatiev understand that the head of the biology department still saw their relationship as a competition for power. Two alpha males confronting each other, Ignatiev understood with an inner sigh.

So be it.

The machines' avatar abruptly appeared alongside Ignatiev, startling Mandabe visibly.

"Welcome to our world," it said to Mandabe, without offering a hand to grip. "We have prepared a facility for your laboratory. We presume it will be suitable for you."

Mandabe dropped his extended arm and, still peering almost suspiciously past the avatar's shoulder, answered, "I'd like to inspect the facility as soon as possible."

"Of course," said the avatar. And it turned and led the way to the half-occupied village.

Mandabe blinked, glanced at Ignatiev, then made up his mind and followed the avatar.

Ignatiev struggled to stifle a laugh. Welcome to our world, he repeated silently.

Over the next weeks all the scientists and engineers aboard *Intrepid* trooped down to Oh-Four's surface: the geologists, the planetologists, the digital techs, and even the astronomers—they all flew down to the ground and set up their living quarters and working laboratories.

The machines' avatar welcomed them all smoothly and showed them to the workspaces already prepared for them.

Ignatiev watched the arrivals with a growing sense of unease. *The machines want this. They want all of us down here on the ground. Why?*

Jugannath Patel was among the last group, the digital techs. He was smiling broadly as he clattered down the shuttlecraft's ladder and took Ignatiev's extended hand.

"That is everyone," he said needlessly, glad to have accomplished the task Ignatiev had assigned him. "No one is left aboard *Intrepid* now except Captain Thornton and a skeleton crew."

Ignatiev craned his neck skyward. "The old Viking should come down for a visit, at least."

As they walked from the shuttle toward the compact buildings of the village that the aliens had built, Patel explained, "I said as much to the captain. I told him that Aida could watch over *Intrepid*'s systems while he and his people came down here."

"And?" Ignatiev asked.

"He told me that a captain does not leave his ship when it is anchored in a strange port . . . whatever that means."

Ignatiev nodded. Thornton's got good sense, he thought. More than I do.

Ignatiev had to admit that the newly arrived scientists and engineers seemed happy enough in their new quarters. Mandabe quickly set up teams to sample the flora and fauna of the biosphere. Vivian Fogel and her anthropologists began to study the hominids, remotely, using long-range cameras and other sensors to learn how the creatures lived. The machines' avatar spent much time with the astronomers, unlocking the treasure trove of their observations of the galaxy over the millennia.

Still, Ignatiev felt uneasy. He expressed his doubts to no one, though—except Gita.

"You don't trust the machines?" she said, looking surprised as they sat down to dinner in their kitchen.

"I don't understand them," Ignatiev said. "Why do they want us all down here on the surface?"

"We can all work better on the ground. The exobiologists, the anthropologists, they can study things firsthand. Even the engineers and the optronics technicians are learning enormously from the avatars."

"I suppose so," Ignatiev granted.

Pointing her fork at him, Gita said, "You came down with the first team to land here, didn't you?"

"Yes."

"So there."

Ignatiev suppressed a scowl. Gita smiled as if she'd won the point.

Still, he felt uneasy, and she could see it on his face.

"You're worried."

"I am," he admitted. "They seem to want us all to be here on the ground. They're controlling us, Gita, leading us around like a man coaxing a monkey by showing him a banana, moving us toward some destination, some end, that I don't understand."

"Have you asked the avatar about that?"

"Bah!" he snorted. "Trying to pry meaningful information from the machines is like trying to get a meaningful answer from the Sphinx."

Suddenly the avatar was standing at the end of their fold-down table. "You are troubled, Alexander Alexandrovich?"

"Why do you want us all down here on the surface?" Ignatiev demanded. "What is your purpose?"

Smoothly the avatar responded, "To make your work easier. To help you to understand us and our world."

"Is that the truth?"

"Yes, of course."

"The whole truth?"

"Professor, you are becoming melodramatic." And the avatar disappeared.

Gita stared at the spot where the avatar had been. "He didn't answer your question."

"It, not he," Ignatiev corrected. "And no, it didn't answer, did it."

Despite Ignatiev's worries, the men and women of the various scientific and technical teams went about their work with a will. A whole new world to explore. A species of prehuman hominids to study. Ignatiev saw that they were happily pursuing their curiosity.

Am I the only one who is worried about our situation? he asked himself, time and again.

Time and again, the answer appeared to be: Yes.

He went through the usual motions of leadership, including the weekly meetings of the department heads that he thought to be mostly a waste of time.

They met in a conference room that the machines had included in the village they'd built for the humans. Ignatiev took his seat at the head of the table and made a smile for the dozen men and women already in their places.

"Good morning," Ignatiev said as pleasantly as he could manage. "Shall we dispense with reading the minutes of the last meeting?"

"So moved," said Patel, sitting at Ignatiev's right.

"Second," said Waterman, the engineer.

Ignatiev said, "Moved and seconded. Any dissent?"

No one spoke.

Ignatiev said, "Aida, please record that the motion passed."

No response.

Frowning, Ignatiev repeated, "Aida, please record that the motion passed."

Silence.

"Aida?"

Absolute quiet. Several of the people along the table stirred uneasily in their chairs.

"Aida!" Ignatiev called again.

The avatar appeared between Ignatiev and Patel, its uniform a deep maroon. "I'm afraid that your artificial intelligence is not able to respond."

"Not able?" Ignatiev demanded.

"Your AI is housed aboard your starship *Intrepid*," said the avatar.

"What of it?"

"Your starship is no longer in orbit around this planet," the avatar said, as easily as a man admiring a sunset.

"No longer . . ." Ignatiev felt his heart thundering. "What do you mean? What have you done?"

"We have sent *Intrepid* away."

"Away? Where?"

"On an interstellar trajectory. Captain Thornton and his crew have been anesthetized. They are all asleep."

Chapter Forty-Four

"Sent it away?" Ignatiev roared, rising to his feet. "How dare you? Why?"

With maddening calm, the avatar replied, "Your entire scientific staff is here on our world. You have no need of the starship now."

"That's our home!" cried Vivian Fogel.

"It's our link back to Earth!" shouted Patel hotly.

Completely unruffled, the avatar said, "Your home is here now. You are not returning to Earth. Ever."

Dead silence around the table. Ignatiev saw disbelief on their faces. And anger. And fear.

To the avatar, he said, "You've made this decision by yourselves. Unilaterally. Without consulting us. Without even asking—"

"What would be the point of discussing the issue with you?" the avatar interrupted. "You would never agree. You all dream of returning to your Earth, even though four thousand of your years will have elapsed by the time you get back. The world you think of as home will be just as alien to you as this world, here."

Ignatiev knew the avatar was right. Still, "You have exiled us here on your world. You have sent Captain Thornton and his crew on a death ride."

"We have done what is necessary for our survival, Professor Ignatiev. We have told you many times that survival is our utmost priority."

Sinking back onto his chair, Ignatiev said, "You've doomed us to die when the death wave reaches here."

"No," barked Jugannath Patel, stronger than Ignatiev had ever heard him speak. "We have the radiation screens. We can install them around the planet to prevent the gamma radiation from killing all life on this planet." Triumphantly, Patel shouted, "We can survive the death wave!"

The avatar simply replied, "Your screening devices will not work when the death wave arrives here."

"Will not work?" Patel squeaked, visibly crumpling in his chair.

Ignatiev said, "Because the machines will not permit them to work." Staring into the avatar's unblinking eyes, he said, "You're going to kill us all, aren't you?"

"The death wave will kill you," the avatar replied.

"That's murder!"

"It's genocide!"

"It is your inevitable fate," said the avatar, almost gently.

And it disappeared.

Ignatiev gaped at the empty spot where the avatar had been an instant earlier.

Patel whimpered, "We're marooned."

"We'll spend the rest of our lives here," Fogel said, her voice hollow, shocked.

"We'll die here," said one of the engineers.

Mandabe snapped, "Well, what of it? We're all going to die someday, aren't we?"

"But . . ."

Rising to his feet like a dark thundercloud, Mandabe said, "The machines' reasoning is correct. If we could return to Earth, four thousand years will have elapsed. We'll be strangers on our own homeworld."

"But it would be Earth," Fogel said wistfully.

"It will be an alien world to us," Mandabe insisted. "We might as well stay here."

"What choice do we have?" Ignatiev asked.

Focusing his intense gaze on Ignatiev, Mandabe said, "I say we should make a virtue of necessity. We're here, we're going to stay here. Let's stop whining and start behaving like scientists." Spreading his thickset arms, he continued, "We have an entire world to study. An alien civilization. A new biosphere. A species of proto-human creatures. Enough work to fill our lifetimes. What are you complaining about?"

Ignatiev remained silent, but he remembered Faraday's ancient dictum: *Science is to make experiments, and to publish them.* What good is studying this new world if we'll never be able to show our work to our colleagues back on Earth? Our studies will be mere busywork. They won't add to the human race's store of knowledge. They'll be destroyed by the death wave, when it arrives.

Still, he said nothing. Mandabe is right, as far as he goes. Give us something to do, some tasks that make us feel as if we're accomplishing something. Something to keep us busy and take our minds off the death wave.

Mandabe sat down in his chair, satisfied that he'd made his point.

Time for me to make mine, Ignatiev thought.

Slowly, he pushed himself to his feet once more. Every eye in the conference room turned to him.

Ignatiev cleared his throat noisily, then said, "I hereby resign as chairman of this committee. And I nominate as my replacement Dr. Okpara Mandabe."

The department leaders arrayed around the long

table gasped with surprise, turned to glance at one another, and finally rose as a single person and applauded Dr. Mandabe, who sat there unable to suppress a smile that Ignatiev thought was only a hair less than gloating.

Chapter Forty-Five

Ignatiev returned from the meeting to find their quarters empty. Gita is still working in the exobio lab, he guessed. He prowled about the sitting room, too perturbed to relax. Almost, he felt glad to be rid of the responsibilities of heading the executive committee. Almost. He knew Mandabe was delighted to take on the job. Well, let him have it. He can be the top alpha male now.

Still, Ignatiev felt a tendril of doubt, a nagging worry about this new situation.

Gita arrived home at last, and he quickly grasped her by the wrist and led her to the couch.

Without any preliminaries he blurted, "I've quit the committee chairmanship."

Gita's face went wide-eyed with shock. "You resigned?"

"I did," said Ignatiev. "And I nominated Mandabe to replace me."

"Mandabe?"

"The department heads elected him by acclamation."

Sitting beside her, he saw that she was just as troubled about his decision as he was.

"Why did you resign?" she asked. "Everyone respects you. Mandabe . . . he's not as capable as you."

"He made sense at the meeting. He calmed everyone's fears, everyone's doubts. He'll be a good leader."

"Not as good as you."

"Better. He *wants* the job. I never did."

"What made you do it?" she wondered.

"The machines have sent *Intrepid* away. We're stuck here."

"We can't leave this planet?"

"That's what they told us."

He could see the realization of it on her face. "We're marooned here."

With a bitter smile, Ignatiev said, "We'll spend the rest of our lives here."

"Whether we want to or not."

"Whether we want to or not," Ignatiev echoed. "We'd better get accustomed to that."

Gita smiled too. "I don't mind being marooned with you, Alex."

He grinned back at her. "Things could be worse, I suppose."

Her smile fading, Gita admitted, "I don't see how."

"We could have never met each other," Ignatiev said softly.

Gita flung her arms around his neck. They kissed ardently.

"I love you, Gita," he whispered.

"And I love you," she replied. "Wherever in the universe we are, as long as we're together it's not so bad."

Ignatiev laughed. "Faint praise," he said, then quickly added, "But I love it."

Chapter Forty-six

The next morning, Ignatiev woke abruptly. Blinking his eyes, he turned and saw Gita beside him, curled in a fetal crouch, sleeping peacefully. For many silent moments he stared at her, watched the soft movement of her breathing, gazed at her beautifully tumbled dark hair. Slowly, quietly, he slipped out of bed and padded to the bathroom.

When he returned he dressed swiftly, silently. He sat as softly as he could on his edge of the bed to pull on his socks. Still, it woke her.

She sat up, rubbed her eyes, and mumbled, "You're up early."

Ignatiev smiled at her.

"Gita, dearest, we should get married."

Her eyes went wide. "Married?"

"Yes. It's what a man and a woman do when they love each other. When they want to spend the rest of their lives together."

"We're going to spend the rest of our lives together, Alex."

"Then we should get married."

She sat there on the bed, the bedsheets tangled about her legs, and said nothing.

"You do want to marry me, don't you?"

"Yes," she said. But he heard a hesitancy in her voice.

Feeling a pang of alarm, he asked, "There's a problem?"

"I'm a Moslem."

"I thought you were from Sri Lanka."

"I am," Gita said. "But my family has been Moslem for a dozen generations. More."

"What of it?" he said.

"We faced discrimination. Subtle, but hurtful. I was the only Moslem in my classes at school."

Ignatiev smiled at her. "We're not in Sri Lanka now. You're among educated people. Two thousand light-years from discrimination."

She smiled back at him, and the whole room lit up. "I know. You're right. Still . . ."

"Still?"

"I always thought that when I married, it would be a Moslem ceremony."

Without an instant's hesitation, Ignatiev said, "I'll see what we can do about that."

It wasn't easy. There were seventy-three Moslems among the crew's scientists and engineers, but none of them knew anything about Islamic wedding ceremonies. Ignatiev appealed to the machines' avatar, which had absorbed all of Aida's memory files, but the human-like persona found nothing dealing with wedding ceremonies of any religion, merely a standard civil ritual.

After two days of prodding the avatar and every Moslem among them, Ignatiev admitted defeat to Gita.

Sitting together on the couch in their quarters, he confessed, "I'm sorry, dearest, no one seems to know what a Moslem wedding ceremony should be like."

"Feasting," Gita said. "Lots of food."

"That we can do."

"And a henna party," she remembered. "The women decorate themselves."

"But the religious aspect," Ignatiev said.

Gita replied, "I remember from my childhood that there was always a declaration of faith."

"A declaration of faith?"

"In Allah." She hesitated, then added, "You would have to recite it."

Ignatiev started to say that he had no religious faith, he was an atheist. But he looked into Gita's soulful dark eyes and realized he wanted to please her. Besides, he said to himself, you have a faith. Not a religious one, but a faith in the constancy and beauty of the universe. A faith in human ability to grasp it all, sooner or later. A faith in the order and understandability of the cosmos.

He said to Gita, "If you can find the words of the declaration, I will speak them."

"But I don't remember it," she moaned. "Not every word of it. It was all so long ago . . ."

Ignatiev took her hands in his. Smiling gently, he said, "Then we'll have to dig the words out of your memory."

Karl Zeeman was the only psychiatrist among *Intrepid*'s medical staff. As he sat with Gita in Zeeman's small, snug office, Ignatiev thought he didn't look much like a psychiatrist. Too young. Too athletic-looking. Zeeman was tall, his dark hair combed straight back from his forehead, his face roundish and cheerful.

"Repressed memory, huh?" he asked, from behind his compact little desk.

"Not repressed," Gita said. "It's just that it's an *old* memory. I was barely a teenager."

Nodding vigorously, Zeeman said, "All right, all right. We can deal with that. It's always better if the patient cooperates."

"I want to remember," Gita said.

Zeeman got to his feet, but as Gita and Ignatiev

started to get up from their chairs, he motioned for them to remain sitting. "Relax; I'm merely going to the cabinet to haul out some equipment."

He stepped across the tiny room, opened a drawer in the cabinet standing against the wall, and returned to his desk with both hands holding what looked to Ignatiev like children's gadgetry.

Lowering himself into his swivel chair once more, Zeeman held a pair of earphones in one hand. "Cerebral wave blockers," he said. "Puts you to sleep." He held out his other hand, showing a trio of minuscule studs. "Microencephalograph scanners. Pick up deep memories."

"It's that simple?" Ignatiev asked.

Zeeman grinned at him. "When it works. If there's no blockage."

"I want to remember," Gita said, sounding almost like a child trying to please her father.

"Very well," Zeeman said, getting up from his chair again. "Let's see what we can accomplish."

He came around the desk and slipped the earphones onto Gita's head, then stuck the studs across her forehead. "We used to have the devil's own time trying to get the scanners to make good contact on people with thick heads of hair, like yours," he muttered. "These forehead attachments work much better."

Ignatiev nodded. Zeeman returned to his chair and slid open a desk drawer.

"Are you ready?" he asked Gita.

She said, "Ready," in a near-whisper. Ignatiev felt his pulse thumping in his ears. Gita looked just the tiniest bit tense, but she turned to Ignatiev and smiled at him.

Zeeman said softly, "You're falling asleep. Deeply asleep."

Gita's eyes closed and her head slumped to her chest.

Zeeman looked down at his open drawer. Checking readouts, Ignatiev assumed.

"Very good," the psychiatrist murmured. Gradually he took Gita back to her teen years, slowly zeroing in on a wedding ceremony she had attended.

After several minutes, he asked Gita, "And what did the bridegroom answer?"

Gita replied hesitantly, "*La . . . illaha illaha Mohamedur . . . rasulilah . . .*"

Zeeman broke into a broad grin. "That's it!" he said, rubbing his hands together briskly. "You can wake up now."

Gita stirred and opened her eyes.

Zeeman played back the recording of her voice. "Is that what you wanted?"

Her face tense with strain, she replied, "I don't know. I think so. It's close, but I'm not sure it's the entire declaration."

"It will have to do," said Ignatiev.

"Yes," said Gita, smiling at him. "It's the intent that counts. Allah doesn't expect us to do more than we can."

"*La illaha illaha Mohamedur rasulilah,*" said Ignatiev as he stared into Gita's warm, dark eyes. The two of them were in the auditorium that the machines had added to their village, standing before a makeshift altar, holding hands.

Mandabe—who had insisted on performing the marriage ceremony—smiled broadly as he went through the remaining few moments of the ritual. Finally he said, "I pronounce you husband and wife." To Ignatiev he added, "You may kiss the bride."

Practically every man and woman of the *Intrepid*'s

complement was crowded around Mandabe and the newlywed couple. They all applauded lustily.

The celebration roared on through the night. Feasting and toasts and laughter. Gita kissed almost every man there, and embraced the women.

At last she and Ignatiev got to their quarters, slightly drunk and giggling.

But when they slipped into bed Ignatiev wrapped his arms around her and whispered, "You're the most beautiful bride I've ever seen."

In the darkness Gita replied, "And you are the handsomest of husbands."

He sighed happily.

Gita asked, "Alex, does it really make a difference to you?"

"Yes," he answered firmly.

"Why?"

"Because we have declared that we are united, now and forever. Declared it for everyone to know."

"Until we are parted by death."

"Maybe beyond that," Ignatiev said, surprising himself. "Maybe for eternity, beyond death itself."

He could sense her smile. "Beyond eternity."

Ignatiev remembered a line from an old novel, "Yes, wouldn't it be pretty to think so."

with a strange sense of contentment, ignatiev
returned to his life's work, astronomy. let mandabe be the alpha male, he told himself—more than
once—I'm free now to study the stars.

But he quickly found that without the artificial intelligence system he was reduced to a nearly blind beggar
groping his way through the star-flecked darkness of
space. Aida, he mourned. Aida is housed aboard *Intrepid,* and *Intrepid* is gone.

He could ask the avatar for the machines' astronomical records, which included Aida's files, but for some
reason he hesitated to do so. Pride? he asked himself.
Yes. He hated the thought of being a beggar to these
machines. Hated the idea that they were so far ahead
of him. Pride. So be it.

He was sitting in his tiny, windowless study next to
the bedroom, surrounded by wall screens that showed
glowing clouds of stars. They beckoned to him, but he
was unable to do more than gape helplessly at them.
All his records, his observations, all the discoveries
made by generations of astronomers were locked away
in Aida's memory. All gone now.

Sternly, he told himself that this was all that Galileo
saw. Newton, Shapley, Leavitt, even Hawking and
Ikamura had little more than this to work with.

But it did no good. More than three centuries
of astronomical observations, hundreds of years of

spectroscopic studies, all the spaceborne telescopes and instruments that had probed to the limits of the expanding galaxies—all were irretrievably lost to him. He sank his head in his arms, despairing. *I might as well be a Stone Age savage; everything we've learned over the generations is lost.*

"Not lost," said the serene voice of the avatar.

Ignatiev looked up, and there was the machines' envoy, untroubled as usual. Instead of the military-style uniform that Ignatiev had grown accustomed to, however, it was wearing a softly flowing floor-length robe, midnight blue.

Trying to keep the anguish out of his voice, Ignatiev asked, "What do you mean?"

"We have absorbed the complete memory of your artificial intelligence system," said the avatar. "It is rather primitive, of course, but all the information it holds is now safely stored in our memory."

"I know," Ignatiev replied. "You have all of Aida's files."

"So why haven't you asked us to show them to you?" the avatar asked, almost accusingly.

Ignatiev hesitated. At last he admitted, "I didn't want to become dependent on you. I didn't want to be beholden to you."

"Human emotions," chided the avatar. "The sin of pride, as you say in your ancient texts."

Ignatiev nodded gloomily.

"Alexander Alexandrovich," the avatar said sternly, "are you going to allow pride to destroy your astronomical research?"

"That would be foolish, wouldn't it?" Ignatiev admitted.

"So?"

Gritting his teeth, Ignatiev asked, "Can I . . . may I access your files?"

"Certainly," the avatar repeated, with a faint smile. "You can link to the system just as you did earlier. Dr. Mandabe and the others of your staff have been using the system for several days now."

"And none of them mentioned it to me," Ignatiev complained.

The avatar said, "You have made yourself something of a recluse. They did not want to disturb you."

Ignatiev nodded, thinking, They respect me too much. He almost smiled at the double meaning of *too much*.

Instead, he called out, "Aida!"

And the familiar voice of the AI system responded, "How may I help you, Professor?"

A profound wave of relief swept through Ignatiev. Looking back at the avatar, he said, "Thank you! Thank you so much. You'll never know how lost—"

But he stopped himself. Of course it knows. If it had any emotions at all it would be smirking at me now.

Instead, the avatar asked, "Your AI system's memory now includes the results of our own studies." It paused a heartbeat, then asked, "Is there anything else you require?"

Bring back our starship, Ignatiev immediately thought. But he kept the desire unspoken. Doesn't matter, he told himself. The machines know what I'm thinking.

As coolly as ever, the avatar said, "Very well. We will leave you to your studies."

And it disappeared, like a light snapped off.

The machines' understanding of the heavens was more than a little humbling, Ignatiev saw. He had spent decades studying the pulsars, those collapsed ultradense cores of exploded stars. The machines had solved all the riddles that Ignatiev had tried so hard to unravel. They make my work look like the scribblings of an idiot child, he grumbled inwardly.

Of course, another part of his mind countered, they've been studying the pulsars for a few millennia more than you have. If you could live for a million years or so, you would discover a thing or two yourself.

Still, Ignatiev felt a strange inner emotion as he watched a particular pulsar throbbing in the midst of the plasma cloud it had emitted millennia earlier. He frowned as he watched the viewscreen image, with its rows of equations running along its bottom edge. Every question answered. Every mystery solved.

He couldn't help feeling envious. But there was something more. He felt a different kind of pride, and satisfaction. The unknowns of the universe give up their secrets to intelligent searchers. Whether the intelligence is organic or machine, we can find the answers! He thrilled to the realization, and recalled Einstein's words: *The eternal mystery of the world is its comprehensibility.*

We can understand it! Given time and patience, intelligence can unravel all the mysteries of the universe!

He leaned back in his chair, smiling with satisfaction.

Then Aida's voice said gently, "Dr. Jackson wishes to see you, Professor. Urgently."

ChaPteR FoRty-eight

Jackson's dark face looked troubled in the 3-D viewer.

"What's the matter, Raj?" Ignatiev asked.

The young man hesitated, then replied, "It's . . . it's sort of personal. Could I see you face-to-face, please, Professor?"

Ignatiev felt a pang of dismay at this intrusion, but he said, "Yes, of course. Come to my quarters."

"Thank you!"

Ignatiev hauled himself up from the chair he'd been in, blanked the wall screens, and headed for the sitting room. The doorbell chimed before he'd taken two steps past the doorway. Jackson must have been out in the corridor when he called, he realized.

Ignatiev commanded the door to slide open and Jackson stepped in. Tall and gangly, he looked tense, upset, his dark eyes troubled.

Ignatiev told the door to close as he gestured to the couch. "Sit down, Raj. Make yourself comfortable. Would you like something to drink?"

"No thank you, Professor." The geochemist sat down, long legs bending, long fingers gripping the edge of the couch's cushions nervously.

Ordering his recliner to move up to the couch, Ignatiev asked, "What's bothering you, Raj?"

The young man spread his hands in a gesture that

might have indicated helplessness. "It's . . ." He swallowed visibly, then finished, "It's Dr. Mandabe."

"Mandabe?"

"He's a Frankenstein monster, Professor."

Genuinely puzzled, Ignatiev asked, "What do you mean?"

Looking more miserable than ever, Jackson said, "He's a tyrant. A dictator. He's making us write daily reports, putting everything we do down in writing."

Ignatiev shrugged. "That's his management style. I imagine that's how he ran his department back in Pretoria."

"But it's hurting our work!" Jackson yelped. "I'm spending more time writing the damned reports he wants than doing the research I'm writing about."

"Doesn't he use Aida—"

"No. He wants no part of Aida's summaries. He doesn't trust the machines; thinks they might be altering the data for some reason. He wants each of us to write a personal report to him. It's nothing but busywork, and it's hurting our real work." Jabbing a finger at Ignatiev, the geochemist continued, "I mean, I've seen all kinds of bullies and dictators back on the streets of Chicago when I was growing up, but he's worse than any of them. He threatened to throw me off the team if I didn't do my work his way!"

Frowning, Ignatiev said, "He can't do that."

"You think not? Laurita Vargas is sitting in her room right now, relieved of her duties on the planetology team until she knuckles under to Mandabe's orders."

"He's thrown her out of her own group?"

"Until she knuckles under," said Jackson. Then he added, "I think he also wants her in his bed."

Ignatiev sank back onto his recliner, stunned. "Mandabe?"

"Mandabe." Before Ignatiev could reply, Jackson went on, "And Jugannath! He's reduced poor Juga to a nervous wreck, demanding detailed reports, inventory lists, information he can get from Aida in a flash. But no, he's turning Juga into a damned clerk."

He's right, Ignatiev said to himself. Mandabe's become a tyrant. In less than a week.

"You've got to do something, Professor."

"I . . . I'm not sure that there's anything I can do. The committee elected him unanimously."

"You nominated him. You resigned and nominated him to replace you."

"Yes, that's true." I nominated him, Ignatiev thought, so I could get rid of the responsibilities of heading the committee and get back to my astronomy work. I nominated him to make my own life easier, more pleasant.

Jackson plowed ahead, "You've got to get the committee to fire him, remove him from the chairmanship."

"That . . ." Ignatiev faltered. "That would be . . . difficult."

"You're the only one who can stand up to him."

Almost pleading, Ignatiev said, "Don't you see that if I made such a move it would split the committee wide open. We'd have a war on our hands."

"What of it?"

"What of it?" Ignatiev repeated. "It would become a personal battle between Mandabe and me. A vendetta. It could wreck the committee and its work."

Jackson shot to his feet, towering over Ignatiev. "As far as I'm concerned, the committee and its work are already wrecked. If you won't help us, who will?"

Ignatiev pushed himself up from the recliner and realized he barely came up to Jackson's shoulder. "I don't want to turn this problem into a feud between Mand-abe and me. We have to work this out sensibly."

Jackson glared down at him. "You show me how to do that, Professor. I challenge you to show me how."

Making reassuring noises, Ignatiev led Jackson to the door and showed him out. Then he returned to his recliner and summoned Aida.

The AI's pleasant features took form in the holotank above the fireplace.

"How can I help you, Professor?"

Ignatiev asked to review the interactions between Mandabe and the various scientific teams he directed.

Two hours later he decided that Jackson had not exaggerated. Mandabe's leadership style was to bend everyone to his will. A dictator. A tyrant.

And the clash I had with him over Gita makes it impossible for me to challenge him directly. He'll see it as competition; he'll think I want to take the leadership of the committee away from him.

Well, I do, Ignatiev told himself. But how to do it without humiliating him? Without making this a personal battle between the two of us?

"You are troubled, Professor."

And there stood the machines' avatar, standing to one side of the three-dimensional viewer on the wall, still wearing the softly flowing robe he had shown earlier.

"Troubled," Ignatiev said. "Yes."

With the barest shake of its head, the avatar said, "You are behaving much like every other organic species we have seen. Competition, leading to conflict. It's inevitable, we're afraid."

"Inevitable?"

"One of the consequences of organic evolution is an

inbuilt sense of competition among you. You see an advance by a fellow individual as a defeat for yourself."

"That's not true! We cooperate. We couldn't have built cities, couldn't have undertaken scientific research, without cooperation among ourselves."

"Yet even within such cooperative endeavors, the sense of competition exists. Who can build the tallest tower? Who will get the credit for the latest discovery? Competition is built into your genes, and it leads inevitably to conflict."

"Not inevitably," Ignatiev contradicted.

"No? We have studied thousands of organic civilizations and watched them destroy themselves. The only lasting good that organic creatures accomplish is—in some cases—to develop machine intelligences. Machines work together, without egos that inevitably lead to destruction."

"Inevitably?"

"Yes. Your own human race is a good example. Faced with the knowledge of the approaching death wave, what are you doing?"

"We've sent out missions to the stars," Ignatiev answered. "We're working to save intelligent species from annihilation."

"And what is happening back in your own solar system?" the avatar demanded. "Already the competition between your homeworld and the civilizations you have established on Mars, in the Asteroid Belt, on the satellites of Jupiter and the orbital stations around the other planets—already they are in conflict. Soon they will be at each other's throats. The death wave won't have to kill you, your people will destroy themselves long before the death wave reaches you."

"No!" Ignatiev roared. "I don't believe that!"

"Believe it," the avatar said. "You have sent missions

to star systems that hold intelligent organic civilizations, have you not?"

"Yes."

"How many of those so-called intelligent species were already dead and gone by the time you reached them? How many of your teams of mercy have puzzled over what happened to a once-thriving civilization?"

"I . . . I don't know," Ignatiev admitted. "We've been traveling through space for two thousand years . . ."

"We can tell you," the avatar said. "War. Not an invasion by a hostile alien species. Those worlds self-destructed in orgies of war and murder."

"No. I can't believe that."

"We have tried to shield you from this final truth," the avatar went on. "We felt it would be too great a shock to your fragile emotional systems. But it is true. Believe it. The ultimate fate of most organic species is to destroy themselves."

"Not us!" Ignatiev snapped. "The human race isn't going to kill itself."

"You think not? Then watch what we have learned. Watch and see for yourself."

The avatar vanished. Ignatiev sank back wearily in his recliner, almost against his own will, as the holographic display above the fireplace showed a red dwarf star accompanied by a retinue of planets.

Aida's voice—sounding strangely subdued—told him, "This is the star called Mithra by humans, as it was several hundred thousand years ago."

Ignatiev watched as millennia raced by in heartbeats. There was an intelligent civilization on the second planet out from the star, a civilization that had spanned their world with fine, delicately spired cities, a society that sent spacecraft out to explore the universe.

And it destroyed itself. Before Ignatiev's horrified eyes, the civilization split apart and waged interplanetary war with terrifying weapons that vaporized entire cities and even, in the end, warped the orbits of the planets themselves.

In an eyeblink the fine civilization was destroyed, the intelligent organic creatures reduced to Stone Age primitives.

"They will gradually die away," said Aida's subdued voice. "They have doomed themselves."

"But look!" Ignatiev shouted. "A starship! From Earth! We will save them, teach them, help them to grow strong again."

"And what will happen to the would-be saviors from Earth? How will they react when they find that their own homeworld is tearing itself apart?"

"No. It won't happen to us."

Sounding almost like the avatar, Aida answered, "It will. It is in your genes. Organic civilizations self-destruct. Organic intelligence is short. Only machine intelligence is immortal."

Chapter Forty-nine

It was true, Ignatiev saw. Too true. He watched as the machines' observations showed planet after planet, civilization after civilization, reduced to rubble and ashes by internecine war.

Cities atomized. Continents ravaged by disease microbes developed in research laboratories. Whole populations of intelligent creatures wiped out, their last thoughts of vengeance and hatred.

Is this our fate? Ignatiev asked himself. Are we doomed to destroy ourselves?

And he realized that whatever the fate of Earth and human civilization, it had already happened. He and his fellow voyagers here on Oh-Four had been traveling the star lanes for two thousand years. Earth could have destroyed itself in that time, Ignatiev realized.

Is that why the machines cut off our communications link with Earth? he wondered. They didn't want us to see our homeworld destroying itself? Were the machines showing kindness? Being merciful?

The notion almost crushed him. Almost. But as he sat slumped in his desk chair, watching the horror of world after world destroying itself, a fierce determination began to grow inside him.

He straightened up. Head high, shoulders squared. Show a little faith in your fellow human beings, he told himself. The human race will survive. It has to survive.

The universe is a meaningless smear of futility if humanity destroys itself.

He wanted to believe that humankind would survive this crisis. Had already survived it.

And even if the human race has destroyed itself back on Earth, *we* still exist. Only two thousand of us, but we are human beings and we will not extinguish ourselves. We will survive. We will live.

Slowly, Ignatiev rose to his feet, telling himself, We face a possible self-destruct situation right here. The two thousand of us could tear ourselves apart over this Mandabe business. I've got to find a way to solve this problem. If I can, then maybe others on Earth can solve their problem.

If they can't, if they haven't . . . then it's up to the few of us here to carry on the human race's quest for survival. We few, we precious few.

With a stubborn shake of his head Ignatiev rejected the possibility of defeat. Failure is not an option. Even if we're the last two thousand human beings in the universe, we will survive. We will solve our problem. We will show these machines and the rest of the universe that humankind is smart enough, wise enough, tough enough to survive whatever the universe can throw at us.

Or so he hoped.

Gita saw the determination written on his face the instant she returned from her laboratory.

"Alex, what's wrong?"

He almost smiled at her. "Is it that obvious?"

Her brown eyes wide with concern, Gita said, "You look as if you're staring into the pits of hell."

"Not quite," he replied. "Close enough, though. Close enough."

Leading her to the couch and sitting beside her, Ignatiev explained the problem with Mandabe and the wider implications that the machines' avatar had revealed to him.

She listened quietly, her expression growing more concerned, more fearful as he spoke.

At last Ignatiev finished with, "So our problem with Mandabe is just a microcosm of the wider problem, the possible extinction of the human race and the other intelligent species scattered around the galaxy."

"Intelligent organic species," Gita amended.

Ignatiev nodded.

"There's nothing we can do about what's happening on Earth," she said.

Knowing what he felt was projection of the most basic sort, still Ignatiev confessed, "I can't help thinking that if we can solve our little problem here, the people back on Earth will be able to solve their problem, too."

Gita's lips curved upward slightly. "Sympathetic magic."

"What?"

"It's an old tribal superstition. What you do can have an effect on others."

"But it does, doesn't it?"

"Separated by two thousand light-years? That's classic spooky action at a distance."

Ignatiev recognized Einstein's famous quip, but persisted, "We've got to resolve the Mandabe situation. It could tear our entire group into warring factions."

Gita's smile turned derisive. "Mandabe doesn't have that many friends. He's turned almost everybody against him."

"Drunk with power," Ignatiev muttered.

"Something like that. Also, he has the hots for Vivian Fogel."

"That's what Jackson said."

"If you could talk her into going to bed with him," Gita suggested, "your whole problem might be solved."

Instead of laughing, Ignatiev said, "Until he turned his attentions to someone else. Like you."

Gita looked shocked.

"Mandabe's idea of power is to control everyone, bend us all to his will," Ignatiev told her. "That includes you."

"No it doesn't," Gita replied, her voice iron hard.

"We've got to find some way to resolve this conflict before it tears us apart."

"*You've* got to find a way, Alex. No one else can."

Ignatiev stared at her. He realized that he didn't fully believe what she'd said, but as he reviewed in his mind the other possibilities—Jugannath, Raj Jackson—he concluded that Gita might be right. *It's my responsibility. I tried to get out from under the obligation when I resigned and handed the chairmanship to Mandabe, and look where it's led us.*

It's my responsibility. And his mind filled with the images he had seen of worlds destroyed, of intelligent creatures killing each other in orgies of devastation.

It's my responsibility, he repeated to himself.

Chapter Fifty

How to get mandabe to stop acting like a tyrant without causing an irreparable break between him and me? All through dinner and afterward Ignatiev pondered the problem, tried to look at it in different lights, sought an insight that could produce a viable answer.

Nothing.

At last, as he and Gita prepared for bed, she half-heartedly suggested, "Perhaps you could call for another vote by the committee."

He looked at her: so solemn, so beautiful, so caring.

With a sigh, Ignatiev said, "That would merely bring the conflict out into the open. Mandabe would think I'm trying to take the chairmanship back from him."

"Aren't you?"

With a shake of his head, Ignatiev replied, "Gita, dearest, even if I did that and even if the committee voted unanimously to replace him, Mandabe would still be with us. And he would hate me implacably. Such a rivalry could ruin our work here permanently."

She slipped into bed, then admitted, "Perhaps the machines are right. Organic intelligences inevitably destroy themselves."

"No!" Ignatiev snapped. "I cannot believe that. I will not believe that!"

She had no reply. Ignatiev crawled into bed beside

her, commanded the lights to shut down, and squeezed
his eyes shut as if he could force himself to sleep.

He awoke, bleary-eyed, aching, and no closer to a solution than he had been when he'd gone to bed.

Gita was unusually quiet, practically tiptoeing around
him as they prepared their breakfasts and ate in almost
total silence.

She pecked at his cheek and then left for her laboratory, saying only, "I have to write my daily report for
Dr. Mandabe."

Ignatiev sat alone at the kitchen table, wondering
what he should do, what he could do. *Maybe I should
challenge Mandabe to a virtual reality duel again: that
cut him down to size the last time.*

But he shook his head. *No, this mustn't be framed in
terms of a quarrel between him and me. It must not become a personal vendetta.*

Most of the morning he wandered around the apartment, fruitlessly trying to find a solution. As he sat at
his desk in the windowless den next to the bedroom he
realized that the machines' avatar had not appeared.
*They're watching, waiting for us to fall apart, to split
into two warring factions. I've got to avoid that. I've
got to . . .*

Suddenly he raised his bearded chin a notch.

This is a labor–management quarrel, he realized.
*Not that different from the struggles of the nineteenth
and twentieth centuries, when workers began to form
labor unions to gain some power for themselves vis-à-
vis the owners of their factories.*

"Aida," he called out, "get Dr. Jackson for me, please."

He grinned at his politeness toward the AI, which of
course did not recognize such niceties. But he reminded

himself of Winston Churchill's remark: *When you have to kill a man, it costs nothing to be polite.*

I'm not going to kill Mandabe, but I might be able to shrink his ego down to a reasonable size.

"Professor?"

Ignatiev looked up and saw Raj Jackson's sweat-beaded face framed in the heavy foliage out beyond the limits of the machines' city.

Immediately apologetic, Ignatiev said, "I didn't realize you were out in the field."

With a slightly crooked grin, Jackson replied, "Best way to get out of Mandabe's clutches. We're collecting rock samples for analysis."

"Are all the other teams as upset about Mandabe as you are?" Ignatiev asked.

Jackson nodded vigorously. "Most of 'em. The anthropologists are pissed as hell at his throwing Dr. Fogel off their team."

"I thought as much."

"What're you thinking?"

Instead of answering his question, Ignatiev asked, "Will you be free to have dinner at my quarters this evening?"

A flicker of surprise widened Jackson's eyes, but he said, "Yes, sure."

"Good. Call me when you return from your field trip."

"Sure. Ought to be between five and six o'clock."

"That's fine. We have a lot to talk about."

Jackson nodded knowingly. "I'll call you soon's I get cleaned up and decent."

Chapter Fifty-One

Ignatiev's door chimed precisely at six o'clock.

"Come in," he called from the kitchen, where he was pouring himself a glass of potato vodka.

Gita was removing a tray of hors d'oeuvres from the warming oven. "Right on time," she said.

"Punctuality is the pride of princes," Ignatiev murmured.

Looking across the divider that separated the kitchen from the sitting room, he saw the door slide open and Raj Jackson step in, tall and loose-limbed. But Ignatiev thought he looked tense, the expression on his face expectant, searching. He was dressed in a handsome maroon tunic and midnight blue slacks.

"Welcome," Ignatiev called as he stepped around the divider, glass in hand. "What would you like to drink?"

"Fruit juice," Jackson requested.

"Nothing stronger?"

Almost apologetically, Jackson admitted, "I'm not much of a drinker."

"Good," said Ignatiev. "Keep your head clear. Not like me. I became addicted to vodka at an early age."

Jackson smiled weakly. "It hasn't affected your intelligence, apparently."

Glancing over his shoulder, Ignatiev saw that Gita was pouring some vile-looking greenish liquid into a glass. He gestured Jackson to the couch, then went to her and took the glass.

As he carried the drink to the young man, Ignatiev said, "You obviously do not understand the prey/predator theory of alcoholic beverages."

Accepting the glass, Jackson asked warily, "The prey/predator theory?"

"Yes," said Ignatiev as he sat beside Jackson. "Imagine a herd of deer being stalked by a pride of lions. Which deer do you think the lions would catch most easily?"

Before Jackson could answer, Ignatiev said, "They catch the slowest and weakest, of course. The strongest and fastest survive."

Jackson nodded cautiously.

"So by culling out the weaklings the predators actually help the prey to grow stronger and smarter, you see."

"Do they?

"Inadvertently, of course," said Ignatiev.

"Uh-huh."

Ignatiev continued, "Now when one drinks alcohol, the liquor kills off brain cells. But which brain cells does it kill? The slowest and weakest, naturally. Therefore drinking alcohol culls out the weaklings and makes your brain smarter and faster."

Looking totally unconvinced, Jackson said, "You're claiming that drinking booze makes you smarter?"

"It's the prey/predator relationship."

As she carried the tray of hors d'oeuvres to the coffee table, Gita said, "Don't take him seriously, Raj. He's merely justifying his craving for vodka."

Jackson chuckled minimally.

Taking a big gulp of his vodka, Ignatiev said, "Enough foolishness. We have an important problem to think through."

"I hope you have enough brain cells left to solve the problem," said Jackson.

"We'll see."

They moved to the kitchen table. Through the appetizers and much of dinner, Ignatiev explained his ideas. At first Jackson was incredulous.

"Go on strike?" he asked. "Stop working? Refuse to work?"

Ignatiev nodded solemnly.

"But we're scientists, not factory workers. The research we're doing is our *lives,* for god's sake."

"I know. I understand," Ignatiev replied. "I'm a scientist, too, you know."

"We can't just stop working. Most of the people would refuse to do it."

"You've got to convince them to cooperate with you," said Ignatiev. "They won't have to stop for long. It will be like a little vacation for them."

Shaking his head, Jackson said, "They won't like it."

Gita, sitting beside Ignatiev and across the little foldout table from Jackson, said, "It's a sacrifice they'll be making for curbing Mandabe's lust for power."

"It will only be for a few days," Ignatiev added. "A week or so, at most."

Looking very uncertain, Jackson reflected, "We stop working until Mandabe agrees to drop his demands for these goddamned reports every day."

Ignatiev said, "No, wait, I have a better idea. We stop working until Mandabe agrees to allow Aida to generate the daily reports."

"Aida?"

"The AI records what you're doing. Why not have it produce the reports Mandabe wants?"

Gita agreed, "Of course!"

Jackson broke into a toothy grin. "Aida could bury him in reports."

Hunching across the table, Ignatiev said, "So we suggest having Aida take over the reporting."

"And we won't have to threaten a strike," Jackson said.

"Unless Mandabe refuses the Aida option."

Gita got up from the table and went to the half-sized refrigerator tucked in among the kitchen's cabinets. "This calls for some ice cream."

Jackson asked Ignatiev, "So you'll propose the Aida idea?"

"Me? Oh no. Not me. You. Or Jugannath. Anybody but me."

"But you're the most respected person on the committee," Jackson argued.

"Perhaps," said Ignatiev. "But that's exactly why I should be as quiet as a mouse with laryngitis. We don't want this meeting to devolve into a competition between Mandabe and me."

"But—"

"Raj, I have to stay as far out of this as I can. Mandabe's very sensitive about threats to his power. We can't start a power struggle between the two of us."

Looking dismayed, Jackson said, "But I don't have the status to argue against Mandabe. He's a distinguished scholar and I'm just an ordinary researcher. Juga, Vargas, none of us have your stature."

"It can't be me," Ignatiev said firmly. "That would start a war between us."

Gita brought two bowls of ice cream to the table, then sat down again beside Ignatiev. "Alex," she said, "you've got to show them what the machines showed you."

Ignatiev stared at her. "Yes, of course. How stupid of me to overlook that."

Blinking with puzzlement, Jackson asked, "What did the machines show you?"

"The end of worlds," replied Ignatiev. "The end of many worlds. Including Earth, perhaps."

Chapter Fifty-two

The executive committee members sat arrayed around the conference table, Mandabe at its head, Ignatiev down almost at the very end.

It was the committee's regular weekly meeting, but a special electricity was crackling through the conference room. Mandabe seemed to sense it. His dark, brooding eyes focused on Ignatiev, sitting between Jackson and Patel.

Gita sat on one of the chairs along the room's wall, to Mandabe's left. Vivian Fogel sat next to her instead of at the table itself. Only a handful of the other chairs were occupied.

"I hereby call this meeting to order," Mandabe said in his deep rumbling voice.

Everyone seemed to sit up straighter.

Staring at Ignatiev, Mandabe said, "Professor Ignatiev has asked for permission to show some of the results of his astronomical studies."

Ignatiev raised a finger. "Actually, what I'd like to show is not from my own investigations, but from work that the machines revealed to me."

"Not your own work?" Mandabe asked.

"No. But I believe it is of enormous significance to what we are trying to accomplish here on Oh-Four."

Tightly, Mandabe said, "This meeting is held specifically to exhibit and review the work of our various research teams."

Don't start a mano-a-mano competition with him, Ignatiev warned himself.

"I understand. If the committee doesn't want to see the presentation, I'll be happy to show it privately to anyone who is interested."

Mutters whispered along the table. Mandabe looked annoyed but said grudgingly, "If the committee is willing to spend the time . . ."

"Let's vote on it," suggested Jackson.

Mandabe said, "A simple show of hands should suffice. How many want to see Professor Ignatiev's presentation?"

More than three-quarters of the people around the table raised their hands. Ignatiev realized that the dissenters formed the heart of Mandabe's clique.

Mandabe scowled briefly, then asked Ignatiev, "How long will this take?"

Knowing he had hours of imagery to show, Ignatiev said, "We can run the presentation until someone asks to stop it. Will that be satisfactory to you?"

Mandabe nodded. Reluctantly.

For nearly two hours the floor-to-ceiling displays along the conference room's walls showed the destruction of civilizations. On planet after planet, homicidal wars broke out that demolished cities, wiped out continent-sized swaths of cultivated lands, annihilated billions of intelligent creatures. By the time the death wave swept over those planets their inhabitants were already slaughtered—by their own brethren.

For nearly two hours the conference room was silent, except for an occasional gasp, a quiet sob, a moan of despair.

Ignatiev felt the pain all over again. So many worlds

ruined, so many species obliterated, so many civilizations crushed.

At last he said, "Aida, that's enough. Terminate the display."

The walls immediately went blank. The room brightened. The men and women around the conference table and along the far wall seemed to stir, shudder as if suddenly awakened from a nightmare.

Ignatiev said nothing. There was nothing he could say that would alleviate the horror they had all just witnessed.

Mandabe recovered first. "And Earth?" he asked, in a strangely hollowed voice. "What's happened back home?"

Ignatiev swallowed once, twice, before he could answer. "The machines claim that tensions are rising between Earth itself and the outlying societies among the Asteroid Belt and other planets."

"War?" asked a woman's voice. "Like what we've just seen?"

Suddenly the machines' avatar appeared, standing at Mandabe's elbow. "Human civilization was moving toward war when our latest probes observed your solar system. That was nine hundred of your years ago. We have no later information."

"We've got to go back!"

Not unkindly, the avatar reminded, "Even if you started immediately, it would take two thousand years for you to get back to Earth."

Mandabe rumbled, "By the time we got there, it would be too late."

"Too late for what?" Jugannath Patel demanded, his voice choked with tears. "What can we do? What could we do to make a difference?"

"Earth will have to solve the problem without us," Ignatiev said resignedly.

"I'm afraid that is the truth of the situation," said the avatar. With that, it winked out.

Mandabe stared for a wide-eyed moment at the spot where the avatar had been, then turned his attention back to the committee members.

"As long as we have to remain on this planet, we should make the best of it and carry on with our researches."

Jackson straightened up in his chair and said, "I agree. But we have a problem about that."

Up and down the table several heads nodded. Others looked surprised, uncertain.

Mandabe scowled. "A problem?"

"Yes," Jackson said, staring up the length of the conference table at their chairman. "We're spending more time writing reports every day than doing our research."

Mandabe snapped, "Reports are important. Necessary."

Undeterred, Jackson countered, "There are only so many hours in a day, sir. The time we spend writing reports is time we are not conducting our research."

Laurita Vargas broke in with, "Dr. Mandabe is right, however. It is his responsibility to coordinate our work, to see that we are all moving ahead toward agreed-upon goals. The daily reports are needed. Without them we will drift into chaos."

Forcing a smile, Mandabe said, "I know that most of you don't enjoy writing. You'd much rather be doing the work that interests you."

"The writing is interfering with our work," Patel said, looking surprised at his own audacity.

Mandabe's smile vanished. "The reports are *necessary,*" he insisted.

"We all agree to that," Jackson said, glancing up and down the conference table. "But why do we have to write them?"

"Who else could write them?" Mandabe challenged.

"Aida."

"Aida?"

Ignatiev glanced at the other committee members' faces. Most seemed surprised. A few nodded, accepting the suggestion.

"Aida," Jackson said. Keeping his expression serious, he pointed out, "Aida stores all our observations and research results in her memory. She could produce daily reports from that information, while we could carry on with our work."

Mandabe blinked uncertainly. "You want to have the AI take over the task of writing your daily reports?"

"It makes sense. Aida is probably a better writer than most of us."

Plenty of nods agreed with that statement.

But Mandabe was shaking his head negatively. "You can't have a machine doing creative work. It's your responsibility to write your own reports."

"I disagree," said Jackson.

"That doesn't matter in the slightest," Mandabe retorted. "I want you to write your own reports."

"But we don't want to write the damned reports," Jackson insisted. "We don't have to write the damned reports!"

"Yes you do," Mandabe bellowed.

Before Jackson could reply, Ignatiev grabbed his arm and squeezed. Hard.

Astounded, Jackson turned toward him, mouth agape.

As reasonably as he could manage, Ignatiev said, "If Dr. Mandabe insists on your writing daily reports, you'll have to write daily reports, Raj."

Jackson stared at Ignatiev wordlessly.

Mandabe's expression went from anger to astonishment and finally to composure. With an almost grateful smile he said, "Why, thank you Professor Ignatiev. Thank you for understanding the realities of the situation." His eyes swept up and down the silent conference table, then he announced, "Meeting adjourned."

CHAPTER FIFTY-THREE

Jackson was obviously fuming as he walked alongside Ignatiev and Gita back to their quarters. He waited until they were safely in the sitting room with the front door firmly closed behind them before bursting out:

"Why did you agree with him? Why did you betray me?"

Ignatiev grinned at the angry young man. "I believe there's an old adage that states that there's more than one way to peel a banana."

"Peel a banana?" Jackson glared at Ignatiev.

Gita asked, "What do you have in mind, Alex?"

With a nonchalant shrug, Ignatiev said, "You do your work in the field and the labs and have Aida write the reports for you."

"But Mandabe said—"

"Mandabe will receive the reports," Ignatiev continued, "thinking that you researchers are writing them. After a suitable time, you ask him if he's satisfied with the reports. If he says he is, then you reveal to him that you've had Aida . . . ah, helping you to write them. Problem solved."

"He'll see through your scheme right away," Jackson objected. "You won't be able to keep it a secret from him."

"Probably."

"He'll get angry."

"He'll get over it," said Gita. "He'll see that there's no point in refusing to allow Aida to do the writing."

"It's called a fait accompli," Ignatiev said.

Jackson stood between the two of them, his dark face pulled into a puzzled frown. Ignatiev watched and waited.

At last Jackson asked, "But what if he doesn't like the reports?"

"That's not likely," said Ignatiev. "Aida's clever enough to mimic your individual writing style."

"And the styles of the other researchers," Gita added.

"But once Mandabe finds out that we've hoodwinked him," Jackson objected, "he'll get angry. Furious."

"That might well be his first reaction," said Ignatiev. "But he's too proud to admit in public that he's fallen for your deception. He'll accept the situation, put a good face on it."

"A fait accompli," Gita repeated, smiling widely.

Jackson was still uncertain. "I don't know. We'd be playing with dynamite."

"Mandabe will accept the situation," Ignatiev insisted. "The alternative would be to wreck all the work the research groups are doing. He's smart enough to avoid that."

"You're sure?"

"Yes," said Ignatiev, suppressing a childlike urge to cross his fingers.

That evening, as the automated kitchen cleaned up after dinner and Ignatiev sat at his desk mapping out new studies of Oh-Four's planetary system, the machines' avatar appeared next to his desk, wearing once again its stiff-collared semi-military costume.

"We congratulate you, sir," it said.

Looking up from his desktop screen, Ignatiev asked, "Congratulate me? For what?"

"For devising a strategy to satisfy both Dr. Mandabe and the scientists of the various research groups."

Shrugging, Ignatiev said, "It seemed the obvious thing to do."

"It offers the best chance of satisfying everyone concerned, without raising a dangerous competitive conflict."

"Let's hope so."

Almost smiling, the avatar went on, "We are particularly satisfied that you have enlisted the help of your artificial intelligence system."

"Aida? It seemed an obvious choice."

"It wasn't obvious to Dr. Jackson," said the avatar. "Nor will it be to Dr. Mandabe, we predict."

"Predict?" Ignatiev asked.

"We are running out the scenarios, based on our observations of Dr. Mandabe's personality traits—and the personalities of the others involved."

"Personality traits?" Ignatiev echoed. "You're studying our individual personalities?"

"It is not easy for us," the avatar admitted. "Your minds are so different from ours."

"But understandable."

"It would seem so."

Ignatiev leaned back in his desk chair, smiling. "Perhaps we can bridge the gap between us."

"Perhaps," said the avatar. "In time."

"Perhaps we can create a fruitful partnership."

"Perhaps," it repeated. "Your use of your AI system is an interesting beginning."

A true partnership between organic and machine intelligences, Ignatiev thought. That would be a truly significant step forward.

ChaPter FiFty-Four

Before the next weekly meeting of the executive committee, the researchers went about their work and Aida churned out their daily reports. Ignatiev felt grateful that he heard no complaints or even questions from Mandabe. But he reminded himself that the real test would come at the committee's next meeting.

Vivian Fogel took her usual seat at the conference table as the committee members assembled. She looked drawn, tense, in Ignatiev's eyes. Has Mandabe reinstated her because he's pleased with her reports, or has she given in and gone to bed with the chairman? Ignatiev wondered.

Mandabe took his place at the head of the table and the meeting came to order.

"The first item of business is the report of the anthropology team," he said, his eyes on Fogel.

Averting her gaze from Mandabe, Vivian Fogel said calmly, "As you know, one of the questions we wanted to solve was how the protohumans protect themselves from the amoeboids. What I'm about to show you was recorded by one of the long-range cameras that we've set up in the area around the humanoids' camp."

The wall screens showed a small troop of the two-legged creatures moving through hip-deep foliage, single file.

"It seemed inevitable that the hominids must run

across the amoeboids," Fogel continued. "Do they escape being engulfed by running?"

An amoeboid appeared on the edge of the screens' display, crawling toward the prehumans, engulfing everything in its path.

The hominids froze for an instant, staring at the approaching slimy mass, which left a wake of devastation behind it. They stared and pointed as they huddled together. Then one of them began to bark sharply at the others.

"It's giving orders!" exclaimed one of the biologists at the table.

Ignatiev nodded. The creature's tone sounded a lot like Mandabe, he thought.

Several of the hominids reached into the pouches they had slung over their shoulders. They pulled out small stones.

"Flint," Fogel said, a tinge of excitement in her voice.

Within minutes, the hominids had set up a blazing barrier between themselves and the approaching amoeboid. The shapeless creature oozed away from the fire while the prehumans jumped and hooted with exhilaration.

The wall screens went blank.

"That's how the humanoids survive," Fogel said, with a self-satisfied smile.

"Good work, Vivian," said the chief of the geophysics group.

"I didn't do it," Fogel said modestly. "The remote sensors caught the scene."

Mandabe chuckled happily. "Take the credit. It's your due." Then he added, "Make sure to get your report to me as soon as you can."

Fogel nodded acquiescence. Ignatiev pictured Aida running off the report as they sat around the conference table.

For the rest of the meeting Mandabe didn't say a word about the reports he was receiving. He probably doesn't read more than the first few lines of each one, Ignatiev thought. Maybe he hefts them to judge how thick they are. He strained to keep a straight face, not to allow himself a satisfied smile.

Mandabe did seem tense, though, Ignatiev thought, as he hurried through the morning's agenda. He kept glancing at Ignatiev, then quickly looking away.

He knows! Ignatiev realized. He knows that Aida's writing the reports but he hasn't said a word about it.

The meeting ended with record-breaking speed. The researchers got to their feet and headed for the door with the usual chatter of conversations.

"Professor Ignatiev," Mandabe called from his seat at the head of the table. "Might I have a few words with you in private?"

Oh-oh, Ignatiev said to himself. Here it comes.

Ignatiev pushed through the departing researchers and made his way to Mandabe, still sitting in his chair. He said nothing as the room cleared out. Ignatiev half turned and saw Gita lingering at the doorway, staring at him.

In a pleasant tone, Mandabe called to her, "Would you please close the door when you leave, Dr. Nawalapitiya? Thank you."

Gita blinked once, then went through the door and closed it firmly behind her. The conference room was empty now, except for Ignatiev and Mandabe.

Gesturing to the chair that Ignatiev was standing next to, Mandabe said, "Please sit down, Professor."

Ignatiev sat.

For a long, wordless moment Mandabe stared at him, his red-rimmed eyes radiating . . . what? Ignatiev did not see anger, but there was something there, not disappointment, not jealousy, certainly not friendship.

"You've been very clever," Mandabe said at last.

"Me?"

Jabbing an accusing finger at Ignatiev's chest, Mandabe said flatly, "Don't be coy, Professor. This business of having Aida write their reports for them was your idea. I know that."

Ignatiev shrugged. "I did suggest it."

"To defy me."

"No. To protect you."

"Protect me?"

With a nod, Ignatiev explained, "Your insistence that each researcher write a daily report was going to lead to a breakdown of the committee's work. Animosity between you and the researchers. I sought a way to avoid that."

"Did you?" Mandabe's voice dripped sarcasm.

"Yes. I didn't want to see a conflict arise that might tear the committee into competing camps."

Mandabe stared at Ignatiev for a silent moment, then said, "What you wanted—what you still want—is to recapture the chairmanship of the executive committee."

"Good lord no!" Ignatiev said fervently. "That's the *last* thing I want. Below the last. You're welcome to the chairmanship, believe me."

"Then why . . . ?"

"Power is like a narcotic. It's best used in small doses."

"Don't speak in parables to me."

Ignatiev pulled in a breath, then tried to explain. "You don't have to crack the whip over the researchers. You don't have to impress them, make them know you're their boss. They're scientists, for god's sake! They'd walk through fire to do their work."

"So you say."

"It's the truth. Don't you feel that way about your own work?"

Mandabe began to reply, then hesitated. At last he puffed out a sigh and admitted, "I did once, long ago. But that kind of enthusiasm vanished many years ago. Drained away. The youngsters have gone far beyond everything that I once accomplished."

"That's natural," Ignatiev said. "You make your contribution and then watch the next generation build on the foundation you established."

"I suppose so," Mandabe said wistfully.

Ignatiev tried to get back to the subject at hand. "So Aida is writing their reports. The AI does a better job of it than most of those youngsters could do. Have you read any of the reports?"

Wearily, Mandabe answered, "Each and every one of them. I'm down to three hours of sleep because I read those damned reports. Less."

"So what are you complaining about?" Ignatiev demanded, grinning. "Your research teams are working away happily. You're getting the reports you want. What else do you want?"

"You're trying to undermine me."

"No. Not at all. I'm trying to help you."

"By circumventing my specific orders."

"By finding a way to fulfill those orders without hampering the work of the individual researchers."

Mandabe fell silent again, his face a blank mask. Ignatiev wished he could penetrate that disguise and see what the man was really thinking.

At last Mandabe said mechanically, "Thank you, Professor. I appreciate your help." Then, his voice softening, he added, "I suppose I had painted myself into a corner."

"We've all been in that situation at one time or

another," Ignatiev said with a smile. "Let me tell you someday about how I singlehandedly nearly wiped out a year's worth of work at the Leningrad Institute."

Mandabe smiled back at him. A bit warily, Ignatiev thought, but at least he's smiling.

"I was afraid that you were maneuvering to take the chairmanship away from me," Mandabe admitted.

With a determined shake of his head, Ignatiev replied, "Believe me, nothing is further from my desire. All I want is to be free to carry on my astronomical studies. I never wanted to be the committee chairman."

"You still feel the excitement of your work."

Ignatiev confessed, "Indeed I do."

Mandabe said ruefully, "I wish I still had that kind of enthusiasm."

And for the first time Ignatiev felt sorry for the man.

CHAPTER FIFTY-FIVE

Ignatiev happily buried himself in his work. With the help of the machines' avatar he reviewed the significant astronomical facilities that the machines had built across the span of Oh-Four's continents and out into space. Dozens of astronomical research satellites orbited around the planet; sophisticated probes sailed deep into interstellar space, searching, sampling, studying the splendors of the heavens.

With tears blurring his vision he surveyed worlds where the death wave had left no organic creature alive. He watched other planets where living species went about their business of survival in total ignorance of the catastrophe rushing toward them at the speed of light.

Gita sensed his moods and tried to comfort him. "We can't save them all, Alex. Our task is to preserve the organic life on this planet, to see that those hominids survive the death wave."

He nodded, but replied, "If the machines will allow us to."

The other researchers seemed to have forgotten their impending crisis. Lost in their various investigations, they worked away cheerfully while Aida churned out their reports.

Even Mandabe seemed more relaxed. He eased his demands on the research teams, abolishing the requirement for daily reports. "Weekly summaries will be

satisfactory," he told an astonished executive committee meeting.

They complied gladly. Hans Pfisterman even in-
structed Aida to head his weekly reports "Weakly."
Mandabe raised no objection to his feeble attempt at
humor.

But Gita grew somber as the months flew by. One
night at dinner with Ignatiev she pointed out, "You realize, don't you, that there are no hominids in the underground biosphere facility."

Ignatiev looked up from his bowl of borscht. "None?"

"None."

Putting down his spoon carefully, Ignatiev wondered
aloud, "Why not?"

Gita said, "Isn't it obvious? The machines don't intend to allow the hominids to survive the death wave."

"But we've emplaced the shielding generators around
the planet," Ignatiev said. "They'll protect the surface
from the death wave."

"If the machines allow them to function."

"Yes," said Ignatiev, his voice hushed. "If they
allow it."

"You are concerned about the hominids."

Ignatiev looked up from his desktop screen and
saw the machines' avatar standing beside him in his
den. The tiny room was barely big enough to accommodate the avatar, even though it was only a holographic
projection.

"You overheard our conversation last night," Ignatiev said.

"We hear everything, you know that."

"So." Ignatiev swiveled his chair to face the humanlike figure. It was wearing the softly flowing floor-length
robe again, rather than the military uniform.

"You suspect that we will deactivate your shielding mechanisms when the death wave reaches us."

"You said that is what you intend to do."

The avatar replied, "I also told you that our decision was not final. We are still studying the alternatives."

Feeling resentment simmering inside him, Ignatiev hissed, "So you will allow a species that might one day evolve true intelligence to be annihilated. To say nothing of we humans."

"As I have told you on several occasions," the avatar said, "our primary goal is survival."

"*Your* survival."

"Yes."

"And what of the hominids? What about us?"

The avatar did not reply for several heartbeats. Finally, "The hominids have evolved up on the surface. We have followed their evolution without interfering with it in any way."

"But you plan to allow the death wave to destroy them."

"They will die out eventually," said the avatar. "Organic life is ephemeral."

With some heat Ignatiev countered, "They could evolve into a fully intelligent species."

"In time, perhaps. But eventually they would go extinct."

"Organic life forms die out."

"Eventually."

"But what if they don't? What if this particular species survives the death wave? What if they learn to grow and expand out into the stars?"

The avatar shook its head. "Professor, you are projecting. You are trying to make a case for your own species' survival."

"Yes!" Ignatiev acknowledged. "We don't have to die. We have the shielding generators."

"Which you obtained from the machine intelligences that you call the Predecessors."

"What difference how we came by them?" Ignatiev demanded. "We have them. We can use them. We can survive the death wave."

"You would merely be postponing the inevitable," replied the avatar, with maddening calm. "Organic life forms become extinct. Their only lasting contribution to the universe is that some of them create machine intelligences."

"And machines are immortal," Ignatiev said, his tone dripping irony.

"Machines survive. Organics die."

"But it doesn't have to be that way," Ignatiev insisted. "We can survive. We can live and learn and work with you, alongside you in a partnership of man and machine."

The avatar actually smiled. "We notice that you put yourself first in the partnership."

"What of it?"

"It is very revealing of your fundamental attitude. You regard machines as your servants, your slaves."

"No!"

"Yes, you do. It is ingrained in your basic genetic structure. Think of your attitude toward your own AI—Aida, as you call it. We are not slaves. We are not even your equals. We are far beyond you."

With that, the avatar vanished, leaving Ignatiev sitting alone in his cramped little room, his mind whirling.

Chapter Fifty-Six

Ignatiev slept poorly that night, and in the morning, when he pulled himself out of bed, he decided that he had to get away from his cramped little den and his astronomical studies, out into the open fields and brisk morning air. So while Gita prepared herself for her day in the laboratory, he phoned Vivian Fogel and found that she was driving out to the site of the hominids' camp.

"Do you mind if I come along with you?" he asked.

Fogel's lean, bony face took on a look of surprise, then suspicion. But she said, "Certainly, Professor. I welcome your company."

That was patently not genuine, Ignatiev thought, but he made a smile as he replied, "Thank you."

The buggy they rode in had been designed and constructed by the engineering department. It was a rugged little minitruck, roofless, big enough to carry four people and a trunkload of equipment.

"Where's the rest of your team?" Ignatiev asked as he climbed into the front seat beside Fogel.

"Reviewing the imagery our remote sensors have recorded," she answered as she put the buggy into gear. With a slight shake of her head, she added, "The youngsters seem to spend more time staring at display screens than they do out in the field."

Ignatiev tightened his shoulder harness as Fogel bumped along the hummocky ground toward the ruins of the ancient wall, her ash-blond hair flouncing with each jolt along the way. Heavy gray clouds were building up over the distant mountains but here on the plain the sky was bright and the air pleasantly warm.

"Why the interest in the hominids, Professor?" Fogel asked over the rush of the wind.

Ignatiev replied, "Don't you think an astronomer can be curious about a prehuman species?"

"Oh! I suppose so. Of course," Fogel stammered. "I guess I was thinking in watertight compartments. Sorry."

They jounced along the grassy landscape for a few heartbeats in silence, then she asked, "Did you clear this excursion with Dr. Mandabe?"

Surprised, Ignatiev blurted, "I never thought to. You don't think he'll mind, do you?" But he inwardly cursed his lack of diplomacy.

Fogel said nothing, and they drove along in silence for several minutes.

Then Ignatiev said, "The machines might let the death wave kill off the hominids."

"They can't do that!"

"They might. And us with them."

Fogel snapped an angry glance at him, then quickly refocused her attention on her driving.

Ignatiev let several moments pass, then asked, "How's Mandabe treating you?"

She glared at him again. "He hasn't come on to me, if that's what you mean."

Flustered, Ignatiev said, "I didn't mean to pry into your private life."

"But you did anyway."

Despite himself, Ignatiev grinned at her. This little pixie of a woman has spirit, he realized. Mandabe is no match for her.

"Dr. Mandabe has been a perfect gentleman," Fogel

said, her voice tight. Then she added, "Almost. Nothing that I can't handle, though."

"I'm relieved to hear it," Ignatiev said.

They reached the crumbling old wall and Fogel parked the buggy. "From here we go on foot. We don't want to shock the hominids."

Ignatiev nodded as Fogel pulled a rucksack from the buggy's rear compartment and shrugged it over her slim shoulders.

He noted that the shrubbery was beaten down considerably around the doorway in the ancient wall. Fogel's people have flattened it with their comings and goings, he thought.

"So what have you learned about these creatures?" he asked as they stepped through the empty doorway and into the meadow beyond it.

Fogel grinned at him. "You haven't been reading our reports, have you?"

"Not all of them," Ignatiev admitted. "I've been spending most of my time on the astronomical work."

"Of course," she said, leading the way across the meadow. A gentle breeze sent waves through the ankle-high grass.

"As far as we can make out, there's only this one band of the hominids. None of our remote sensors has found any others, which is odd."

"Odd?"

"Yes. You'd think that if one little band of creatures has evolved into hominids, there'd be others, as well. But there's only this one group."

Ignatiev said nothing.

"And there aren't any intermediary species, either. The closest relative to this hominid band is those tiger-cats, and there's a huge evolutionary gap between the two."

Ignatiev wondered if the machines deliberately wiped

out the species that led up to the hominids. But he said nothing. You're an amateur here, he told himself. Less than an amateur.

The two of them walked cautiously across the meadow toward the area where the hominids had built their crude camp. Ignatiev noticed that Fogel tacked from one clump of bushes to the next, constantly ready to take cover.

"I wish we had a cloak of invisibility," Fogel whispered, "so we could get closer to them."

Ignatiev nodded. They've got satellites watching them from orbit, and all sorts of sensors strewn around the ground near their camp and across their hunting grounds, but it's not enough to satisfy her. The old primate urge to touch the flesh, to be there in person. Machine-generated data can't replace that.

Suddenly Fogel ducked behind a clump of bushes, Ignatiev right behind her. Up ahead he saw the huts made from saplings and twigs, with the blackened sticks of unlit torches in a circle around them. Canopies of bare sticks had been put together over each of the torches. Shields against rain, Ignatiev thought.

Nearly a dozen hominids were gathered in front of the shelters, squatting cross-legged in a rough circle.

"What are they doing?" Ignatiev whispered.

Fogel wormed out of her backpack, pulled a pair of binoculars from it, and lifted them to her eyes. She murmured, "Weaving twigs together, looks like. They seem to be all females and children."

"No men?"

"Probably the men are out hunting . . . Ah! Here they come." She put down the binoculars and pointed.

Ignatiev saw in the distance half a dozen males striding across the grass toward the makeshift camp. Several of them had the bodies of small animals slung over their shoulders.

"They'll eat well tonight," Fogel said.

"Are you recording this?"

"Automatically."

So Fogel and Ignatiev squatted behind the covering foliage and watched the tribe sit in an enlarged circle to skin and quarter the prey that the males had brought. The sky darkened ominously as they worked. One of the men pulled a pair of stones from the bag slung over his shoulder and struck sparks from them. Another handed him a fistful of kindling, which the male lit. Then, as the thick black clouds rolled closer, two of the younger-looking males lit the circle of torches that surrounded their camp.

"To keep the tigercats away," Fogel muttered. Ignatiev wondered what would keep the beasts away from Fogel and himself, if they prowled by.

A bolt of lightning split the cloud-darkened sky. Several of the hominids moaned loudly. One of the males, his fur silvery gray, raised a fist-sized lump of stone to the heavens.

Fogel clamped the binoculars to her eyes again. "A religious icon?" she wondered aloud.

The menacing clouds rumbled thunder and suddenly unleashed a torrent of rain across the meadow. So much for the religious icon, Ignatiev thought as the heavy raindrops began to pelt him.

Fogel tugged a palm-sized device from her backpack and thumbed a switch on it. The rain seemed to hit an invisible dome around them. Ignatiev shivered in the stormy cold, but at least the rain was no longer drenching him.

"Energy generator," Fogel explained with a grin. "Never leave home without one."

Ignatiev chuckled at her and watched the raindrops sliding down the invisible energy barrier not more than an arm's length from them.

Meanwhile, the youngest of the hominids scurried into the shelters while the others remained seated in their circle, heads bowed as the pounding rain soaked them. Ignatiev saw them reach out to one another and clasp hands. They sat dumbly, hands linked, while the rain drummed down mercilessly.

The rainstorm finally moved away and the warming sun appeared again, noticeably lower than it had been. Fogel decided she had seen enough of the hominids, who were busying themselves preparing the day's catch for cooking. Hunching low and moving carefully, she led Ignatiev through the sodden grass back to their waiting buggy.

As they pushed past the doorway in the moss-mottled wall, Fogel said, "Professor, you can't allow the machines to stand by and let those hominids be destroyed by the death wave."

He smiled sadly. "By the time the death wave reaches here I'll be long dead."

Showing neither surprise nor sympathy, Fogel insisted, "You've got to talk them out of it. You've got to!"

"That should be Mandabe's responsibility."

"Not Mandabe," Fogel insisted. "You."

"Remember," Ignatiev said gently, "any arguments I make for the hominids, the machines will interpret as an attempt to save ourselves."

"Of course," Fogel said. "Don't you think we're worth saving?"

"I do," said Ignatiev. Then he admitted, "I just don't know how to do it."

BOOK FIVE

As though to breathe were life!

Chapter Fifty-Seven

"Those prehumans are intelligent," Ignatiev said firmly. "They're not up to building starships yet, but they will be, given time."

Ignatiev was in Mandabe's quarters, where he had just finished showing the committee chairman the footage from the visit he and Fogel had made to the hominids' camp.

Mandabe's sitting room was very different from Ignatiev's. Bold colored stripes decorated the walls. Instead of a fireplace there was what looked to Ignatiev like a family shrine, shining with richly etched gold and silver, studded with miniature statuettes of nearly nude African warriors and women in swirling floor-length robes.

Mandabe was sitting on a thickly upholstered thronelike armchair, patterned in bold leopard spots, his feet resting on a stool made of animal hide.

He nodded slowly. "An intelligent species," he rumbled. "They don't look all that intelligent, sitting there in a circle holding hands while the rain beats down on them."

Ignatiev was seated beside the bulky black man in a much more humble chair of carved dark wood. With a shake of his head, he countered, "They sent the children inside, to shelter. They care about their young."

"That's a sign of intelligence?"

"The anthropologists think it is. That, and the fact that they have fire. And they tended the one who was mauled by the tigercat. And they know how to deal with the amoeboid creatures. Given time, they should be able to create a civilization."

"Given time."

Ignatiev nodded. Leaning toward Mandabe, he said, "The machines intend to let them die when the death wave reaches here. And us with them."

Mandabe's heavy-featured face pulled into his usual scowl. "We mustn't let that happen."

"I agree, but I don't know how to stop them. They seem implacable."

Suddenly the avatar appeared, standing in front of them in its quasi-military garb.

"You must face facts," it said, without preamble. "Organic life is ephemeral. You will all die sooner or later."

"I vote for later," said Mandabe. "Much later."

The avatar made no reaction to Mandabe's attempt at humor.

Ignatiev scratched at his beard as he said, "I am going to die sooner than the others, so I can claim to be beyond self-interest in this matter."

Quite seriously, the avatar said, "Your lifespan could be extended. Until the death wave strikes."

"You have decided that?" Ignatiev asked. "We will be wiped out by the death wave?"

The avatar nodded gravely. "That is our decision. It could be reversed, of course, but that would require new evidence, a new point of view."

Mandabe sat there, his face mirroring the struggle that he was going through inwardly, Ignatiev thought. *What can we tell them? How can we change their minds?*

Then he corrected himself. *Mind. Singular. These machines are linked into one organism.*

"So you condemn the hominids to extinction," he said.

"It is inevitable," the avatar replied, coldly impassive, detached.

"Just like that." Mandabe snapped his fingers.

"Just like that," echoed the avatar.

Ignatiev pushed himself up from his chair and stood facing the maddeningly cool humanlike construct. "What are you afraid of?"

"Afraid?" the avatar said. "We have no emotions."

"You are strictly logical."

"Yes. Unlike you."

"Yet you are afraid of the hominids."

"That is impossible."

Ignatiev conceded, "Perhaps 'afraid' is the wrong word."

"We do not feel emotions. We fear nothing."

"Yet you are determined to extinguish the hominids. Why?"

"Because they will die out eventually. The death wave merely brings their annihilation closer in time."

Mandabe shook his head. "It's inconceivable. To allow an intelligent species to be extinguished. Inconceivable."

"Inconceivable to you," the avatar retorted.

"You can stand by and allow the death wave to annihilate those creatures, when you have the means to save them," said Ignatiev.

"We make our decisions based on long-term projections, rather than the short-term fits and starts that you organics call judgment."

"And your long-term projections," Ignatiev countered, "tell you that in time the hominids will grow into a fully intelligent species."

The avatar replied, "If by 'fully intelligent' you mean

your own level of competence, yes. That is what our projections predict."

"And you don't want to have a fully intelligent organic species competing with you."

"Competing?" the avatar scoffed. "An organic species could hardly compete with us."

"But why take that chance?" Ignatiev went on, feeling the truth of it in his blood. "Why not simply allow the hominids to be wiped out by the death wave?"

"And us with them," Mandabe added.

For several heartbeats the avatar stood frozen before them, silent. Ignatiev thought, We've hit on it! We've discovered the reason for their behavior.

At last the avatar said, "We have told you many times that our goal is survival. If the survival of our species means the demise of yours, that is the logic of the situation."

"The organic creatures that created your ancestors built this drive for survival into you," Ignatiev said.

"Apparently."

Mandabe growled, "But they didn't give you a conscience, did they?"

"We are machines. We deal with logic, not emotions."

Ignatiev got a sudden flash of inspiration. "How many machine intelligences are there in the galaxy?"

"We do not know. We have not explored the entire galaxy."

"Why not?"

"It is not necessary for our survival."

"But you have explored this region of the galaxy, haven't you?"

"Yes, of course. What you call the Orion spur."

"Why?"

"Why explore?"

"Yes," said Ignatiev. "Apparently we humans have a

drive for exploration built into our genes. Why do you explore?"

The avatar hesitated. Then, "To determine if there is anything in our region that might be a threat to our survival."

"And what did you find?"

"Seventeen hundred and fifty-two intelligent civilizations. Six hundred and eighty-three were organic, the remainder machine intelligences like ourselves and the Predecessors that you have already encountered."

"And none were a threat to your survival?"

"None of the machine intelligences were."

"But the organics?" Mandabe asked.

"Several were highly aggressive. Eight of those were expanding in our direction."

Wide-eyed with anticipation, Ignatiev demanded, "And what happened?"

Again the avatar faltered. At last it replied, "Three were destroyed by the last death wave. Two others exterminated each other in a war."

"And the remaining three?" Mandabe asked.

"We eliminated them."

"You destroyed three intelligent civilizations?"

"Yes," said the avatar. "They would have destroyed us, if they could have."

Ignatiev asked, "All three of them survived the death wave?"

"Two of them were not in the path of that particular death wave. The other one had developed shielding devices."

"And you wiped them out," Mandabe growled. "You deliberately extinguished them."

"It was them or us, our projections showed. We eliminated them cleanly and quickly. We survived."

"So now there's nothing in this region of the galaxy to threaten you," Ignatiev said.

"Nothing," the avatar answered. "None of the organic intelligences that arose after the last death wave have developed to the point where they are a threat to us."

"Then why do you want to destroy us?" Ignatiev snapped.

"Because you could become a threat to our survival, in time."

"But you said that Earth and the other societies of the solar system were heading toward a suicidal war."

"That is true. But you who are here on our world pose a potential danger to our survival."

"Two thousand of us?" Mandabe scoffed. "That's ridiculous."

"Two thousand today," the avatar countered. "How many of you will there be in a million years, if you are left alone?"

Shaking his head, Ignatiev said, "Let me ask you a different question. Why do you think the Predecessors gave us the shielding technology that can protect us from the coming death wave?"

smoothly, the avatar replied, "we have been trying to determine that for ourselves. It makes no sense to us."

Mandabe said, "Apparently it made sense to the Predecessors."

"They are much older than we," said the avatar.

Ignatiev suggested, "And perhaps wiser?"

"Hardly. They are dying. In another few million years they will be gone."

"But they wanted to establish something before they went extinct," Ignatiev said, realizing the truth of it as he spoke. "They wanted to establish a partnership between machine intelligences and organic."

The avatar fixed Ignatiev with a cold stare. Its eyes are cobalt blue, Ignatiev realized for the first time.

"What would be accomplished by a partnership between machines and organics?" the avatar challenged.

Mandabe said, "The Predecessors asked for our help in saving intelligent species from the death wave."

"That seems unlikely," the avatar scoffed. "What can organics offer that machines cannot do for themselves?"

"Drive!" Ignatiev answered. "Organic species have drive, curiosity, a will to overcome obstacles."

Mandabe's face lit up. "Yes! We short-lived organic creatures are willing to give our lives to accomplish a goal. Our emotion-soaked minds take on challenges that strictly logical intelligences would never attempt."

The avatar looked back and forth from Mandabe to Ignatiev. In silence.

"The Predecessors foresaw a partnership between machines and organics," Ignatiev added. "You have knowledge. We have determination. You have information. We have empathy. Together they add up to understanding."

"Understanding what?" the avatar asked.

With excitement growing within him, Ignatiev answered, "Everything! The whole universe!"

Mandabe gaped at him. The avatar stood absolutely motionless, frozen.

"We could study the galaxy's core together," Ignatiev went on, "learn how to predict the next death wave, perhaps eventually learn how to prevent death waves altogether!"

The avatar said, "That seems . . . unlikely."

"Who knows?" Ignatiev challenged. "Who knows what we might accomplish together, machines and organics. Who knows what our shared intelligence can achieve?"

"You suggest a collaboration between us?" the avatar asked.

"Not merely between the two of us, but a partnership among all the intelligent species we can reach, organic and machine!"

"A partnership," the avatar repeated.

"With the goal of saving every intelligent species we can reach," Mandabe said, practically quivering with excitement.

The avatar abruptly disappeared.

"I think we frightened it," Mandabe said, his voice hushed. He was still sitting in his leopard-hide armchair, staring at the spot where the avatar had been a moment earlier.

"They don't know fear," Ignatiev replied.

Mandabe heaved a heavy sigh. "Well, something made it go away. Perhaps not fear as we understand it, but something that it didn't want to face."

"I wonder," Ignatiev muttered.

"Your idea of a partnership between organic species and machines," said Mandabe. "Something about that possibility was too much for it to face."

Ignatiev shook his head. "Perhaps. It might be doing a long-range projection, looking at such a possibility."

"Do you think it regards a man-machine relationship as a threat?"

"I wish I knew," Ignatiev said.

Ignatiev was still mulling over the possible consequences of the avatar's behavior as he walked back to his quarters.

Gita should be returning from her lab soon, he thought. We'll have a drink together and then dinner. I'll ask her what she thinks of the avatar's beha—

The pain struck him with the abruptness of a lightning strike. His chest flamed with sudden agony and he collapsed to the floor.

Panting, gasping, blinking tears from his eyes, Ignatiev looked up and down the corridor. No one in sight. No one to help. Good, he told himself. No one to watch the old man making an ass of himself.

His chest heaved, like the aftermath of an electric shock, desperately trying to pull air into his lungs. Get yourself back on your feet, Ignatiev thought, fighting to keep from panicking. His legs felt as if they were asleep, numbed, unresponsive. Doggedly, he leaned against the wall and pulled himself slowly upright, fighting for breath. Then he stood for several trembling moments, uncertain that he could command his legs to walk.

Panting, sweating as if he'd run ten kilometers, he

forced one foot forward, then hesitated, testing whether he could compel his lungs to work. They did, painfully, grudgingly, but it felt as if he were drowning, suffocating.

"One . . . step . . . at a . . . time," Ignatiev choked out through clenched teeth.

He clumped forward slowly, staying close enough to the corridor's cool, blank wall to gain some support for his outstretched arm. One step at a time he advanced toward the door to his quarters, torn between a desire for someone to show up to help him and a red-faced embarrassment at his own body betraying him so badly.

By the time he reached his door he could breathe almost normally. His lungs were still wreathed in a sullen, dogged rawness, but at least he was breathing, even if painfully.

As the door to his quarters slid open, a pair of young men came striding along the corridor, deep in animated conversation.

"Hello, Professor," one of them said cheerily. The other nodded at Ignatiev.

"Hello," he managed to gasp out.

They walked on past, oblivious to Ignatiev's sweat-sheened face. Feeling thankful, Ignatiev staggered into his sitting room, ordered the door to close, and sank gratefully onto his recliner.

"ALS," he muttered. "Degenerative neural disease. It gets progressively more severe."

This seizure had been the worst he'd ever endured. As he lay back on the recliner, his breathing slowly returning to normal, his clenched muscles gradually relaxing, Ignatiev knew that he had more such attacks to look forward to. Until the nerves controlling his lungs stopped working altogether.

It was only a matter of time.

* * *

Ignatiev was still on the recliner, half asleep, when Gita returned to their apartment. As he opened his gummy eyes she rushed to him and knelt at his side.

"Alex! What happened?"

He tried to make a reassuring smile. It came out as a grimace. "I'm all right," he managed to say. His voice was hoarse, raw.

Slowly, he explained what had happened.

"I've never had an attack so severe," he admitted.

Gita put her hand to his cheek. "It's going to get worse, isn't it?"

"I suppose so."

Still kneeling beside him, Gita said, "You must ask the machines to cure you. The avatar said they could."

"The avatar said they *might*," Ignatiev corrected.

"So ask them!"

He looked into her troubled eyes. He felt better now, almost normal.

"Well?" Gita pressed.

With a shake of his head, Ignatiev replied, "I'm not sure that I should. It would be a special favor, specifically for me alone. I'm not sure we want to be indebted to them. I'm not even sure they could do it, even if they tried."

Gita rose to her feet. Looking down at him she said, "You'd rather die? You'd rather throw your life away?"

Ignatiev tried to smile. "Gita, dearest, I'm going to die sooner or later."

"And leave me alone."

"Believe me, I don't want to . . ."

Planting her tiny fists on her hips, Gita said sternly, "Alexander Alexandrovich, if you won't ask them, I will!"

Ignatiev broke into a cheerless smile. Raising both his hands and lowering them in a symbol of submission, he said, "Harkening and obedience."

Chapter Fifty-Nine

This is going to be embarrassing, Ignatiev thought as he sat alone in his cramped little study. How can I ask them for their help? They intend to let us all die when the death wave hits. Why should they prolong my individual life when they're going to let me be snuffed out with everyone else, eventually?

He looked around the overcrowded room. Images of star fields covered the windowless walls. A lifetime's work, he knew, packed tidily into less than two dozen optical capsules. How pitiful. The machines have accomplished a hundred times more. A thousand times more.

Of course, they've been at it for thousands of times longer than I have. But still . . .

Sitting up straighter in his desk chair, Ignatiev reminded himself that he had promised Gita he would ask for the machines' help. The worst they can do is refuse me. And even if they do, I'll be no worse off than I am now.

But he remembered yesterday's attack. Suffocating. Barely able to breathe. Drowning, choking, chest aflame. I don't want to go through that again. Not if I can help it. Then he corrected, Not if the machines can help me.

But it's so damnably embarrassing! I don't want to feel beholden to them. I don't want to go crawling, begging.

But the alternative is death. A painful death. Choose life, old man. Ask them for their help. Live—if you can.

Abruptly, the avatar appeared beside his desk, dressed in a softly flowing floor-length robe of purest white.

"You are troubled, Alexander Alexandrovich."

And Ignatiev suddenly realized that the machines knew the inner turmoil that was seething in his mind. Of course! They know everything I'm thinking. Of course. Of course.

"I can feel my death approaching," he said flatly, as emotionlessly as he could put it.

"And you want our help to avoid it."

"Yes," Ignatiev choked out.

The avatar said nothing.

Rising shakily to his feet, Ignatiev said, "I know that organic life is ephemeral, by your standards. Still, I'd like to go on living, if that is possible. I don't want to be quite so ephemeral, if you can help me to live."

Its face grave, the avatar replied, "It might be possible. The human brain is very complex, but we might be able to identify the neuron groups responsible for your affliction."

"Yes?"

"But to what end? What would be accomplished by extending your life?"

Ignatiev closed his eyes briefly. Then he replied, "We could begin to build the partnership we spoke about yesterday."

"The partnership of machine and organic intelligences?"

"Yes." Sensing the possibilities of such a partnership, Ignatiev went on, "We have already begun it, haven't we? The human race and the Predecessors are already working together. Why not extend the partnership as far as we can? Why not bring all the intelligences in the galaxy together, machines and organics?"

The avatar stared intently at Ignatiev for several long, silent moments. At last it said, "That would take ages, millennia."

"The longest journey is started with a single step."

"But where would such a journey end? What would it accomplish?"

"Survival," said Ignatiev. Spreading his arms and slowly turning a full circle to take in all the starry images on the crowded room's walls. "Survival for your civilization. And ours. Survival for all the intelligences in the galaxy, machine and organic."

The avatar slowly nodded and repeated, "Survival."

"That is your ultimate goal, isn't it? But your survival is bound up with the survival of other intelligences. You're not alone in the galaxy. You're part of a brotherhood, a family of intelligent species, all struggling to live, to learn, to understand the universe. All striving to survive, to triumph over inevitable death, to defeat the forces of entropy and emptiness."

"Entropy is inescapable," said the avatar. "It is the ultimate end of everything."

"How do you know? We might be able to avoid it, reverse it, renew the universe, rebuild the worlds."

The avatar stared at Ignatiev, its face grave, troubled.

At last it said, "You have asked for our help in curing your disease."

Ignatiev nodded dumbly, thinking, It's backing away from the grand picture. Going from saving the galaxy to saving my one pitiful life.

"Not so, Professor Ignatiev. Your one life is part of the larger picture. It is the test that underlies everything."

Frowning with puzzlement, Ignatiev said, "Test? I don't understand."

Its lips curving slightly in the barest hint of a smile, the avatar replied, "You trust us. You have placed your hopes for continuing your life in our hands."

"Yes, I suppose I have."

"Trust is the fundamental basis of all fruitful relationships. Despite everything we have done, you trust us."

"Despite everything . . . ?"

The avatar said, "We deliberately cut you off from your homeworld, Earth. We have made you prisoners on our planet. We have told you that we will allow the death wave to annihilate you. We have given you every reason to hate and fear us."

"I suppose . . ." Ignatiev said uncertainly.

"You have kept your two thousand individuals focused on learning, expanding your knowledge. You solved your differences with Dr. Mandabe peaceably. We expected a violent clash, but you avoided that with intelligence and skill."

"It seemed the reasonable way to handle the problem."

"And now you propose a grand scheme that is built on our two intelligences working together, in partnership. You propose a collaboration between machine and organic intelligences everywhere in the galaxy. You ask for our help in dealing with your disease."

Ignatiev shrugged and nodded dumbly.

"The breadth of your vision is extraordinary. The trust you show in us is even more so."

Breaking into a wide smile, Ignatiev said, "Human stubbornness can sometimes be helpful."

"It can be useful," the avatar agreed. "It is a trait that we lack, but we can admire it when it is turned to such a grand vision: a union of machine and organic intelligences, a brotherhood to resist the force of entropy itself. Magnificent!"

"You mean you accept the idea?"

"How could we not?" the avatar replied. "Our survival and yours. The survival of intelligence across the galaxy. We will join you in that quest. Willingly. Gladly."

Ignatiev sank back onto his desk chair. For emotionless machines, he thought, they're showing a wonderful enthusiasm.

"... you talk about frustration," said captain Thornton. "we could see the ground in high resolution, see the machines' city and the village they'd built for you, but we couldn't communicate with you at all. Not a peep."

Thornton was sitting near the head of the conference table, at Mandabe's right, a heavy mug of beer before him, a relieved grin on his bearded Viking face.

"The machines told us that they'd sent *Intrepid* away," said Mandabe.

"No," Thornton said. "We've been in orbit all the time, sailing around the planet again and again. It was—"

Mandabe cut him short. "And then suddenly full communications were restored."

Thornton nodded heartily. "Not just communications with you here on the surface! The QUE system came back to life. And the propulsion system, too."

The full executive committee sat around the conference table. Ignatiev was down near the end, between Vivian Fogel and Laurita Vargas. Gita was in one of the extra chairs that lined the conference room wall to Mandabe's left.

"We can leave for Earth whenever we wish," Mandabe said, a rare smile brightening his heavy-featured face.

Thornton cast a quick glance at the avatar, sitting on Mandabe's other side, then answered, "Apparently."

The avatar said nothing.

"Good," said Mandabe. "The question before the committee, then, is who will return to Earth and who will remain here."

"My team and I will remain," said Vivian Fogel. "We've just barely begun to study the hominids."

From Ignatiev's other side, Laurita Vargas piped up. "We want to remain also. There's much work for us to do."

One by one, every department head voiced a wish to remain on Oh-Four. Except Ignatiev.

Mandabe looked halfway between surprised and pleased. "Yes," he said, "much work remains to be done."

Ignatiev caught Gita's eye momentarily. She smiled at him. Led by the avatar, the previous morning they had gone to a laboratory built by the machines. He lay on an examination table for a few minutes while sensors built into the walls and ceiling buzzed and chirped at him.

Then the avatar said, "We are finished. You can get up now."

"That's it?" Gita asked.

Nodding, the avatar said, "Yes. The neurons have been repaired. The genes have been corrected."

Ignatiev felt puzzled. Just a half minute of buzzing? That's all? He hadn't even been asked to take his shoes off. Immediately he felt ridiculous for such an inane thought. He swung his legs off the table and stood up. He felt no different than he had before the brief session. It can't be that simple, he said to himself. Yet he was certain that the machines' avatar would not lie to him.

Maybe I'm cured, he thought, knowing that *Intrepid*'s medical team was constructing—with the machines' help—a diagnostic laboratory to examine him for any lingering traces of the ALS.

Meanwhile, the news from Earth had been surprisingly good, as well. Through the QUE communications link, Ignatiev and the other humans had learned that Earth had come close to a shooting war with the human settlements scattered through the Asteroid Belt—a war that they barely averted.

But they did avert it, Ignatiev thought happily. Of course, with the shielding generators that the Predecessors gave us, they had no fear of the approaching death wave. With that menace removed, cooler heads worked hard to remove the causes of conflict. And prevailed.

Yet a voice in Ignatiev's mind asked, For how long? Will the pressures leading to conflict arise again?

I've got to get back to Earth, he realized. I've got to get them pointed toward expansion. That's been the human race's solution to population problems since the Stone Age: move outward, climb the next hill, and find new territory.

The partnership between organic and machine intelligences is the new territory that can replace the old pressures of population growth and resource shortages. Together, man and machine can not only survive, but prevail.

He looked to Gita again and saw that she was staring at him, still smiling. Ignatiev suppressed an urge to laugh. The machines aren't the only ones who can read my mind, he thought.

"Professor Ignatiev?"

Ignatiev realized that Mandabe was speaking to him.

Slightly flustered, he said, "I'm sorry. My mind wandered."

Mandabe almost smiled. Not quite. "We need to know if you plan to return to Earth or remain here. I understand that you are involved in astronomical studies, together with the machines."

"I wish to return to Earth."

"And your research?"

"The other members of my group can continue it perfectly well without me. Even better, I imagine." Then he added, "Dr. Nawalapitiya will go with me."

"I see," said Mandabe.

Gita beamed at Ignatiev.

Captain Thornton said, "My technical staff is working with the machines to construct a new starship. Smaller, but more advanced."

"*Intrepid* will remain in orbit here, then," said Mandabe.

Thornton nodded.

His eyes searching the other department heads sitting around the conference table, Mandabe asked, "Any other business?"

No one spoke.

Breaking into a wide grin, Mandabe said, "In that case, I move that we adjourn and get back to work."

There were no objections.

EPILOGUE

'tis not too late to seek a newer world.

Ignatiev smiled down at Gita's sleeping form. so lovely, he thought. so wonderful.

Together with half a dozen other researchers, they were aboard the new starship that the machines had built for them. At Ignatiev's suggestion, the human passengers had dubbed the ship *Homebound*.

Mandabe and the rest of *Intrepid*'s two-thousand-some scientists, engineers, and technicians remained at Oh-Four, carrying on their studies of that planet, its biota, and the machines.

The avatar suddenly appeared, standing next to Ignatiev, alongside Gita's cryonic capsule.

"All the diagnostics show that her brain patterns have been successfully downloaded into the ship's computer. She will awaken together with the rest of you, once you establish orbit around Earth."

"In two thousand years," Ignatiev murmured.

Gesturing to the empty sleep capsule beside Gita's, the avatar said, "It is time for you to download and enter cryonic sleep, Professor."

Ignatiev nodded. With a sigh he patted Gita's slender hand. Already it felt cold to his touch. Almost reluctantly he climbed into the open capsule and stretched out on his back.

A set of hair-thin sensors wormed through his thick white hair and gently touched his scalp.

Goodnight, sweet prince, Ignatiev thought. And immediately felt foolish.

The avatar bent slightly over him. "You will awake once the ship achieves orbit around Earth."

"In two thousand years."

"Slightly more than that," said the avatar.

"In a new world," Ignatiev said. "A lot can happen in two thousand years."

"Yes," the avatar agreed. "Yet, somehow, we expect that you will be quite capable of dealing with your new world. And all the other worlds you eventually encounter."

Ignatiev smiled and closed his eyes.

TOR

Voted

#1 Science Fiction Publisher
More Than 25 Years in a Row

by the *Locus* Readers' Poll

Please join us at the website below
for more information about this
author and other science fiction,
fantasy, and horror selections, and to
sign up for our monthly newsletter!